DARK JUSTICE

ANGELA SMITH

Dark Justice

Copyright © 2019 by Angela Smith

Author Name: Angela Smith

Title: Dark Justice

Cover Artist: Steven Novak

Formatter: Katie McGinley

Editor: Tamara Eaton

ISBN-13: 978-1-7323859-4-8 (EBook)

ISBN-13: 9781693399268 (Print)

Thank you for buying an authorized edition of this book and for complying with copyright laws by not reproducing, scanning, or distributing any part of this book in any form without express permission. You are supporting writers and allowing creativity to continue. Scanning, uploading, or distribution of this book without permission is theft of the author's intellectual property. If you would like permission to use material from the book other than for review purposes, please contact angela@loveisamystery.com. Thank you for your support of the author's rights.

This book is a work of fiction. Names, characters, places, and incidents are the product of the author's imagination or are used fictitiously. Any resemblance to actual events, locales, or persons, living or dead, is coincidental.

Author Angela Smith

www.loveisamystery.com

www.twitter.com/angelaswriter

www.facebook.com/authorangelasmith

www.amazon.com/author/authorangelasmith

To Jw. Our story is my favorite love story.

ACKNOWLEDGEMENTS

An author can never complete a book without a lot of help, and I have so many people to thank. To the writing community all across the world, many of whom I have never met. They continue to help me grow as an author.

Thanks to Gary Bunyard, a former coworker, retired prosecutor, and current friend, for helping me with all the legal questions I had while writing this novel.

Thanks to Marc and Melissa Nobles. Marc, for letting me use your music for inspiration and for my book trailers. And Melissa, for putting up with me since second grade and loaning me books when I had none to read.

Thanks to Tabitha and Shelley for helping me with my plot and keeping me sane.

To my sister and best friend, KaSandra. I love you.

And to my niece, Kaley Wingett. Never be afraid to go after your dreams.

CHAPTER ONE

Luke Twelve Years Ago

"All rise for the jury."

I stand, my legs unsteady. The jurors filter in, one by one, their eyes downcast. Those who look, only glance at the prosecutor. Not me or my defense attorney.

Wayne's breath hitches. It's a whispery whoosh, a sound he likely doesn't realize he's made, but it tells me everything I need to know. I almost collapse in defeat.

He thinks they found me guilty. And by their expressions, I agree.

I size up the crowd gathering in the courtroom. Most of them sit on the prosecutor's side. Clint is there. Once my best friend, but now I'm convinced he's a killer. He's next to Lauren. The love of my life and the one I presumed would stand by my side forever. But since she believes I killed her sister, I guess I can't blame her for turning her back on me.

But Clint? Fear curls my spine. He's charming, I'll give him that, but he's an absolute psycho. Nobody in Lauren's family will listen, especially Lauren. And before all this, I wouldn't have believed Clint is the killer. He killed her sister. How do I know she won't be next? How can I protect her if I'm locked in prison for the rest of my life?

The judge drones on about the charge, then asks the jury if they've reached a decision. Wayne shifts and gives me a blink that tells me he wants to make sure I'm aware of what's going on. I'm eighteen, for God's sake. How could anyone my age understand criminal justice?

He's warned me of how you can never predict a jury, but this group of fourteen holds their heads high as if they've never been surer in their lives. Two of them are alternate jurors, so it's up to five men and seven women to decide my fate.

An older gentleman hands the bailiff the verdict. I hold my breath, and the judge reads. "We the jury find the defendant, Lucas Donovan Fuller, guilty of murder."

Gasps fill the room. Chaos erupts, at least in my bones. More like a commotion, nothing too disastrous to alert the judge, and something he's probably accustomed to. He only regards the crowd. A lot of loud talking, crying, and my mother's wails. He's way more patient than me and waits for everyone's reaction to subside.

My muscles grow weak. I badly want to sit and wonder when I'm allowed. I want to reach out to Lauren. Tell her I'm sorry this happened, I didn't do it, she has to trust me, and please, please don't trust Clint. I open my mouth to say these things, but my attorney stations his hand on my shoulder, as if his one palm is going to keep me silent.

He warned me over and over not to react. I'm not allowed to speak. I am barely allowed to move, and I can't look her way, although I shift to do so. The bailiff puffs out his chest and walks closer, as if I'm going to bolt.

"Calm down," Wayne says. "We still have punishment. Don't make a scene."

Why shouldn't I react? This is life changing. My life is over. I'm going to prison. The judge hasn't declared a final sentence but after everyone's testimony, I've started to believe my own guilt. I'm likely going to prison for the rest of my life.

———

Luke Present Day

Luke Fuller's pen scribbled across the page. His heart hammered while he wrote the words, ears filling with the deep drum of his heartbeat as if he was re-experiencing the event. Tired of writing, he shut the notebook and tossed it on the wrought-iron table beside him, along with his cap and shades. He stood and opened the grill to check the ribeye.

Food would be ready in a few minutes, and all he needed was right here. A little salt and pepper, paper plates and plastic forks to eat with, and a cooler full of drinks. Even a hundred feet from the river, the bullfrogs' croaking put him at ease.

A sound he never expected to hear again.

He closed the grill, grabbed a beer from the ice chest, and lounged on the patio chair. It took a while for his heartbeat to settle. Writing these memories was difficult, harder than he expected, and his body ached from the flashbacks.

The sun descended, a showcase of gold fueled by rain clouds and humidity. He loved the open porch and didn't want a screen to filter him and the outdoors. With bug spray, sleeping out here at night was a dream come true, despite the oppressive mugginess. Lightning flashed in the south, implying the much-needed shower was near. Nothing better than the clatter of rain on the roof.

Even the mosquitoes avoided the Texas July heat, but he'd take heat over the prison cell where he'd spent the past twelve years of his life. He'd take it over that any damn day.

LED lights strung across the porch offered a soft glow to ease him come sundown. He hated the darkness. Too many reminders of prison and the things he wanted to forget. But this darkness out in the country was peaceful, welcoming, different. Almost bearable.

A car drove up, the headlights zipping through the trees. His muscles tensed. He studied the nearby monitor attached to the front security camera. The car parked, the lights shut off. His lungs tightened, burned, then disintegrated when the woman stepped out and sauntered to the back.

She remembered. Friends always came to the back door. But she was no friend.

He blinked, his gut churning. Was he dreaming? Hallucinating after writing those memories? Lauren shone bright in his mind, even the seductive scent of honey and berries he once loved to sample behind her ear.

Her footsteps echoed up the stairs, and she came into view. She was no illusion. He remained sitting, nonchalant and drinking his beer as if he had no care in the world.

His mouth dried. The beer a sour tang. Her presence meant nothing good.

She thought he'd killed her sister. The entire community deemed him guilty before a jury of his peers sentenced him to life in prison. His sisters never stopped fighting to prove his innocence. He was released two months ago thanks to Adrienne and Charlotte and the team of defense attorneys who fought for him.

But he favored prison over the look of revulsion on Lauren's face. A flowing skirt skimmed her knees, the imprinted flowers rivaling the charm of the countryside. Her slender body was as gorgeous as ever, heating him in ways better left ignored. She wore open-toed sandals. He never understood why she chose those shoes while hiking. They had to stop many times during their treks to pluck out grass burrs.

At one time, they didn't mind the interruption.

Her dirty blonde hair was darker, accented by rich caramel, and the image of her ocean blue eyes burned in his memory. Despite the similarities, she wasn't the same woman who once loved him.

He didn't flinch when she pointed the pistol his direction. He continued to sip his beer, his ears tingling with the chatter of June bugs and crickets. If she wanted to shoot him, so be it.

Although he hadn't killed her sister, he was just as much to blame. He had been selfish in spending his time with Lauren and didn't mind leaving her sister alone. He trusted his best friend, had known him since grade school, but ignored his recent questionable tendencies. The town of Terrence was quick to point fingers while the real killer roamed free.

Lauren Twelve Years Ago

Lauren cried in Luke's arms. His strength grounded her while she prayed Elizabeth would be found safe. But she had been found, and she wasn't safe.

Someone murdered her. Her throat slit. Her body—Lauren shook the image away. She hadn't been allowed to see her, so her imagination played havoc with reality.

Reality was, her baby sister, the one she was supposed to protect, the one she was not supposed to outlive, was dead.

She had left her little sister so she could be alone with Luke. Her parents, even throughout their own grief, begged her not to feel guilty. Elizabeth was twelve and pleaded for them to trust her and let her stay by herself. She loved it every time they agreed. She was afraid of nothing.

Lauren would have given her life for her little sister. And whoever stole her life would be punished.

"Is everything okay?"

She flinched at Clint's deep boomy voice. His footsteps pounded into her skull. Luke's arms tightened, but she sensed him shaking his head at his best friend.

She withdrew from her fiancé's warm arms and faced Clint, swiping tears from her cheeks. "No. Nothing is okay. Did you hear? They found Elizabeth. She's dead."

Clint's eyes widened, face blotched in horror. He stepped forward as if to approach, but Luke took her in his arms again and held her, shaking his head at his friend. She snuggled into Luke's chest and breathed in his musk.

She hadn't always liked Clint. He annoyed her. But he tirelessly worked to help find her sister. His father, the mayor, assembled an extensive search party and went above and beyond their duties, then vowed to catch the murderer. Clint had been Luke's best friend since forever, and maybe one reason he annoyed her. She wanted Luke to herself and hated to share.

But she was grateful for his help. His ancestors founded this town, and the ones still alive were powerful. They considered themselves everybody's family.

The door crashed open. Lauren jerked and turned. The sheriff bulldozed in with two of his deputies. Lauren frowned.

"Lucas Donovan Fuller?" the sheriff said.

Luke's hands dropped to his side. He stepped away from Lauren, fists clenched. His face paled. "Yeah?"

Lauren floundered, opened her mouth to say something, but her breath stalled and confusion wracked her brain. Clint tugged at her and she stumbled backward into his hold.

What was happening? This was no time for nonsense.

The sheriff continued. "You're under the arrest for the murder of Elizabeth Cooper."

Her brain stalled. Lips grew numb. Vision blurred as the sheriff slapped the cuffs on him. She opened her mouth to say something, to argue all the reasons the sheriff was wrong. But they hauled him out of the room, and everything grew black.

Lauren Present Day

LAUREN COOPER POINTED the pistol at Luke, knees knocking and thighs quaking. She was proud of herself for keeping a steady grip despite her sweaty palms.

She'd practiced plenty, eyeing her target, strengthening her resolve. Today, Luke Fuller was her target. Maybe her first moving target—although he didn't move, didn't even flinch—and definitely her first human target. Still, she'd often imagined him on the other end of her gun.

What was she thinking? She risked losing her job over this, even facing jail time, for threatening with a firearm. Was it worth it to lose everything she'd worked so hard for? Even worse, to risk her daughter's wellbeing?

Luke had murdered Elizabeth, was released, and now another man accused. But not just any man. Clint Merkel. A close friend. Almost family.

Thousands of times she'd confronted Luke in her dreams. Robbed him of life as brutally as he had robbed her twelve-year-old sister's. More like nightmares. The man she once loved with all her heart. The jury had convicted him, but now he was exonerated. Doubts still clouded her mind. The newest facts couldn't obliterate twelve years of certainty, no matter how credible.

Her spine clenched. She had tossed and turned and cried herself to sleep for years. Her emotions skyrocketed all over the place. Suppressed memories jumbled out of her. Memories of his kiss, his embrace, their shared lives, their plans. In high school, they'd been dubbed Luke and Lauren. She didn't want to plan college without questioning where he'd go. They were a team, a couple and everybody—including her—presumed they'd stay together after high school.

Stupid to give her life away to a man, to halt her ambitions and plans. And then one fateful night the truth had been discovered, and the cops had placed the cuffs on his wrists.

He was still the most handsome man she had ever seen. Still captivated her. The sting of attraction needled through her muscles, her bones, her heartbeat. Her pulsed thrummed into her toes. She fought to stand her ground and reveal nothing about his effect on her.

Thunder boomed. She jumped. The rain began a harsh and fast hammering on the roof.

He sipped his beer, body relaxing as if knowing she wasn't about to pull the trigger. He remained unaffected by the thunder, by the deluge, and by her presence.

"You going to shoot me or not?" He shrugged one shoulder, his drawl tightening the shivers in her stomach. Heat flared under her skin, the familiar anger—the reason she came here—blazed to her core. Him all casual, enjoying a beer while smoke billowed from his fire pit. The spices of the steak tore knots in her throat.

But she wasn't only angry at him. She was angry at herself for letting him charm her.

The storm doused the dusk, but miniature lights lined the porch. She saw every inch of him and the way his gaze slid over her. They had studied each other for hours when they were younger, in love and carefree. The green of his eyes soaked up the earth and emitted the colors of eternity. They were harder, his face bearing a few scars only she might notice.

He dropped his beer to the table beside him. "What are you doing, Lauren? Just shoot me already. I've practically been dead these past years, anyway."

Her throat closed. She refused to imagine what he experienced these last few years.

Luke shifted forward and frowned, let out a rickety cough, then perched his elbows on his knees. He swiped a hand over his face, then continued. "Look. I'm sorry about everything. Sorry you had to go through the loss of your sister and you believed I did it. Sorry I couldn't comfort you. I'm... just sorry."

His wobbly voice shattered her reserves. His movements broadcasted an unexpected nervousness. She let out a whoosh of breath, every fiber of her being sinking into a black hole of misery. Tears rolled out of her, hot and choking. Her grip on the gun wavered but remained clasped in her fingers.

He stood and swaggered toward her. His heavy-booted steps on the wooden planks thudded in her ears. She wanted to back away, but her butt rested against the porch railing and an invisible anchor rooted her to the ground.

She swayed.

Her hands shook, and her best interest was to put down the gun before somebody got hurt. Most likely her.

She lowered the pistol. He stopped in front of her and took it. She was too weak, too helpless to fight. His presence suctioned every bit of her power.

He set the gun on the ground. She jumped as another round of thunder boomed. Rain pounded the roof. Droplets hit her skin, but not enough to matter. She craved the cool refreshment. He stood facing her, his eyes boring into hers. She licked her lips as if drawing sustenance from that one small move, a move that drew his gaze to her mouth.

She swayed again, about to fall. He grabbed her and pulled her into his arms.

"Careful." His words wisped across her ear and trailed down her spine to spool into a reservoir of lust in her loins.

She planted the top of her head against his chest and sobbed as he held her. Her shoulders shook, the tears escaping in violent torrents. She couldn't stop no matter how hard she wanted to.

He smelled like mesquite smoke and musk, along with crisp grass cuttings under Texas sunshine. Stupid, stupid to imagine such things.

The tears were a release. A goodbye she never had a chance to say.

Had she believed he was capable of murder? She refused to listen to his sister when she begged. All the evidence pointed to him. The police, the prosecutor, even the city mayor had convinced her.

How could they all be wrong? Her mind churned with questions. Questions she should have asked before she'd threatened him with a gun.

His fingers skated up her hair, and he tucked a piece behind her ear. She straightened her spine and lifted her head, willing her body to fight the attraction as her tears dried.

"I don't know if I believe it," she finally said.

"What? That I didn't do it?"

She nodded, her limbs weak and trembling.

"Well, if Clint didn't do it, why did he run?"

She wondered the same thing, but Clint being a killer was terrifying, even more so than Luke, considering she'd entrusted her daughter with him.

She lowered her head and sniffled. He placed his fingers under her chin and forced her to look at him.

Not a force but a slow, gentle move. He had always been gentle. Clint had been the edgy one, the one who tested her nerves. And yet after Luke had been accused of murdering her sister, she had turned to Clint as a friend and let him take part in her life. How had he manipulated her? How had she allowed it? Her belly flopped, the drying tears searing her throat.

She'd always felt safe with Luke. Safe, yet vulnerable, because her heart was at risk.

He dropped his hand from her chin and finger brushed her hair. Her neck tingled. She longed to savor his mouth on hers after all these years.

"I've imagined being in front of you, begging you to listen." His voice was a slow deep penetration to the core of her being. Something impossible to pull away from. "I did not kill your sister, and as much pain as I knew you were in, it broke my heart you never gave me a chance."

She lifted her chin higher and stared straight into his eyes. "And I imagined having the chance to stand in front of you and kill you."

A strangled sob escaped him. His eyes flickered. Her body grew warm with regret. Regret for her words, regret for refusing to hear him out so many years ago, and regret for wanting him so much she hurt.

"You've got that chance now. Why don't you take it?"

Pain ripped Luke's heart. His body ached with the need to touch, taste, and experience Lauren. An eternity had passed, although it seemed like only yesterday.

He wasn't sure which one of them came to the other first, but the fiery touch of her lips almost brought him to his knees. He planted his hands under her ass and pressed her closer. Their tongues warred and tangled. When she didn't pull away, he lifted her skirt, his fingers penetrating her heat.

She was hot and wet. Thunder boomed and rain pounded on the roof. She rested her spine on the deck pole and opened her legs wider, groaning when his finger slipped inside, in and out. Her hands gripped the back of the pole and she lifted her head, exposing her neck. He sucked the skin beneath her ear.

He dropped his shorts, thrust aside her thong, and entered her. She lifted one leg around his waist. He clasped his hand on her thigh to hold her steady.

He almost caught himself, almost pulled away and fled from her presence. He'd choose a bullet over the torment of her leaving him again. But she pressed against him and let out a soft moan and when she returned his kiss, it was impossible to pull away.

The pressure built too hard, too fast. He slowed down to prolong the tidal wave of pleasure, but her hips moved in sync with his and he couldn't focus, couldn't find his grounding.

The mating was over within moments. She convulsed around him and he exploded into her, a torrent of longing for more pouring out of him in droplets of sweat. They stilled. Realization dawned in her eyes and with it came panic and regret. He released her and meant to talk, soothe her, tell what he so longed to say, but without warning she fled from the porch.

He reached out, wanted to ask her to stop and give him more time, give him the benefit of the doubt she had refused. But his tongue tightened in his throat and the sound emerged in a raspy groan.

He had never stopped loving her. Her image kept him sane in prison. He had held onto the memories, even when faced with no choice but to let her go.

Night descended, elevating the darkness in his mind. She disappeared, and he stood helpless. The storm raged beyond his porch. Her headlights lit up, then the car rumbled away.

He pulled up his shorts and planted his forehead on the deck pole, squishing his eyes closed. Moments before, her body had pressed against this same pole. Anguish tore through him, deepening the wound of his regrets.

Smoke billowed out of the grill, the charred beef's stench saturating the earthiness of rain. Her pistol remained on the floor. A brutal reminder of why she'd come.

He hadn't raped her. He hadn't. But he might as well have. He hadn't controlled his intentions and had taken advantage of a vulnerable situation. His actions could create a hell of a wildfire if she were to cry rape. Many people still considered him guilty.

Her included.

CHAPTER TWO

LAUREN FLED, tripping her way down the wet steps. The rain pounded the earth, matting her hair and disguising the tears in her eyes. But nothing disguised the burn.

No escaping the guilt, no escaping the longing she felt when she looked into his eyes.

Massive puddles erupted from the hard and unrelenting rain. Mud coated her feet by the time she reached the car. Her hand slipped against the slick handle, and she dropped the keys. She cried out and knelt to grab them before the earth took hold.

She had to get out of here. Fast. Why had she come?

Navigating through the downpour was almost impossible. The storm was a testament to her mistakes. The flashing lightning continued to mock her. She turned from his driveway onto the county road, the tires digging into the sludge to get away. She slowed, taking it easier once she was out of his property. The wipers clunk-clunk-clunked against the windshield. She couldn't see.

The summer storm struck like most in Texas. Hard and fast with a deluge of rain that raised creeks and shut down low water crossings. She had to consider her life. No matter how desperate she was to flee, she'd sit in the car and wait if she had to. But she could make it to the creeks and wait off on the side of the road somewhere. Anywhere but here. They weren't too far to drive.

She gripped the wheel and peered into the dark night, the glow of her headlights a bridge into oblivion. Lightning crackled across the sky, a warning strobe of gloom.

Her heart pounded against her chest, her throat a swampy mess of tears.

Why had she let Luke violate her? The caress of his breath brought back memories of the two of them together.

Who was she kidding? She welcomed his touch, his tongue, his caress. No violation was involved.

For Crissakes, he'd killed her sister, or so she'd believed. The heaviness of doubt still burned. Yes, Clint had run. Why had it been so easy to believe Luke was guilty but she had trouble believing Clint was? Luke had paid for that guilt for the past twelve years.

Her daughter was now the age her sister had been when she was killed.

Their daughter.

She gasped, her breath cutting into her throat and plummeting to her belly. He couldn't know. He couldn't find out about Laramie. She slumped over the wheel, peering into the storm's obscurity.

Her tires slid. She hydroplaned and lost control. Frantic, she steered, searching for her way back on the road. The car slid down a ditch and sideswiped a tree, scraping along the passenger side until it stuttered and stopped.

"No!" she screamed as thunder boom-boom-boomed.

She pushed on the gas to escape. A stupid action. The tires only burrowed further into the mud. She stopped and willed herself to breathe. She was familiar enough with the road and wasn't in a rising creek bed, so she could wait out the storm right here. The airbag hadn't exploded. Most likely, she was just stuck.

She refused to walk back to his house even if it wasn't raining. Besides, she was far enough away staying in the car was best.

Phone service was sketchy out here in the best of conditions, and she wanted no one to know she'd come. Come hell or high water, she'd drive out of this ditch without having to call a wrecker.

Thunder cracked and flashed. She jumped at the sound of the earth being ripped apart. The rain eased into a light mist, and she turned off the engine and the lights to save battery power. She didn't feel threatened. She wasn't stuck in the middle of a snowstorm in frigid temps with no means of getting home, and she wouldn't starve to death. She'd left her pistol at Luke's.

Thunder rumbled again, decreasing in its intensity. Lights streaked across the distance. Lights to a vehicle.

She tensed, grabbing her purse and pepper spray. Probably someone who lived on this road, but one could never be too trusting. Rough edges of panic knifed through her when the Jeep from Luke's driveway stopped behind her.

His body was a dark shadow as he trudged to her car, his face lined in concern, then relief when he knocked on the window and saw she was okay.

At least, that's what it appeared to be from her perspective. He went for the door when she wasn't fast enough opening it.

"Are you okay?"

"I'm fine. Slid off the road and hit a tree. The car is stuck."

"The Jeep might get you unstuck, but it'll be difficult right now with the mist and the darkness. I can call a wrecker for you."

"No. No, thank you."

"Were you planning on staying out here until morning then?"

"If I have to."

Rain misted over him. He stood behind the open door, one hand bracing the frame and the other on the roof. His body offered a canopy, but cold sprinkles stung her skin.

"I have a friend who drives a wrecker. He'll do it for free. From the looks of your car, though, you'll need to file an insurance claim."

"It isn't about the money."

"What is it about?"

Realization dawned in his eyes. "You don't want anyone to know you came out here tonight."

"Not part of my plan, no."

"Part of your plan was to shoot me."

She shook her head. She dreamed of facing him with a gun, but she could never take a life. Why had she done it? Why risk everything?

"Look, I don't plan on telling anyone if you don't, but we need to get you out of here. We can check on the car in the morning, or I can call my friend who won't ask questions. We'll get it to a body shop and get it looked at. But right now, why don't you let me take you home? Or at least come back to my house so we can talk without rain and lightning."

Going back to his home was a terrible idea, but she didn't want him to know where she lived. Maybe have him drop her off at a convenience store and walk the rest of the way. Laramie was staying overnight with a friend, so she didn't have to worry about her until tomorrow.

But she worried all the time now. When would Clint come out of hiding? Could he kill her daughter, the child he had claimed to protect as a godchild, so easily? As easily as he had killed her sister?

Had he, in fact, killed her sister all those years ago and gotten away with it for so long? Another man had gone to prison. A jury had heard evidence and convicted him. And now she was standing in the middle of the dark with that same man, and her heart was pitter-pattering way too clumsily to be fear.

"If you're hungry I've got steak, although it's a bit crispy now," Luke said, his voice pulling her out of her trance.

The rain grew heavy again, a steady downpour with thunder skulking in a low growl.

"Besides, the creeks are probably up by now, so we'll never get across them if you don't decide soon, and I'm not leaving you here alone." He rambled, and she remained quiet, her thoughts a jumbled mess. She hadn't thought things through. Dismissed any consequences when she drove out here with a pistol.

"Okay. I'll let you take me home for now," she said.

"As long as the creeks haven't risen," he said.

She knew about the creeks. They swiftly rose, but receded soon after the rain stopped. She clenched her hands and sighed. "If so, we can go back to your house to gain perspective, but I'm taking back my pistol and if you get anywhere near me, and I mean even as close as you are right now, I'll shoot you."

She had come here to scare him. Show him she was highly capable with a gun and had moved on with her life. Did she think to win a showdown with him so he'd know he didn't intimidate her and she would never let him get close to her and her family again? Never let him have an advantage over her. Or maybe some sick part of her longed to see him again.

But the truth was, she still questioned whether he had murdered Elizabeth, and she'd spent the last twelve years of her life wishing he was dead.

Luke Twelve Years Ago

"Mr. Benoit You may call your next witness."

"The state calls Lauren Cooper."

My breath hitches. My chest explodes. Stars ricochet in my head and when I do finally gain my breath back, it's a silent gurgle. I swallow tears, but my throat is too raw to accept them. They turn into squeamish worms in my windpipe. I blink, blink, blink until my vision clears and I keep my jaw clenched to prevent any noise from erupting. I refuse to share my grief with the twelve men and women who are deciding my fate.

Lauren is on the witness list, but this is the first time I've seen her since I've been in jail. Six months. That's how long it took the state to prepare my case, although my attorney tells me it's quick, almost too quick. He says these things can take years.

But it hasn't been quick for me. He'd probably think differently if he was the one in jail. Since Lauren is a witness, she isn't allowed to sit in the courtroom and watch. A relief, since the compelling testimony of their witnesses says nothing good about me. I'm almost convinced of my own guilt.

She struts into the room, head held high. My whole body tenses. My fingers clench the pen I'm holding before I drop it and it plunks to the desk. The sound is an amplified ping in my ears. I want to stand, call out to her. My defense attorney grips my arm and slides a note my way. *Stay cool.*

I swallow. Wayne Evans has been more than a defense attorney. He's been an anchor, a coach, and he trained me on how to react and, more specifically, how not to react. I have to hope for the best.

The judge swears Lauren in. "Do you promise to tell the whole truth and nothing but the truth so help you God?"

She nods once. "I do." She sits, and then squirms in the seat, clasping and unclasping her hands. I know her well enough to notice the slight tremble in her lips and in her hands. She doesn't glimpse my direction. My heart knocks against my ribcage. I call out to her in my mind. *Lauren, babe, look at me. I love you. You know I didn't do this.* We previously had that type of connection, but her doubt has severed our bond.

The prosecutor asks questions, and I have to force out the jumbling of my thoughts so I can hear. I lean forward and divert my whole attention to the girl I love. Have always loved and will always love. We planned to spend our lives together.

There's no room in my heart for resentment with her, but I channel plenty to the prosecutor and the criminal justice team representing the County of Terrence. They told Lauren hellacious things about me. If it's anything like I've heard in court, I don't blame her for hating me.

"Can you tell us how long you've known Lucas Fuller?" Mr. Benoit. Tall, ball-headed, with an engaging personality and a bulldozer mentality. He never gave me a chance.

His blue eyes are piercing, a harsh sterility mixed with compassion and an element of devotion. As if he could play this game until everyone else bowed out from exhaustion. As Lauren would have said, he gives me the heebie-jeebies.

"Oh, I, for years, really. We've grown up together since kindergarten."

"Have you ever been in a serious relationship with Lucas?"

She nods, then squints her eyes. "Yes. We dated."

"How long have you dated?"

"Since, oh, like serious dating? I mean, we've known each other so long." Her gaze lowers and she fiddles with the cuffs of her sweater. She fidgets when she's nervous.

"How long have you been serious?"

She glances up, her watery eyes the only sign the questions affect her. I wonder what they mean, and I'm sure she does, too. When had she fallen in love with me? Or when had she given herself sexually to me? Probably the same. Her gaze darts at me for a second. A split second, but she looks away too soon. "Two… two years I guess."

"Has Lucas ever been physically abusive?"

Her jaw clenches. "No."

"Mentally abusive?"

She shakes her head. "No."

The muscles in my body unkink. Will this help her realize I could never do the things they say I did?

"What about Elizabeth? Has he ever abused Elizabeth?"

Her hand flutters to her chest, then falls to her lap. "No." She shrugged. "I mean, she had a crush on him. Like, you know, a schoolgirl crush. And he thought it was cute."

"He thought it was cute?"

"Yeah. He teased her about it sometimes."

"Teased her about it?"

"Sometimes she annoyed him."

"She annoyed him?"

My attorney stands. "Objection your honor. She's answered the questions, and he's baiting her now."

"Overruled."

I've learned from this trial overruled means the judge does not abide by my attorney's objection and the prosecutor is allowed to ask. Good. I'm curious to hear what she has to say.

"So, he teased her about her crush?"

My attorney stands again. I resist the urge to pull him down by the arm. "Objection. Ask and answer, and leading. She's already answered and now he's leading her."

The prosecutor stands. "Your honor, I'm trying to learn about the relationship between Lucas Fuller and Elizabeth Cooper."

"He's not asking—" Wayne says.

"Mr. Benoit. Rephrase your question and stop repeating hers."

They both sit. My tense body is ready to explode. I can't take this anymore. I am tempted to jump up and shout I'm guilty just to get it over with, and to wipe off the pain on Lauren's face. Not that it would work since she already thinks I'm guilty.

"Lauren, how did Lucas tease your sister?"

"Oh, he called her squirt. And told her he had to wait until she was older to marry her. Things like that."

I cringe. Jurors' eyes turn on me. I squirm in my seat. An innocent way to make Elizabeth laugh and feel better. I grew up hearing plenty of funny name-calling and empty promises. But in the light of trial, it paints me as a deviant and opens a landmine of accusations.

I hang my head. Nothing I do will restore the love in her eyes. Her sister is gone. Brutally murdered. The years I potentially face in prison won't ever wipe away the memory of Lauren's grief. The months I've spent in county jail awaiting my trial date never compares to Lauren's suffering. I long to be by her side, loving and supporting her and helping her get through this. Instead, I am a pariah. This entire town—one I loved so much—has turned against me.

"Was he wearing a cap the day you learned Lauren was missing?"

She nods once, blinks, and says, "I... I believe so. Yes. He always wore that cap."

I wasn't wearing my cap. I had lost it, and she had even asked me about it. But now she doesn't remember.

"May I approach the witness?" the prosecutor asks the judge, then does so at the judge's permission. "Ms. Cooper, do you recognize this photo?"

She gasps. Any color remaining on her face drains. "No."

"Have you ever seen anything like that in your boyfriend's bedroom?"

"No." Tears fill her eyes, and my heart breaks. Wayne's co-counsel—I can't ever remember his name—literally has a death grip on the table next to my arm. As if he's getting ready to grab me when I bolt up.

Another objection from my attorney, but I'd like to know what the hell Mr. Benoit is showing her. The judge lets him continue.

"This is nothing compared to what was found in his room," Mr. Benoit says. "But we can't show those photos or we'd be breaking the law too."

"Objection, your honor," Wayne says. I tune out the rest of the prosecutor's questions and the debate between my attorney and the state's. I can't pay attention anymore. I've lost the fight. Even if I'm found not guilty, I can never regain the love of my life.

"Pass the witness," Mr. Benoit says.

My ears perk. My spine clenches, but I straighten in my chair. A swampy marsh clogs my breath, blocks my air, and stifles my pulse. Lauren glowers but doesn't give me the time of day. She angles her body as if doing everything in her power to avoid my gaze.

"Lauren, may I call you Lauren?"

She nods, then says, "That's my name."

Wayne chuckles, but it's quiet enough I'm sure I'm the only one who hears. That's the woman I love. The spitfire Lauren no one can break once she makes up her mind. My already broken heart crumbles at the thought. She's already decided my guilt.

"You and Luke planned to go to college together didn't you?"

She cocked her head. "At one time, yes."

"And what did you plan to study?"

"He wanted to be a doctor while I majored in psychology."

"Interesting. So you had big dreams?"

When Lauren nods, Wayne reminds her to speak up for the court reporter. "I suppose," she says.

"You wanted to study psychology?"

"Yes, sir."

"So you enjoy studying people?"

"I enjoy helping them. But I hadn't decided on a doctorate."

"Do you consider yourself a good judge of character?"

"I did, before."

"So you're saying you are not a good judge of character? I mean, you didn't even know your boyfriend's true nature after all these years?"

"Objection." Mr. Benoit stands, and I almost stand with him. Wayne warned me he'd have to be harsh, but this is ridiculous.

I have so many questions to ask Lauren. So many. But Wayne has pissed her off.

She finally looks at me, her gaze frigid, her eyes a hard flint. "I guess I'm not," she answers cooly before the judge can make his ruling.

"I pass the witness."

She looks away. A sliver of glass cuts into my jugular. My emotions are too raw, too new. I miss her like crazy, and I miss Elizabeth too. Never having a chance to say goodbye sucks. Never having a chance to grieve sucks worse.

Mr. Benoit leans forward, something he always does when he's trying to make a point. Who cares. I have nothing left to lose.

"What's the last thing you remember about Elizabeth?" he asks.

"She was standing at the curb, waving goodbye."

"And do you feel guilty about leaving her?"

"Every day." She hangs her head and sobs.

Luke Present Day

The creek roared over the roadway on the first low water crossing. The next two would be worse.

He'd predicted they'd be up because of how hard and fast it had rained, but no point in telling her so. Better to see for herself. She considered him a murderer, so being with him couldn't be easy. Too bad. She chose to confront him.

They reached his home. She walked up the steps and across the porch, her gaze pointed to the ground. Eyeing her pistol, she snatched it up and slid it into her purse.

"I'm sorry," Luke said, his voice croaky and clipped.

She turned to him, eyes flaring, but she didn't speak.

"I'm sorry about what happened," he continued, offering a head nod in the direction they'd had sex, as if further explanation was necessary.

"Let's pretend it never did." She swiped her hand across a chair to check for moisture and sat, clutching her turquoise purse.

Why was he apologizing? She was the one who came to his house and threatened him. He'd spent the last twelve years of his life—the most important years of his life—

behind bars for a crime he didn't commit. And although he refused to despair over losing out on his twenties—college, first job, first house, kid—adjusting was damn hard sometimes.

LED lights glimmered across the top of the railing, but the light also cast shadows, and the shadows were tough to endure.

He remained standing and shoved his hands in his pockets. "I want you to know... I mean, I don't know what protection you use, but there's nothing to worry about from me."

"Nothing to worry about?" Panic stretched her words high and tight.

"I mean, I don't have any diseases, in case you were wondering."

"Oh, so you've been checked?" Sarcasm rolled off her voice. That and something else impossible to name as her body remained tense on the seat.

"I see a doctor like anyone else. And I've never had sex with a man to answer your unasked question."

She shifted in her seat and glared at him, her nose flaring. He didn't mind making her uncomfortable. This was her fault. She'd chosen to come here. Many people assumed the worst about prisoners. They were raped, brutalized, perhaps part of a gang. And while he had been in plenty of fights and had to choose his acquaintances wisely, he handled himself just fine. He quickly learned who to have in his corner.

"What happened changes nothing," she blurted.

"Never expected otherwise. Consider what happened between us a commencement ceremony."

"This is no beginning of us."

"No. But it's a beginning of my life. And an end to us. A goodbye we never had."

Smoke billowed out of the grill. The charred steak spoiled the fresh rain-soaked air. He had been setting aside the steak and potatoes when a commotion echoed the earth and car lights cut through the trees to the east where she had driven. He'd reacted in terror, racing to figure out what had happened and see if she was okay.

"Want something to eat?" he asked. "I can't promise this steak will taste good, unless you like it blackened, but the potatoes are good and I've got salad."

"I'm not hungry. Thank you."

He opened the ice chest and pulled out a beer, forcing himself to blow this off as if none of it mattered. It might not be best to pretend nothing happened, but that's exactly what he planned to do. "What about a beer?"

She nodded. "Sure I'll take a beer."

She took the bottle, and he sat. The rain died. Crickets announced a safety to emerge, their chirrups a pulsating energy around them. The creeks would recede in an hour or so, but for now he enjoyed his drink.

Although he shouldn't try, his instinct was to put her at ease. She believed she was alone with a killer and a man who had recently violated her.

He'd thought to never see her again, taste her, or hear her voice. She'd been his inspiration even while in prison and the small photo pinned to his wall kept him from slipping too far under. At times it would have the opposite effect and make him spiral into depression, but the hope of her smile always helped.

He was no stalker. Pictures of his family, his sister and his old pets had also hung on the wall near his bed. Something to help him remember his humanity.

She had been a huge part of him. They planned to marry, start a life together, and continue their education together. Maybe one day even have children together. Yes, that was the past and he couldn't live in the past, but neither could he destroy his memories. He didn't want to.

"So what did you end up doing with your life?" he asked. Lauren had huge aspirations, and he wondered if she'd pursued her dreams. She'd loved to paint, but her main goal in life was to help others. Psychology interested her, and at one time she had planned on becoming a psychologist.

"I'm not here to make small talk," she spat.

"Oh right, you're here to kill me."

Her shoulders tensed, the shadows creating an ethereal aura around her. But he wasn't dreaming, and the waves of hostility pouring from her body were palpable.

"Well, I hope you continued to paint," he said. She had been a talented painter, her art stirring him into a slow ride to oblivion.

She drank her beer, leaving his question unanswered.

"You want another?"

"Sure."

He stood, grabbed another beer out of the ice chest, twisted off the top and handed it to her.

"Thank you," she said, her voice a low garble.

He settled in his seat and kicked up his feet on the opposite chair. He rested his head on the chair and closed his eyes. This had been his intention all along, sleep outside until the heat became too unbearable. But the rain had eased the temperature, and a slight breeze stirred the air. Those conditions this time of year usually roused humidity, but tonight was beautiful.

Minutes passed. He didn't drift off. More like a meditative state. The river flowed near his home, and the music of nature put him at ease.

"I didn't continue to paint. Not really."

Her voice startled him. He jumped and straightened. Beer sloshed over his torso. She ducked her head to hide her smile. He hated that she hid her humor when she once laughed.

Another piece of his heart broke.

Lauren didn't know why she spoke. She should have let him doze off. She wouldn't be sleeping tonight, not until she had her car and was home.

She didn't want him to know about her personal life. Best if he didn't know about her job, about Laramie, or about what she did for fun. She barely recognized what she did for fun anymore.

"I'm sorry," he said. "Why didn't you?"

Lauren shrugged and sipped her beer. "My life is too busy to worry about such nonsense."

"Painting isn't nonsense."

She picked at her shirt, bare of anything to pick besides the memory of his closeness. "Mine is," she said, keeping her head lowered and away from his gaze.

"No, it isn't. It never was."

Ridiculous to resort to self-pity to earn his approval. They weren't kids anymore. The only goodbye she had wanted to share with him was to see him buried. The dirt slapping over his grave, the moist soil mingling with the sweat and her tears. She was being harsh, unforgiving, but she had suffered hate and confusion and resentment for too long. The last thing they needed now was to pretend they were friends.

Even if she forgave him.

"You shouldn't stop doing something you love just because life gets in the way," he said.

How did you become such an expert in prison? She wanted to ask, but clamped her mouth closed. She denied telling him she hadn't painted because she focused on giving her child a good life, or her last painting was paint-by-number when Laramie was young enough to enjoy it.

An hour later, she rode with him in his monstrous Jeep to check the creek beds. Her pulse thrummed under her skin. The creeks rose swiftly, but soon receded once the rain stopped.

They crossed the first creek, the water roaring, and she gripped the *oh-shit* handle. His doors and top were off and she felt she'd fall out at any moment, even with the seatbelt.

"My lifted Jeep made it, but I don't think your little SUV would."

"Probably not," she said.

The river roared nearby. It reminded her of static on a television, a perpetual surge over rocks and gravel and road. But this was hushed, stable, and calming.

They approached the second, and he parked his Jeep off to the side and turned on his hazards, then jumped out to check the waters.

"This one is way too deep." He climbed back in. "Sorry. Maybe another hour if it doesn't rain again."

A cold knot of dread bunched in her stomach. Another hour would be past midnight. She shouldn't have come here, but now she must face the consequences.

They made it back to his house and once again sat outside. A tingle rushed up the back of her neck, face and ears. She fidgeted in her seat and scoured the dark night as awkwardness consumed them.

"If I'm keeping you from something, like sleep," she said, her voice shaky, "then you don't have to babysit."

"You could sleep here tonight," Luke said. "I planned on sleeping out on the porch anyway."

"No." She stood. "I'm going to walk back to my car, now. See if I can start and move it." She hated to ask—Luke owed her nothing—so she said it as a statement. He could accept it, or not. Offer to help, or not. She wasn't sure she even wanted him to. She hated the dark, but she had a flashlight on her phone, and her phone had enough charge.

He stood along with her. "You won't be getting that car out of the mud by yourself."

"How can you be so sure?"

"I'm sure. But if it'll make you feel better, I'll take you to your car and see if we can get it unstuck." He pointed behind him, toward the trees and the darkness. "I need to take a piss first."

"Don't you have a bathroom for that?"

"Yup. But I'm not going to use it." He turned to walk off the deck, then stopped and eyeballed her. "If you need to, though, you remember where it's at."

She nodded. She needed to but didn't want to ask or go inside his house. Still, better than going roadside.

He strolled down the steps, and she admired his confident swagger. That hadn't changed, not really. He'd always had that style, now edgier and more unrefined. She peeked at the deck post where earlier they had tangled together, then pivoted to the door. His brand burned on her skin, the memory of the two of them an image she'd rather forget.

She stepped inside his home and took a reeling breath. Nothing much had changed. Touches of his mom and two sisters consumed every inch. The photos, the plants and the decorative washboard wall-hanging his mother had bought at a garage sale. She gulped back a cry at the memory of Cindy, gone way too soon. He was in prison when she was diagnosed with cancer, and although he'd missed the terrible stages of her disease, he'd also missed her funeral.

Lauren had missed it too and cried for days. She'd loved Cindy like her own mother. His sister Adrienne had reached out time after time to plead his case, but she refused to talk.

She'd missed so many moments with a family she loved. Her almost in-laws.

Cindy had died before Lauren moved back and never knew she had a grandchild. The town continued to grow, and although Terrence hadn't lost its small-town charm, many newcomers and changes made it easier to get lost in the shuffle. Easier to escape the past. Easier to blend in.

Another gulp of tears, and Lauren realized she was standing in the living room looking at the pictures on the wall. She shuffled to the bathroom and locked the door.

Melancholy. Only melancholy. She had to get her life back to normal before she exposed too many secrets.

CHAPTER THREE

Luke Twelve Years Ago

I CAN BARELY WAIT for tonight.

I've already proposed to Lauren—and she said yes—but I'm more nervous now than I was when I slipped the ring on her finger.

I've got news, and I'm not sure how she'll take it.

I pick her up at our allotted time, and my pulse jumps when she saunters out the door and waves. I would greet her, but she's told me a million times it annoys her. And I relish sitting in the driver's side, watching her approach. Although she is anything but high-maintenance, I have a feeling she loves it, her one time to strut across a runway. Lord knows she's got what it takes to be a model.

I spot her little sister playing in the yard and hope we can get out of here before she badgers us. She's a cute kid, but she'll beg to go with us and Lauren will eventually relent.

"Hey, Luke," Elizabeth says as she approaches.

"Hey, Squirt."

"What you up to today?"

"Taking Lauren out for some adult time." I cringe. My words came out wrong. What I meant was she wasn't welcome and please don't invite yourself. But I never have the right words for Lauren's little sister.

"Lizzie, doll, we have plans today," Lauren says. She pats her on the head and gives her a kiss on the cheek. "Go back inside and play. Mom will be home soon. You promise you're okay to stay alone?"

"I told you a million times I don't mind being alone. Although maybe I should lie and say I do. Does that mean I can go with y'all?"

"Not this time," Lauren says, and I breathe out a sigh of relief. "Love you. See you in a bit."

Lauren grabs the Jeep's 'oh-shit' handle and vaults into the seat. It's easy to do with no doors, but having no doors sucks when I want my hands all over her body. Which is all the time. Makes it harder to hide my intentions from the outside world, and her parents like to peek out the window when I bring her home at night.

"Bye, Lisa," I say and wave.

"Bye."

She is standing at the curb waving as I turn the corner. She's a cute kid. A sweet kid. Her name is Elizabeth, but she prefers to be called Lisa. Lauren calls her by her full name or Lizzie, and I generally call her Elizabeth because that's what Lauren prefers.

"Too many L words," she once claimed. I argued Lizzie was an L word, but she didn't budge from her opinion.

I take Lauren on a drive through the country. It's June in Texas, blistering hot, and I've lost my favorite cap so I have nothing to protect my head.

Her skirt reveals long legs, a lacy blouse I'll unbutton later, and red polish on her toes with the sexiest strappy sandals. A strand of hair escapes her ponytail and coils down her back. I reach over to tuck it behind her ear, then I squeeze her leg and slide my hand up to rest against her inner thigh. Our gazes meet and she gives me a smile that makes me want to give up everything for her.

She bumps her forehead to mine and curls her fingers through my hair. My body heats and tightens. "You aren't wearing that stupid cap," she says.

"Hey, what's wrong with my cap?"

"I prefer to see your beautiful hair."

"I lost my damn cap," I say.

She chuckles. "Good."

We run around town for a while, grab a sweet tea at the beer barn, and take a drive through the back roads. She claims she isn't hungry or in the mood to swim, so we drive to Cedar Falls to shop at the outdoor mall. She declines a movie at the theater, and I'm ready to tell her my news, so we go to my home.

I pull into the driveway but continue off the road into the pasture and down the hill to the river, a hundred feet from the house and covered by trees. I park near a large rock, tempted to go off into the sand where we can really be alone, but it's illegal. Later, we might swim, but for now we sit and enjoy the view. Birds dip in and out of the water. Water ripples over the rocks.

This has become our special spot. It's far enough away from my house where we have privacy but still on my property where we aren't trespassing. The river's grousing roar reminds me of a mating call and soothes my chaotic nerves. Shade trees make the temps bearable. The sun is crisp, sparkling like a fine bottle of champagne, and ducks swim along the sandbar.

Things couldn't be more perfect.

"What did you want to tell me?" Lauren asks. I had

already told her I had news I wanted to announce before we went out to dinner. My nerves are a jumbled mess. I should have packed us a picnic lunch. That would have been romantic.

Instead of telling her, I reach over to the glove compartment, where I remove the acceptance letter from Columbia University. I hand her the letter. Her eyebrows squinch together and she takes the paper.

"What's this?" She reads, then drops the page in her lap. "I... I... don't know what to say."

Congratulations, maybe? I say nothing. My breath is heavy, and she faces forward. Her profile is vicious. My pulse skitters. She needs time to absorb, but I should have handled this better.

"Wow," she says. "This... this... I mean, I didn't know this was your dream."

My gut ties in knots. I expected a better reaction although I don't know what. She's the first person I've told. Not even my parents know yet. "It's not Harvard, but Columbia University is not something to balk out when it comes to my doctorate."

"No. No, of course it isn't. But it would have been nice to know."

"To know what?"

"To know you applied. That you were interested."

"You knew I wanted to be a doctor."

She finally faces me. Her fists clench in her lap. "Of course you want to be a doctor. But you never said you applied to New York almost two thousand miles away. Don't you think I should have known?"

When I don't reply, she lowers her gaze and fiddles with the ring on her finger. The sparkles are a beacon of hope. We will get through this like we do everything else.

I don't reply. My breath tangles with my voice and rubs

my throat raw. I don't know what to think or how to respond, but I expected excitement. She knows how much I've yearned to be a doctor, eventually to specialize in oncology since my mother has battled cancer and has been in remission the past three years.

"This has been my dream…"

"New York has been your dream?"

"It isn't about New York."

Her laugh is a choking snigger of sound and fizzles on impact. She yanks off the engagement ring and tosses it at my chest. It falls, and I fish for it in my lap.

"What about this?" she asks. "Doesn't this mean anything to you?"

"Of course it does. You can apply there too. We can make things work."

"If you wanted me to go, you would have told me you applied and we could have applied at the same time like we have everywhere else."

"I never thought to be accepted. I'm still not sure we can afford it." My parents had put aside money, but even with scholarships I'm doubtful it'll be enough.

Her head rests on the seat. "Just take me home."

"Lauren."

"Now. I want to go home. I don't want to talk to you about this anymore. You don't get it. At all. And I need time to process. I need time to myself."

I sit there a moment, reach out for her, but she slinks away. What can I do? Annoyance clips my desire to make things right with her. She should support me. Love me. Why does she need time to think? It's not a big deal. A couple thousand miles isn't anything when you're in love, and any college would welcome her.

I take her home. She doesn't relax on the ride. I stop in

the driveway and draw her in for a kiss, but she jerks away and hops out of the Jeep.

"Lauren," I call, her name the afternoon's mantra.

She ignores me, and I let her go. She doesn't get angry often. I don't get angry often. But sometimes, we need our space. Now is one of those times. The Jeep idles until she's safely inside, then I pull away, my rage flaring.

She could at least support me.

Eventually, she will. We have a connection. Once she settles down, she'll reach out to me and be sorry and we'll figure out what to do. I don't have to go to Columbia, and I refuse to go anywhere that risks our relationship.

A breeze stirs the air, into the door-less Jeep and patters into my pulse. The summer chill comes quick and fragile. Anything could happen. I don't want to fight. I want to turn back, tell her I'm sorry, and beg her to listen. Tell her never mind if she accepted the apology.

But I'm allowed to be mad at her for a while longer.

Luke Present Day

Luke escorted Lauren to the passenger side of the Jeep to make sure she didn't need help to get up the lifted vehicle. She managed fine the first time, but being a gentleman was ingrained in him, even if there were no doors to open. He kept his four doors and top off since a carport covered it to keep it safe from the elements.

He didn't invade her space, and she pulled herself up by the handle before settling in the seat. He strolled to the driver's side, fired up the engine, and shifted it in gear.

"I see you finally got your dream Jeep," she said.

He nodded then, realizing she couldn't see him in the dark night, said, "Yup. My first purchase as soon as I got released."

"Did you buy it tricked out like this?"

His lungs expanded at her memory, and he took a deep, satisfying breath. "No. I bought an old used one and put a lot of work into it. Still not finished yet."

"Looks nice. You do any off-roading?"

"A little, yeah."

He'd love to ask her to go off-roading with him. In the old days, he owned a used two-door Wrangler they had taken on many adventures, but he'd always dreamed of upgrading and promised her they would travel and explore the world.

They had fun on their road trips together. He wasn't trying to impress her now, but his heart lifted at her compliment.

His mind had no room for *if-only*, but the memories tugged at his heart. They were good memories and had kept him grounded in his darkest days. He breathed in the rain-soaked air, but the Texas humidity came out with the heat, and the mosquitoes.

Lauren slapped at her arm.

"Sorry. I should have grabbed bug spray."

"It's fine. This shouldn't take long."

He stopped, the headlights pointing at her car, and flicked on his hazards. She continued to sit while he grabbed a flashlight, trudged to her vehicle, and turned on hers. No sense taking any unnecessary risk.

He pulled the cable out of the Jeep's winch and connected it to the rear of the Escape's chassis. If he was a different man, he'd take his time and prolong their visit, but he wanted out of her presence as fast as she wanted out of his.

For different reasons. She wanted out of his because she thought he was a killer. He wanted out of hers because she stirred in him longings he couldn't afford to have. Longings for a normal life, to talk with her about their lives now, their lives then, and their future dreams. Her scent, like honey covering a fresh bowl of strawberries, incited his hunger to taste her skin. Every hitch of her breath made him hard.

He backed up, pulled the vehicle out of the mud and parked near the road, then jumped out again to unhook. He skirted the Ford to check on things. The passenger side needed repaired and she couldn't open the door until then. He fired up the engine and listened to make sure nothing sounded too uncertain, but everything else seemed safe for her to drive home. She approached but kept her distance. Her lips trembled.

She didn't cry, though, despite her somber expression. She lowered her gaze, and he longed to trace his fingers along her jaw and kiss away her anxieties.

Few people drove on this ranch road, especially at night. He parked the vehicles off to the side, but as much as he'd love to stand here with her and invent all kinds of reasons to check her vehicle, he didn't want to risk someone out this late hitting them.

"You're good to go, but I'll follow you to the creeks until I know you crossed all three."

She finally looked at him, her eyes gleaming with tears. He wanted to take her in his arms and hold her, tell her prison hadn't hardened his heart. It had changed him, taken pieces of him, but he was a man capable of compassion.

"You don't have to do that," she said.

"I will anyway."

She climbed inside but rolled the window down before she shut the door. He fixed his forearms on the opening. "You should take this to a body shop. Jim's Auto Body has a good reputation. You'll have to file an insurance claim and it'll go against your collision. They'll ask how it happened."

"I don't plan on filing a claim."

"Are you going to drive around with it damaged like that? You need to make sure you have no underlying damage."

"I'll just pay for it out of pocket."

He let out a low whistle. "That will be a pretty penny."

"How would you know?"

"Well, I didn't completely lose my senses in prison."

She blinked a slow, regretful, full-on grievous but also disdainful blink. "Look... I—"

He held up his hand. "You don't need to say it."

Squinting down at her lap, she nodded, her lips trembling again. "I do. I need to say I'm sorry. I'm sorry for coming out here tonight. I'm sorry for..."

"Trying to kill me," he said, his playful voice lightening the mood.

Her lips thinned and she nodded. Her eyes didn't even gleam in laughter.

"We both lived through it. But it's late. So get home. Follow me, and I'll cross the creeks first to make sure they're safe for you."

She didn't argue. "Okay. Thanks for your help."

He slapped his hands on the window frame then turned and trudged away. She waited for him instead of taking off, surprising him by following. He crossed the first creek. His heart tripped after the second because the night was almost over and she would be out of his life. After he passed the last low-water crossing, he stuck his hand out the Jeep and waved to show all was fine. She drove through slowly, then flashed her lights at him. He honked once before turning around.

Pain rose in the back of his throat, his heart a slow descent as it flipped to his gut. Some things hadn't changed. Even as teenagers, this had been their ritual if she had been out to his house late and he hadn't driven her home when she was insistent she was fine to drive herself. And now, like then, he worried for her safety. But he couldn't expect her to let him know she made it home.

He could have told her... so many things. Like how much he knew about fixing wrecked vehicles and why. And how much he'd dreamed of seeing her again. Touching her again and breathing her in again. And his regrets. He never should have taken her like that in her vulnerable state, but he'd probably do it again if given an opportunity.

They had loved each other at one time. He'd worked hard to get over her—he wasn't sure he was over her—but their circumstances were way too serious to renew any relationship.

Luke was sitting on the porch, tying his shoes and preparing to go down to the river, when his cell phone rang an unfamiliar number. The man identified himself as the District Attorney. It took a moment for his brain to catch up to his pulse, but when it did, it whirled.

Why would the DA call him on a Sunday morning? Was he calling to apologize? He wasn't the elected DA back when Luke was sentenced, but the former DA had been awful. He had suppressed evidence on Luke and no telling how many other cases. Luke no longer trusted anyone in criminal justice.

"Do you have a moment to talk?" the man—who had identified himself as Brian Wimberly—asked.

Luke had all the time in the world, even if he did have a lot to catch up on after being imprisoned, but he didn't bother saying that.

"What can I help you with?"

"Well, I'd like to make you an offer."

Luke steeled and held his breath, waiting for the man to continue. If he was expecting Luke to beg for him to ask, he'd wait forever.

"We have an upcoming conference and the speaker cancelled because of an emergency. I know it is last minute, but I'm part of the committee for this conference, and I thought you'd be the perfect candidate. We'd like to invite you to share your story with this group of people, and what you're facing now."

Luke's chuckle emerged in an exaggerated sigh. He'd had offerings from the press to share his story, even one lady who wanted to write his life's account, but he turned them all away with promises to think about it. He refused to allow someone else to write his life's details. "I'm not sure you'd want to hear my story."

"Oh… I… we'd want to keep out the intimate details."

Luke threw his head back and laughed. Guffawed was more like it. He'd like to make the man uncomfortable, served him right. "You want to hear about how the District Attorney withheld evidence that led to my conviction? How the mayor was the father of the man who actually committed this murder I served time for, and he did everything in his power to make sure his son wasn't involved? Bribing the police, the District Attorney, and even his staff? Is that the story you want, or do you want a nice, sweet package of forgiveness?"

The DA hesitated. His breath was loud, sizzling through the speaker. Luke's pulse rose.

"This is a convention for District and County Attorneys and their staff. But we aren't like that. This town had a bad batch, unfortunately, but that was a long time ago. I hope your story will prevent something like that from happening again. Sharing your story could help newbie prosecutors as well as old-timers make sure justice is served and this never happens again."

"I'll have to think about it."

"We pay your travel, meals, and hotel, along with a basic speaker's fee. But we can negotiate with the late notice."

As if his denial had anything to do with money.

"I said I'd have to think about it," he reiterated. He finished tying his laces and stood.

"We need an answer by Monday."

"Tomorrow is short notice," Luke said.

"Unfortunately, we have to fill this speaker soon, since it's so last minute. July eighteenth, in Galveston."

"That is last minute." Two weeks. Luke was finally comfortable in his home again, and he didn't have much ambition to leave.

"Yes, I'm sorry about that. But you get daily meals and hotel for three nights. Why not consider it a nice vacation?"

Oh, cool. After being in prison, the DA expected Luke to jump at the chance to visit the hottest, most humid part of Texas and enjoy the beach.

Luke stepped off the deck and strolled down the path to the river. "You want me to speak for a day and stay for three?"

"Only if you want to. You could leave after the first day."

"You really want me to speak to a room full of prosecutors so soon after my release?"

"I hope you'll tell us the truth and we feel the pain you experienced during this difficult time. I also hope you'll keep the bitterness light. Most of us believe in truth and justice."

"And the American way?" Luke bleated, animosity seizing his throat. Maybe it'd be good to speak to a room full of strangers, people who were supposed to believe in impartiality.

Clint was out there, and if they ever caught him, he faced

a trial. Not near as unfair as Luke's, but Lauren would have to undergo twelve-year-old evidence. Unless Clint took a plea, which was unlikely. No matter what happened, doubters loomed. He hoped law enforcement did everything in their power to find him.

"I'll have an answer for you by tomorrow morning," Luke said, already deciding. He was working on a memoir and had been offered a sweet deal if he ever finished it. Seeing Lauren again complicated things, but speaking at a conference might boost his initiative.

———

Luke strode into work Monday morning, his stomach a bundle of nerves. He had a sleepless night contemplating his decision and called the DA first thing this morning before he changed his mind. Now he needed to talk to Jim.

Speaking at a conference wouldn't affect his job hours. He was part time and set his own hours, but he liked to give his boss plenty of notice. And he needed guidance.

Jim was a good man. He had been a friend of Luke's dad and had stood by his family for years. He hadn't hesitated to hire Luke and didn't worry about losing customers over someone who might not consider Luke innocent. Years of hard labor kept his body permanently slumped, and he had aged hard since he lost his son who had died of cancer around the time Luke went to prison.

Luke had many regrets over losing his friends and family, but not being able to pay his respects to Jim and his wife Claire had been huge.

"How was your weekend, Luke?" Jim approached and shook Luke's hand. Their Monday morning ritual, a handshake, a cup of coffee with chitchat—mostly minor—and then getting to work. Jim had commuted to Austin for years before retiring and opening his own body shop. He didn't want a lot of overhead and had no other employees but Luke and another part-timer who sometimes worked weekends, along with the painter and his prepper to paint all the vehicles. Jim preferred to keep his shop small.

Luke never should have told Lauren about this place but chances were, she would take it to one of the larger shops in town. He had every intention of telling Jim, just in case.

But first, coffee.

"I have a few things to tell you, actually. Let's get that cup of coffee first, shall we?"

"The wife is in there, already screeching and squalling. I know it's hot in this shop, but we're probably better off here."

"Okay. I'll go grab us both a cup and be right back," Luke said. Claire wouldn't screech and squall for long with Luke nearby. She was a lot like her husband, put everyone's needs ahead of her own and loved and supported him like no other. Most people who knew them envied their relationship.

He walked into the office and grabbed two large Styrofoam cups. "Morning, Claire."

"Luke." She stood and rubbed his head as if he was a young child. They had known each other for as long. "Good morning. Have you had a chance yet to talk to Jim?"

"Not yet, no. Well, just a hello. Why? Is something going on?"

"No, no, not at all. He's got a few new vehicles coming in today, but I can't stay. I've got an appointment. I think he was afraid to ask you for more help today."

"Now, why would he be afraid to ask for my help?" Luke poured the two cups and left Jim's black but added cream and sugar to his own. He'd had plenty of bad coffee in prison and had no intentions of drinking dreck ever again.

"Oh, you know Jim." Claire rummaged through papers on

an old metal desk. Clean and organized, except for a scattering of papers she kept tidy.

Luke kissed Claire on the cheek. She wore her white hair short, at the nape, and her makeup was classy and natural, but the hoops in her ears hung past her hair length. "I know you, too, and I know you will be back as soon as you can to help Jim. Don't stress. We've got it handled. I hope everything is okay."

"Sure. Why wouldn't it be?"

"You mentioned an appointment."

She waved her hand and stuck the papers she had been rummaging through in a file folder. "Bah. Just a yearly thing. And you're right, I'll be back before you know it. Now get that coffee out there to Jim so you can start your gossip session."

Luke grinned and grabbed the two cups. She followed him to the door, opened it for him and shooed him out, then waved a kiss at her husband before shutting it behind her.

"Is she still squawking?" Jim asked.

Luke handed Jim his coffee and took a sip of his own. "No. But she mentioned you had a few vehicles coming in today and you don't want to ask for my help."

"Oh, did she now?"

"She did. Any truth to that?"

"Maybe a little. Did she also mention one of those vehicles is Lauren's?"

Luke's heart sunk. Now they were getting to the heart of the problem. "She didn't. But I was going to tell you that was a possibility."

Jim's face went blank, his eyebrows posturing into thin lines. "You knew?"

Luke sat his cup of coffee on his tool chest and grabbed his keys to unlock the cabinet. He needed something to do besides stare at Jim. He had planned to tell him about

Lauren's wreck, but he had no intention of going any further with his story.

"I ran into her Saturday. She had a wreck, and I happened to be nearby. I told her this was a good body shop and thought nothing more of it."

"You didn't tell her you work here?"

"No. I didn't tell her I work here. But look, I don't want any awkwardness and I'm sorry I—"

"Well, it's not your fault. And I could always use the business."

"If you don't want to work on it, we can give it to Kyle."

"Nonsense. You're the best body man I've got."

"Well, besides Kyle, I'm the only body man you've got."

"Still the best I've ever known."

"Yeah but—"

"No buts." Jim held up his hand, a stop gesture, then grabbed a wrench out of Luke's toolbox and tinkered. Luke didn't normally like anyone touching his tools, except for Jim. "I don't want to hear it. There is no conflict with working on her vehicle."

"There are plenty of conflicts to working on her vehicle," Luke said.

Jim rocked back and forth on his heels. "Name one."

"Well, she still thinks I killed her sister. So there's that."

"She's already brought the vehicle. I'm not about to call her and tell her you work here. She'll find out soon enough."

Luke searched the lot but didn't see Lauren's Ford. Jim opened his shop every morning at seven AM, but Luke didn't start until eight. Never one to sleep in, he was usually here by seven-thirty. This time, he was glad to have been running behind and missed seeing Lauren.

He slapped the wrench against his hands. Jim was always tinkering and never able to stand still for long. "She still has to file the claim. She wanted me to take a look at it and give her and estimate before she did file a claim. Says she'd rather not."

"Oh. Well, how about we write up a cheap estimate and I pay for the rest?"

Jim's eyebrows squished together. His brows, thick and dark brown despite the rest of his graying hair, always spoke of his emotions before he did. "I'm not sure that's a good idea."

"Why not?" Luke asked.

"I don't think it's a good idea to get involved."

Luke drained his tepid coffee and grabbed his drill driver. "You're right. I know. Look, I've got that old Chevelle I've got to get in paint by Wednesday, so unless I plan to stay here all hours of the night, I've got to get busy."

Jim dropped the wrench and patted him on the shoulder. "Okay. Sounds good. Nothing else happened over the weekend you want to gossip about?"

"No. Nothing important."

Jim nodded and went to work. Luke turned away, musing in his thoughts.

He would tell his boss about speaking at the conference later.

CHAPTER FOUR

Lauren Twelve Years Ago

Lauren journeyed with unsteady legs into the prosecutor's office and sat on the chair beside her parents. The DA had already introduced himself as Dan Benoit when he greeted them in the lobby. She had already met the Victim Coordinator, who had walked them through the court process, handed out paperwork, and offered counseling among many other services.

Two months had passed since Elizabeth's death and Luke's arrest, but they had been the longest of her life. She refused counseling, but every day she wondered if she shouldn't find someone besides her parents and her friends to talk to. Most of her friends were preparing for college and although Clint had stood by her, she hated to concern him. Luke had been his best friend, and he hurt also.

Mr. Benoit sat at his desk, a large Banker's box with Luke's name scripted on the side with a Sharpie. Lauren's stomach churned, the box taunting her.

"Thanks for coming in. I've asked you here to let you know the status of Lucas Fuller's case and the evidence we have on him and talk to you about what happens next. The trial starts in November."

"November?" Lauren screeched. "That's only three months away." Impossible to prepare herself in such a short time. Then again, judging by the last two months, three would drag.

"Defense filed a motion for speedy trial and I believe I've got everything I need to convict. There's no doubt he killed her. His blood was all over the place. His knife. His cap. A torn piece of his shirt. He almost admitted it."

Her ears rang with the news. "He almost admitted it?"

"Officer Johnson believes he would have if his defense attorney hadn't saved him. But we still have evidence and witnesses."

"What kind of witnesses?" her mom asked. Her mom, who had fluctuated between being a basket case or being a rock. Everyone's emotions scattered from one extreme to another. Today, her chin was lifted, shoulders straight, her hands clenched in her lap, determined to see the man who killed her daughter was punished.

"Witnesses say they saw Elizabeth walking along the road and Luke picked her up."

"Adrienne told me she saw Lizzie with Clint," Lauren said.

Her mom's eyes grew wide and desperate when she turned her head to look at her. Her chin trembled, eyes watery. "You've been talking to Adrienne?"

"Not really. But she called me to try to talk."

"Adrienne will say whatever she can to save her brother," the DA said. "She's also the one who found Elizabeth."

Chills wracked Lauren's body, then a wave of heat so intense, she grew dizzy. Her mind swarmed. How angry had

Luke been when she left him that afternoon? Angry enough to kill? She had known him for years. How could he have killed her sister? Sure, Elizabeth annoyed him sometimes, but she was a cute young kid who liked to be the center of attention, and sometimes he didn't want to give her the time of day.

Her dad studied her, brows lowered and posture rigid, but she squirmed at her mom's squinty gaze. She hadn't meant to upset them.

"I plan to prove Adrienne knew where to find Elizabeth because Luke told her," the prosecutor continued.

Lauren flinched, her blood running cold. She shook her head over and over. "No." No, no, no, how could Luke do this to her? To her family? Impossible to believe he had. And yet, impossible to believe he hadn't. All the evidence pointed to his guilt.

"I'm sorry, Lauren. I really, really am. I know this is hard for you. Clint told us something too."

"What did Clint tell you?" her father asked, the first time he spoke since they sat.

"He said Luke liked to look at pictures of young girls."

"That's not true!" Lauren screeched. She had known him for years. Wouldn't she know this about him?

"We found proof. In his room."

She vaulted up, the chair bouncing on its legs before settling on the ground. Her chest tightened, lungs hardened, a swarm of darkness surrounding her. Luke wasn't the man she thought he was. He had lied, kept secrets from her. He'd applied to a college she didn't know about. And if he liked looking at young children? Is that what drew him to be a doctor? They had a healthy sex life—too healthy sometimes—but she was naïve in the ways of men's preferences. And there were plenty of times she wondered if she was enough for him.

Lauren's legs tightened, nausea bubbling in her throat. She felt like throwing up. "I can't talk about this anymore."

"Lauren." Her mom stood and reached out. Her face was pale, lined in wrinkles. Lauren felt worse for stressing her mom out even more than she already was, but didn't they understand her grief? She had lost her sister and her boyfriend at the same time.

Lauren trampled to the window and peered outside. The courthouse loomed across the street. The office was part of an annex of other county buildings. Several shops and eateries circled the main square. She hadn't been inside the courthouse since she was a child on a school field trip, but she and her friends loved to stop at the cafes and coffee shops. So did she and Luke at one time.

"I'm not sure she's ready," her dad muttered, but she heard every word as if he was talking through a bullhorn. "I'm not sure any of us are."

"I wish we could get him to plea," Mr. Benoit said. "But he refuses, and I don't think his attorney is going to convince him."

Luke had lied about college. They had planned to take the summer off and start a year late. They didn't want to hold off getting married, but they didn't want to put off college either. Meanwhile, he was applying to a different university two thousand miles away. Luke was smart. He wanted to be a doctor, and she planned to major in psychology even if she didn't go after her doctorate. She wasn't smart enough to apply to Columbia or any of those fancy universities, but they could have made things work.

Luke was smart, and he was smart enough to kill and think he could get away with it.

Mr. Benoit continued, and she focused on his words. "We need to rush this as quick as we can while we can. People's memories fade. Evidence gets tainted. If Lauren can't testify—"

She reeled around and interrupted. "I'll testify." She would do anything necessary for her sister's justice. Even testify against the boy she once loved.

Lauren Present Day

LAUREN MADE it to work the next morning, her belly in knots. Nobody knew what she had done this weekend, how tempted she'd been to take Luke's life, but she cringed at every hello.

She'd never been a great liar.

How was your weekend?

Well, I almost killed a man. Contemplated it and even pointed the gun at his chest. Then we screwed against the deck pole.

Not her best choice when she was the Victim Coordinator for the District Attorney's Office.

Her body tensed when Brian called her into his office. Throat tight and legs a gluey mess, she flitted to the back of the building. He usually came into her office to discuss cases. Everyone knew things were serious when he called you to go to him.

"Good morning," she said, way too cheerfully. She flounced in and shut the door. Might as well try to feel cheery. Fake it until you make it and all that.

A young girl's death by a local man had been huge news, and his release had been nationwide for a while. The District Attorney's Office covered four counties, and back then the office was located in the next county over, forty miles away. No one in the office had worked under the previous DA and most people hadn't grown up here or had first hand knowledge of the case, so no one pieced Lauren and Elizabeth Cooper together. She'd kept that part of her life off limits and didn't have many personal conversations about her past with her coworkers. Brian was the only one who knew before he hired her, and he swore to keep her secret.

"Good morning," he replied. "Please sit. I have something to tell you."

Oh God, did he know what she did Saturday night? Had Luke called the cops? Threatening him with a gun on his property was a crime. She could be arrested, taken to jail.

She sank into the hard leather chair. Two months ago, when he had something important to tell her, she'd learned the man accused of murdering her sister was being released. She thought she could deal with it, and maybe she could have until she learned he was back home, staying in the house he had grown up in. Why had she confronted him? Why had she obsessed over it until she finally confronted him? And why, even after seeing him, was she obsessing over the next time she might see him again?

She had no idea how to explain any of this to Brian.

Brian was in his mid-fifties, sharp witted and unrivaled in a jury trial. Unrivaled most anywhere, really. Fit and trim, his dark hair was thick but short, sprinkled with a heaping of salt at his temples, and his leathery brown eyes were soft enough to persuade anyone to his side. He was a career prosecutor and loved everything about his profession.

And although he was kind, he was a bulldog and knew how to apply mental pressure.

She fidgeted and cleared her throat. "What is it?" she asked, urging her shoulders not to hunch.

His fingers formed a steeple, his elbows on the desk and he leaned forward. A moment's hesitation. "I've asked Lucas Fuller to speak at our conference."

She shot out of her chair in a half-stand, half-squat, and gripped the sides. "You what?"

He held up his hand. "Sit down. Relax."

The chair squeaked when she sat, releasing the pressure within the leather as if belching out her burdens.

"Mr. Long cancelled, and I needed a quick replacement. The board and I agreed he'd make a good candidate, but I wasn't sure he'd agree. He did."

"He did?" Her voice squeaked.

She urged herself to breathe and counted the pictures on the wall behind him. Three tense and lifeless pictures. One of him standing with two other attorneys she didn't know, one of him speaking in a conference much like the one he'd asked Luke to speak at, and one of him sitting at the bench in the courtroom. All done in black and white. No personal mementos or photos of his family. He claimed he liked to keep those out of business so nobody knew enough about him to make him vulnerable.

As if he was a superhero. She trusted Brian, despite his intimidation tactics, but this blank slate of an office ramped up her frazzled nerves. He chewed on his lower lip, his eyes hooded, seeming to draw away from her as if he didn't appreciate her reaction.

Well, tough luck. How else was she supposed to act when he told her the man accused of murdering her sister was speaking at the conference? She looked forward to the event but now wanted to avoid the place. Did he expect her to react with the calmness and professionalism she'd displayed throughout her six years working for him?

"Do you have a problem with the speaker? We're professionals here, you know."

She swallowed her resentment, her *unprofessional* backlash.

Brian was a good man, a good boss, and a great District

Attorney. Nothing in her job had ever been as personal as this, and it hurt he considered this okay. Hurt he thought she should be fine and just deal with it *as a professional.*

"Of course I have a problem with the speaker. Is that even a question?"

"You could always cancel," he continued, but she'd never consider that. She was teaching a workshop with a colleague and had been looking forward to it. Why should his speech be more important than the class she was to teach on victims?

"You want me to cancel?" she asked, hurt and anger screeching her voice. "I'm teaching a class and you want me to cancel? Why should I? Is that what you want?" Her words babbled way too fast.

She would avoid Luke. The hotel was big enough, and no one could tie them together unless he said something, which she doubted.

"No. Well, I thought you might prefer to—"

"No."

"Oh, ok. That's fine. That's great. I'm glad you're okay with it."

"I'm not okay with it," she said, her voice deadpan.

His face flushed and his lips tightened in a smile. To him, any uncontrolled emotion exposed a weakness. "You don't have to speak with him. I'm not sure he'll stay the whole time or just the first day. He might not even recognize you."

Oh, he would recognize her. Even if she hadn't appeared on his porch and threatened his life.

"Why don't you tell me about him? Why you think he'll make a good candidate? Why you think he's innocent."

"Lauren—"

She held up a hand to stop his interruption. "I know, I know. Last time you told me, I didn't want to hear it. But I'm ready now." Last time they talked about Luke was when he told her Luke was being exonerated, and she was too upset to listen.

He pointed to a large box in the back corner of his office. "There's the file if you want to review it."

She shook her head, dread foaming in her throat. She didn't want to see it. Not everything anyway. She'd seen plenty of gruesome pictures in her career here, but she couldn't handle seeing crime scene photos of her sister.

He unfolded his hands and grabbed a pen, twiddling it between his fingers. "The investigation was sloppy. The sloppiest I've ever seen. But the prosecution was sloppier. Everyone involved deserves to lose their license. If the mayor was alive, he deserves to be behind bars for corruption. The crime scene was tainted. The mayor lied, and several witnesses who had vile things to say about Clint were either never questioned, or never put on the stand. The cops here thought they had their boy. The mayor helped convince them they had their boy. If the knife belonging to Luke hadn't been discovered, several other things belonging to Luke were scattered throughout the property for officers to find. Things his best friend could have easily filched. Most were never tested for DNA. The biggest find, of course, was the knife. The blood on that knife belonged to Elizabeth Cooper and Clint Merkel. The sweat in the cap belonged to Luke Fuller and Clint Merkel. The prosecution team destroyed evidence, and the mayor offered donations to his elected officials. One of them admitted to the cover-up."

"But why?"

"Because Mayor Merkel was a big deal in Terrence County. Not only was he the mayor, but he owned several businesses around here and hugely supported the elected officials and the cops. You were too young to remember or know about all those galas the mayor threw. He was rich.

Had no business being a mayor. His concern wasn't the town of Terrence."

Lauren chewed over everything he said. Her parents accepted the facts they were told and moved on. But she had worked for this office too long to even fathom anyone that corrupt. The bad guys, yes. But those whose entire job revolved around seeking justice?

"That's a lot of people to be involved for someone not to crack and say something," she said.

"Most of them did their job and went home. They did what the sheriff and district attorney told them to do. Any of the reports by the officers contradicting anything they had to say was never brought to light because they were never put on the stand and the defense attorney didn't know about them. The investigator hoped to be sheriff one day. And the mayor was running the show."

Lauren rubbed her forehead and gave a light head shake. Brian was on his second term as DA and had been DA for over six years. She'd started working for him soon after, but she remembered the previous DA, Dan Benoit, and his first assistant, Patrick Ratliff. She also remembered Patrick running for election, and how brutally Brian defeated him. Brian had cleaned house.

"What about the witnesses they say saw my sister walking down the street and Luke picked her up in his Jeep?"

"One of those witnesses was elderly and died a few years back. The other was questioned again by his attorneys in the exoneration process. He claimed he couldn't say it was Luke, but a man wearing the cap Luke often wore. He also said it wasn't Luke's Jeep, and he didn't recognize the vehicle. Didn't even remember if it was a Jeep. And the cops were so adamant they confused him. His testimony was skewed."

"What about photos of naked girls?"

"How often did Clint go into his room?"

Lauren's face burned. Too much information to process. Her stomach revolted.

"How often did you? And how often did you find any signs?" Brian stood and grabbed the file box, dropping it on his desk where it thunked. He rummaged through it, but she refused to view this file. After all these years, she'd never been tempted.

He pulled out a folder and skimmed through it, then slid it over. "Here. There's nothing gory in here. Just witness statements and synopses. Even one from Adrienne, his sister. And one from you, which pretty much states you were together up until about six p.m. But did that ever get brought up in trial? No. The autopsy clearly showed she died somewhere between two and four that evening. One friend stated she had seen Elizabeth go with Clint sometime at about eleven that morning.

"There was another box of items. Evidence that never got sent off to be tested for DNA. And some that did, including the knife that came back with your sister and Clint's. As you know, DNA has changed a lot over the years. When I was first asked for the file from his appellate team, I gave them everything I had. Ultimately, the DNA on those items were tested and linked to Clint Merkel. Nothing but the sweat on his cap linked to Lucas Fuller."

She opened her mouth to speak but couldn't get past the garble.

"Nothing," he reiterated. "Why don't you look it over if that'll make you feel better?"

She slid in the chair and rested against the back. The phone rang, and he picked it up to tell the receptionist he was unavailable to take calls at the moment.

Brian hung up and swiped a finger over his mouth. "I could keep telling you things and make you sick to your stomach. It's a huge cluster fuck. Sounds like a drama TV show. But nothing about this is fiction." He tapped the folder. "It's all in the file here. Even my notes. I know you think his sister's engagement to the FBI agent started this, but they don't have that much control. Plenty of attorneys make it their life's mission to help prison inmates. Several of them have looking into his file for years and filing motions to help him. I handed everything I had over to them the day I started my tenure, way before his sister's friends got involved."

That would have been nice to know too, Lauren thought. "And you didn't tell me this because…"

"Because it wasn't information you needed to know at the time," Brian said, voice glib and cocky. But she knew how far to push him, and she hadn't pushed him far enough yet.

"Why didn't his defense attorneys do a better job?"

"They got paid to do what they did. Defend someone accused of murder. I don't think his family had money to hire private investigators. They got good attorneys for a small amount of money, but those attorneys were from the big city. They thought they'd swoop in, wow everyone with their charm, create enough doubt in the jurors' minds to get their man a not guilty, and move on. We see that all the time, don't we? Their tactics didn't work in this small town."

Yes. Everything Brian said was true. Although she hadn't watched the entire trial, she'd seen plenty of others in the past six years of her career here. How a jury responded to evidence was unpredictable.

Part of the reason she wanted to help others as a victim coordinator was because of Rebecca, the victim coordinator who worked with her during Luke's trial. Rebecca had retired and moved on, and Lauren never reached out to her, but everything Rebecca had done to help her family had touched her. She'd grown interested in helping others and in learning about the criminal justice system. And now, here she was. The murder stole her sister, took away the love of her life, and set her career path.

"I don't doubt that Luke didn't do it," she admitted. Her confession eased her soul. She had believed it for a while, even two days ago when she planned to take his life, and she still had questions and doubts. If Brian had only talked to her more about this, she might never have confronted Luke. Her vehicle wouldn't be in the body shop, getting fixed. She might not ever accidentally run into him in town.

"I believe he is innocent," she continued. "But I don't understand how the people responsible, the people in office at the time, were able to get away with murder. Quite literally. And they are walking the streets, living a happy life."

"I wouldn't say a happy life. Mr. Benoit lost his license and will never practice law in the state of Texas. I heard rumors he's down in Mexico somewhere. His first assistant is now an alcoholic and can't get a job doing anything but janitor work somewhere near Houston, and that's only if he can hold a job down long enough. And the sheriff died of cancer, like Mayor Merkel."

Chills rolled over her skin. "Not that I wish that on anyone."

"Karma is a bitch," Brian said. "And don't forget how much this town has grown and changed. Things were much smaller back then. Much different. We had the good ol' boy system for a long time. It's getting better, but we still have that problem to an extent. I struggled with being a newcomer."

"Luke wasn't a newcomer," she said.

"No, but he was lower in the approval rankings. High in the popularity rankings from what I hear. Probably one reason Clint framed him. Lucas did well in school. Planned to get out of here and be a doctor. He was a likeable person, but he didn't kiss ass and never amounted to Mayor Merkel and his son. But then, I'm not telling you anything you didn't already know."

Lauren lowered her head and gave it a slight shake. The town was growing, but it still remained small and many of the locals bucked at growth. The founder was a Merkel, who had named it after his wife's maiden name of Terrence. He was the great-great-grandfather to Clint Merkel. The county, also named Terrence, had a population of over fifty thousand, with several small towns constructing the county.

Yes, Terrence had changed, yes it was growing and good things were happening, but the love of her life had spent the last twelve years of his life behind bars. Her stomach clamped into an edgy twitch, her mind rushing.

No matter how she had reacted Saturday night, resorting to violence wasn't her nature, but pulling the trigger on Clint would be easier knowing he had no morals. She had pointed a gun at an innocent man. She might have even shot him if she hadn't already had such doubts. But now she was obsessed with righting things with Luke. Not in her relationship. No, nothing like that. But for him. In his life. To give him peace he deserved.

But she couldn't afford to get too close. She couldn't afford for Laramie to find out.

Brian took the folder and slid it back in the box. "If you ever want to look it over, it's here. You're welcome to make copies and take it home."

"I don't know if I can ever open that door," she said. "I'm better off leaving it alone."

He set the lid on top and slid the box off his desk, dropping it in the corner. The lid—more of a topping than anything else—was banged up from overuse and barely fit over the bulging box. The hours pored over that file and yet they hid the truth was a face-slap. She had reviewed files when helping attorneys prepare for trial. But the previous prosecutors had sentenced an innocent man to life.

"If you change your mind, I haven't put it back in storage yet, just in case. And I'd rather keep it away from prying eyes. But I hope now you understand why I thought Mr. Fuller was the best speaker for our conference."

She had no idea if he was a good speaker, but now she was curious.

"I only hope you will go and hear him out."

"Why?" she asked, needing to understand why this was so important.

"Because I think it will help you. Clear you of your past regrets and the doubts you harbor. Not necessarily doubts about him, but about yourself and the judgments you've placed on yourself."

She reeled from his comment, but he was right. Although some memories deserved to stay buried, she needed to stop being so hard on herself. She'd put her life into raising her daughter and into being the best victim coordinator possible to help other victims. Brian had constantly worried she would burn out, and she wondered if Saturday's incident was a sign she was close.

She swiped a finger across her brow. "You don't even know what he's going to say yet."

He folded his hands together again, a sign he was listening and contemplating but had something positive in response. "No. No, I don't. He might burn down the entire criminal justice system. I don't know. But it wasn't just my decision. All the other members voted for him, unanimously. Prosecutors want a chance to hear what he has to say in the aftermath of such an egregious injustice."

CHAPTER FIVE

Lauren Twelve Years Ago

THE MORNING of Luke's verdict, Lauren woke with the same nausea she had experienced since his arrest. But the anxiety of trial hadn't caused the sickness.

For months, she had rushed out of bed and hurried to the toilet, believing she was full of worry and stress. Something was wrong. The truth dawned on her in a shimmer of early morning light. Her mind rebelled at the thought. Luke's baby? No. She could not be pregnant with a murderer's child. Her reflection in the mirror paled. He could never know.

She had kept it a secret for too long.

"Honey, are you okay?" came her mother's voice.

Lauren stood to wash her face and brush her teeth. "I'm okay." She would tell her parents later, but today wasn't the day. She had to get to the trial and make sure they convicted Luke, the man who murdered her little sister.

"I'm fine," she repeated although her mother was gone.

ANGELA SMITH

She combed her hair. Already felt better. If only she could convince herself it was something she ate.

They sat on the hard benches in the courtroom and listened to the closing arguments. She steeled her spine. She refused to look into Luke's eyes, avoiding him whenever he stared. When the jury came back two hours later, the longest two hours in her eighteen years, she held her breath waiting until they pronounced the verdict. "Guilty."

She collapsed against Clint, her friend. He wrapped his arms around her, and she buried her face in his chest. "It's over," she said.

But her little sister was gone. Moving away from Clint, she grabbed her parents' hands and as a group they hugged one another.

But it wasn't over. They announced the verdict, but the punishment took the rest of the wind out of Lauren. Life in prison wasn't long enough for the bastard who had killed her sister.

An officer cuffed him. They waited until he left before they exited the courthouse. The news reporters yelled out questions.

Her father put his arm around her mother. "What happened to Elizabeth should never happen to another child. We ask for privacy. Thank you." They hurried to their car.

Hatred blinded Lauren. Why hadn't her father said anything against Luke? Luke had betrayed her. How could she have been so fooled by him? She blamed herself for her sister's death. And she carried the murderer's baby. The secret loomed large.

In the backseat she waited for her father to start the car, but he sat there, her mother leaned her head on his shoulder.

"Mom, Dad. I'm pregnant." The words blurted out of her, unplanned. "It's Luke's."

Things moved quickly after that. Within two weeks, her

parents sent her to live with an aunt in California. She enrolled in college and gave birth to a beautiful baby girl.

She didn't return to Terrence, Texas for another six years.

———

Lauren Present Day

WARM SHIVERS TRAILED the length of Lauren's body while Luke's hands slid across her stomach and cupped her breasts. His tongue lolloped along her neck, his lips nipping her collarbone, while her ass pressed against the deck railing.

Her phone rang, and she jerked back to reality. What the hell? She was a grown ass woman and shouldn't be fantasizing about Luke and his kisses during work. She shouldn't fantasize about him ever.

"Yes?" she answered.

"Jim from the body shop is on the phone."

"Oh, good. Put him through." She had been waiting on Jim's call. She had dropped her car off this morning for him to do an estimate and contact the insurance for approval.

She had hoped not to have to make a claim, but the two-thousand-dollar estimate left her no choice. Stupid, stupid she'd have to pay for her mistakes with an increase in her insurance, but it was her fault. She was lucky she had only hydroplaned that night.

Well, not the only thing. Every time she closed her eyes, she felt Luke's lips on her skin, saw their bodies in an age-old dance of lovemaking. No way to label that incident as lovemaking.

"Hey, Jim," she said.

"Hi, Ms. Cooper. Insurance approved the estimate and a

rental. If you're ready to get it scheduled, we can start on it right away. Come by whenever you can for a rental."

"Yeah, okay, I'll get by this afternoon. Another hour or so if that's okay."

"We'll have it ready for you."

After handling a few other things—phone calls to victims and notating files—she changed into shorts and comfortable shoes, then grabbed her purse. She'd come back for the bag of clothing later.

She stopped at Tamra's desk. "I'm leaving early to pick up my rental car."

"Do you need a ride?"

"I appreciate the ride this morning, but the rental place is only a few blocks away, so I'll walk."

"Are you sure? It's pretty hot out there."

"I could use the fresh air. See you tomorrow."

The heat slammed into her when she stepped outside. The oppressive mugginess slithered on her skin and pilfered her breath. Perfect for erasing Luke's image. She texted Laramie to ask if she wanted pizza tonight. A dumb question. Of course her daughter wanted pizza. She'd live on pizza. Lauren called in the order while she walked. The rental didn't take long, and she collected the food on her way home.

Laramie was sitting outside on the porch wrapped in a towel, her phone in front of her face, when Lauren pulled into the parking lot.

"Hey, Mom. Did you get a new car?"

"I had a wreck, and this is a rental. Can you get the door for me?"

She jumped out of her seat. "Oh sure. Are you okay?"

"Yes. Hydroplaned from the rain. I'm fine. What are you doing outside?"

"Just came from the pool and wanted to finish drying off."

The community pool was two blocks away, and she had a

feeling her daughter was already dry, but she was a lot like her father and loved to be outside. She didn't know who her father was, so she wouldn't know. A new round of guilt jabbed Lauren.

Cool air washed over her when she entered the house. She set the pizza boxes and purse on the counter and turned to her daughter. "Clint is still out there, so be very watchful, okay?" Law enforcement believed he was long gone and they had nothing to worry about, but Lauren still worried.

"I won't let him get a hundred feet of me," Laramie said. She'd never been a huge fan of Clint. "Have you seen the guy they released? The one originally accused of murdering Aunt Lisa?"

"No," she lied. "No, I haven't."

Laramie sat on a bar stool and opened the box of pizza. "I Googled him. There's not much info and I can't find any social media accounts, but a few press releases. He's hot."

"Laramie," Lauren warned.

"What? He didn't kill Aunt Lisa."

"That's what they say," she muttered, although her conversation with Brian improved her mood.

Laramie chewed on her pizza, eyebrows level and nose wrinkled in curiosity. "You know he was barely out of high school when this happened, right? It was summer. He had just graduated and planned to be a doctor. I don't understand how you never knew him. You obviously went to school together."

"Don't talk with your mouth full, Lare," Lauren warned. She didn't want to have this conversation. Her aunt owned the local newspaper and had kept Lauren out of the spotlight then and now. Exonerations in Texas weren't rare, and media attention quickly died. She hadn't researched what information was available on him, but she would continue her denial.

Things were hard enough carrying a baby whose father

was a murderer. And then she'd named her Laramie Elizabeth—after her sister—with another *L*, as if she couldn't break that chain.

"He graduated the same year you did, Mom. It's a small town. I know everyone in my class."

"But you aren't friends with everyone in your class, are you?"

"Didn't you get pregnant with me around that time?"

Way, way too many questions. But this was a lie she could tell well since part of it was true, and she had rehearsed it since before Laramie's birth.

"After the trial, I moved to California to live with your grandmother's sister. We all thought it best if I get away. I met someone, got pregnant, had you, then went to college for criminal justice, with a minor in psychology. He left for the military. Wanted nothing to do with us. I moved to Austin and worked there a few years but didn't want to have you start school there, so I moved back here when I got my current job. We've discussed this."

"And where was my dad?"

"You already know he went to war. Got killed there."

"So why won't you tell me his name?"

"Because he wanted nothing to do with us, and I barely remember him. I moved and went on with my life."

"So, did he die, or are you just saying that?"

"He's dead." Her voice held a tinge of warning and regret. An end to a conversation she didn't want to have. She was a terrible mother for lying about a man who never existed. But in her mind, Laramie's father had been killed. The man she loved had died the day he was arrested. Too difficult to tell Laramie her dad was in prison for murder.

"So do you really think this guy did it?" Laramie took another bite of pizza. "Maybe you should meet him," she said over a mouthful. "Talk to him. Get some closure."

"Don't talk with your mouth full, Laramie Elizabeth," Lauren warned again. "And no, I have no intention of doing such a thing." She grabbed a slice of pizza and chewed. Maybe that would stop the questions, and now her twelve-year-old daughter was playing shrink. Just what she needed.

"Why not?"

"Why would I? Once they find and arrest Clint, and we get to the truth, then I'll have closure. For now, I'd prefer not to talk about it, okay? We need to plan our summer. School will start before we know it."

"Yeah, in six weeks. We're fine. Don't forget my camp at the end of summer."

"We'll see about that."

"What do you mean we'll see about that? I'm not *not* going to go just because that asshole is still out there."

"Laramie!" Lauren shouted.

Her daughter shrugged, then finished her last bite and scooted off the chair. "I need a shower, if that's okay."

"Yeah, okay."

Laramie shuffled to her room, and Lauren's shame intensified. Maybe if she hadn't been keeping secrets from her daughter, she'd be more open to conversation. Laramie was curious, had always been a curious child, and loved talking about things that intrigued her. Lauren hated to shut down her inquisitiveness, but this was a conversation she wasn't ready to have. A subject she might never be ready to talk about.

Would she ever tell Laramie the truth?

Her daughter was only twelve. How old did she need to be to understand? She acted so much older, but she shouldn't be worried about adult matters. She was a good kid, but Lauren didn't think she could understand the things her mother went through and the reasons she lied. She would hate her.

Her chest hitched at the thought of Laramie learning the truth. A whimper escaped, and she swallowed the painful tightening in her throat.

The truth would destroy their relationship. Destroy Laramie's trust. She might want a chance to get to know her father, but Lauren wasn't ready to pursue any relationship with the man who had destroyed her dreams. Even if he wasn't a killer.

CHAPTER SIX

THE WEEK PASSED IN A NON-EVENT. Lauren took Laramie to the movies on Saturday, still in the rental car. Lauren always made time for her daughter, having mother/daughter night at least once a week. That might include dinner and a movie —sometimes at home—getting manis and pedis, swimming together in the community pool, or going out for an adventure. Her daughter was her everything.

Laramie hounded her she should have traded her vehicle off for a newer model instead of getting it fixed.

"That requires money," she explained. "Money that could go toward your college education."

Despite the wreck, her Escape was in good condition, and she only had a year left on the payments.

Wednesday, a week and a half after she wrecked the vehicle, she received the call the car was ready to be picked up. A friend had dropped Laramie off at Lauren's work a few minutes before the workday ended, so they drove to the auto body shop on the way home.

When Lauren strode through the door and saw Luke, she

halted. A panic switch flicked on in her chest, heart pounding in fight-or-flight mode.

Stay. Don't run. She forced her erratic breathing to slow.

Laramie stood beside her. *Laramie*. Why hadn't she picked up the car later, when Laramie wasn't around? Oh yeah, because she never expected to confront Luke at the same body shop he recommended.

Jim Edwards approached. She didn't know him well, but enough to know he was a good man and ran a good shop. He and his wife owned and managed it together. Despite Luke's recommendation, Jim's reputation made it her first choice. Knowing Luke worked here would have changed everything.

Jim was tall but squatty, with a permanent curve to his back, a twinkle in his eyes, and salt and pepper hair. Grease covered his clothes. He rubbed his hands in a towel but didn't offer a shake.

"Ms. Cooper, good to see you again. Your vehicle is ready. You wanna look it over first?"

The shop was full of grease and tools and contraptions expected to be in such a workplace. A sign to her right pointed to the office. That's the direction she should have gone. If only she had known to avoid Luke.

"Um." She wet her lips, swallowed, and ignored Luke's gaze from the other side of the garage. "Who handled the repairs?"

"Oh, that'd be Luke Fuller. Great technician. He's standing right over there if you'd like to talk to him."

Jim pointed, but she knew exactly who Luke Fuller was.

What kind of joke was this? A joke with destiny? How had Luke been the one to repair her vehicle? It was practically his fault she had wrecked. Not directly his fault, but indirectly. She had been running from him and from all the emotions he'd wrought in her.

He should have told her he worked here.

"Luke," Jim called, waving him over. She hadn't answered, so he must have thought that meant she wanted to talk with the technician.

She didn't. She wanted to get into her car and run away. She'd have to force herself to go slow and easy so she didn't wreck. Luke's long strides ate up the distance between them.

"That's okay, we're good to go," she told Jim, but he kept waving Luke over.

She had wanted to talk to him. Tell him how sorry she was about everything that happened. But now wasn't the time. Her whole body shook, weakness assailing her when her daughter gasped beside her.

"Laramie, get in the car," she whispered.

Laramie was busy studying the man coming toward them, blatantly curious. She undoubtedly recognized Luke from her online search.

He stopped in front of them. Lauren tried to turn Laramie away, but Jim spoke.

"Can you go over the Escape with Ms. Cooper? I've got to run. Great to meet you and do business with you, ma'am. You can settle up your deductible in the office there. Claire will take care of you. Or Luke can take care of it, too." He nodded toward the door and offered his hand. "Have a great day, little lady," he said to Laramie. The man walked away, and she stared at his disappearing back, her mouth opening but no words formed.

I don't want to talk to Luke, she wanted to say.

She avoided his gaze and eyed Jim's retreating back as if he was her lifeline. But when she turned back to Luke, his brows creased and his head swiveled between Laramie and her.

She planted her hand on Laramie's shoulder. "Get in the car. I'll be there in a minute." Her voice was shaky, empty, and way too tactless not to sound suspicious. She couldn't

ANGELA SMITH

have him studying Laramie too long. She didn't need him to figure things out. And she damn sure didn't want Laramie questioning anything.

"As you can see, ma'am, we replaced the passenger door and fixed the front fender. The bumper was a bit skewed, and—"

She whirled on him, her eyes flashing fire. "And what else did you do?" Her whisper was a silent but scorching scream, only meant for his ears. But not silent enough Laramie wouldn't hear the irritation. Her daughter continued to stand beside her, but she was too shocked to do anything about it.

He gave a slight headshake as if confused by her outburst. "Excuse me?"

"I'm supposed to get into this vehicle now? After you've touched it?"

He took a step back, his mouth opening.

"I replaced your fender and repaired your passenger door. Your bumper needed a bit of adjustment, too."

Angry fire clogged her throat, her voice an eerie grumbling twang. Laramie stood silent beside her, watching her, observing her reaction. Lauren bit back on her fear.

This was Luke's daughter. Luke's daughter, and he didn't know it, didn't need to know it. She never would have brought her if she'd known he was working here. But now her best interest was to know everything she could about him, including his daily routine and where he worked, so she never had to run into him again.

Best to stay composed and avoid attention. She didn't need her daughter wondering, or Luke studying her daughter too much.

She needed to get out of here.

His gaze flipped to hers, then to Laramie's. She shielded her by shifting ever so slightly in front of her, but the question in his eyes revealed his curiosity.

"Mom?" Her daughter's voice held that tween-angst-trust-no-one-and-question-everything tone.

"Get in the car," she told Laramie, biting back her name. She refused to speak her name in front of Luke, as if that made everything real.

"You have a daughter?" Luke's voice rose in a choppy wave of aggression.

No one besides them was in the shop. What would Jim's reaction be if he knew he'd left her alone with the man who had sired her child and gone to prison for murdering her sister?

Her belly tightened. The car stereo fired up, jolting her back to reality. Laramie had climbed into the car, doing as asked, and a boomy bassy song blared from the speakers. The rumble resonated in her heartbeat.

"How old is she?" Luke asked. Why was she still here, her feet planted into the concrete floor as if stuck? His eyes flashed, lips curled. Her entire body shook. Curled into knots.

She squared her shoulders. "Thank you for the repair," she said, then turned on her heel toward the car.

He caught her by the elbow. She flew around to face him. Nose flaring, eyes burning. Not because she wanted to cry. She wanted to fume. And she was scared, so scared he would find out about Laramie.

"How old is she?" he asked again.

"I don't see where that is any of your business."

If she planned on telling him—which she wasn't—it wouldn't be like this.

She yanked her arm out of his grip, then crawled into the Escape and slammed the door. Curling her hands around the steering wheel, she settled her breath and pulled out of the shop. His gaze dug into her skin. Even when he was out of view, even out of the rearview mirror, her skin burned.

"Well, that was awkward," Laramie said.

"What was?" Lauren asked. Might as well play dumb.

"Mom. I'm not stupid. I recognized that man. I mean, how could I not? And he acted like he knew you."

"Of course he knew me. He went to prison for murdering my sister."

"Why did he grab your arm like that? Shouldn't we report him?"

She'd taught her daughter well. Don't let anyone mishandle you. But now she had to contradict her teaching. "No. No, it's okay."

"Did you know him before all this?"

"We went to school together. Yes."

"You knew him well enough for him to touch you."

"No. He was just trying to stop me. He wanted to apologize."

"Apologize for what? I mean, if he's not guilty, what should he be apologizing for?"

Lauren pulled off the side of the road before she had a stroke. She rubbed her arm, the heat and stress stealing her breath. Five more minutes and they'd be home, but she had to regain control before she went back on the road and her car ended up in the body shop again.

Adjusting the fan on the AC to blow on her heated face, she returned her clammy hand on the steering wheel and noticed Laramie's gaze. Her arm didn't hurt where he had grabbed her, but his touch had branded her.

"Aunt Lisa would roll over in her grave," Laramie said. She had never met Elizabeth, but she always referred to her as Aunt Lisa. She had grown up hearing stories, seeing pictures, but never hearing much about the man who was accused of taking her life. Until now.

Lauren eased back onto the street and drove home.

"Clint would flip, too," Laramie said.

Her daughter's words had her wishing she'd stayed parked. "Don't you dare mention his name."

"Why not?"

"I thought you hated him."

"I do. Especially now."

Laramie barely spoken of Clint after he was accused of murder, but Lauren wondered what was going through her daughter's mind. "You have your grandfather."

"Yeah."

Lauren didn't know if Laramie was hurt or playing her tween manipulation game. Laramie never liked Clint. She obviously had a better perception of character than Lauren did.

"Do you miss Clint?" Lauren asked, turning the SUV onto their street. *Almost home.*

Laramie's gaze flew to hers. "No. I told you he's a creep before this first happened. I always worried you would marry him or something. And look, he turned out to be the real murderer."

Lauren pulled into the driveway and slammed on the brakes way too hard.

"What are you doing, Mom? Trying to wreck again?"

"Sorry."

"You wanna wreck so you can take the car back to that hunky guy at the auto shop?"

"Laramie Elizabeth," she said, her voice a warning growl. Laramie's words messed her up, and her daughter had no idea how they affected her.

Laramie gave an exaggerated eye roll. "What, Mom? He has a lot more charisma than Clint. I can't believe you thought he killed Aunt Lisa. Especially if you knew him. I saw in his eyes he's obviously not a killer."

Laramie was going through another pre-teen tween angst stage. Hate your mother and say incredibly mean things, but then become the sweetest most loving daughter in the entire world.

Lauren opened the door and slid out of the car. "You know nothing about him."

Laramie's footsteps plodded behind her. Lauren unlocked the house, and her daughter asked the most haunting question. "Is he my dad?"

Her heartbeat stopped. She stumbled into the house and dumped her purse on the table beside the door. "What?"

Time to come clean and tell her daughter everything. But she couldn't. Her body clammed up every time she considered admitting the truth, and the lie was digging her further into a black hole. Dragging her into something she couldn't escape.

"Is he my dad?" she asked again.

"That's ridiculous. What makes you say that?"

Laramie shrugged. "I don't know. I saw his eyes. He was curious about me."

"We weren't close enough to have a child together." Another lie, rolling so smoothly off her lips.

She owed Luke an apology, accusing him of messing with her car. Why would he risk such a thing? She didn't know him, not anymore, and for years she thought the man she had fallen in love with was a fraud, a killer. He wasn't the same man she had known. But maybe he was. Kind, selfless, funny, adventurous. Why hadn't she remembered that when he had been accused of murder? How had it been so easy to forget?

"Mom?" Laramie asked.

Lauren stood near the door, her mind drifting. She jerked back to reality. "Come on, let's go figure out what we're going to have for dinner tonight."

"I asked how well did you know him."

"Not that great. Can we stop talking about this now?"

"Why?" Her daughter's mossy-green gaze tore into her. So

much like her dad's. All they had to do was look into each other's eyes and discover the truth.

"Because it's a touchy subject for me and not something I enjoy reminiscing. Okay?" Her harsh voice bleated through her reserves to remain calm. If it got Laramie off her back, so be it.

Laramie stormed into the kitchen and tossed over her shoulder, "Well, I think it's weird."

Lauren followed. "What do you think is weird? That I don't want to talk about my sister's murderer? You've never had a sister, so you wouldn't understand." Lauren flinched at her cruel words, and swallowed her regrets. She was treating her daughter like an adult, speaking to her like an adult, when Laramie was a child, trying to understand way more than she should.

Laramie whirled on her. "You're right. I never had a sister. I never had a father either. As far as I know, some stork dropped me."

"We've talked about this."

"Why don't you tell me the truth, Mom?"

"Laramie, drop it. I've had a long and tiring day. I have a headache and now isn't the time to talk about Elizabeth, okay? It's a hard time for me. Remembering her. Knowing the killer has been out there all these years and so close to our family. Knowing the wrong man went to prison. Okay? It isn't easy to talk about." Her voice cracked, tears filled her eyes, and she rushed to the refrigerator to open it, the cool air easing her tears. Ground beef was thawed and she'd planned on spaghetti, but the cool air from the fridge had her standing longer than necessary.

She refused to break down in front of her daughter.

Laramie approached and wrapped her arms around her waist. "I'm sorry, Mom. I was being insensitive."

She pivoted and took Laramie in her arms, swaying with her. "It's okay, doll. It's okay."

They hugged each other a while, then Laramie pulled away. "Are we going to fix dinner, or not? I'm hungry."

Tears burned Lauren's eyes. She was grateful for her daughter. Grateful for their relationship. She didn't want anything to destroy it, and she was afraid these lies would. But Laramie was too young to understand. No matter how adult she acted, and how intelligent she was as a child, and no matter how perceptive she was, Lauren had to protect her.

Especially from the truth.

―――

Luke strode into the office and slapped five one-hundred-dollar bills on the table where Claire sat. "Did you know she had a daughter?"

Claire held up her hands. "What?"

Luke swallowed his anger. Unfair to take it out on her and Jim wasn't here.

"Where did Jim run off to? I'm sure that was done on purpose."

"Now, Luke." She picked up the bills. "What is this?"

"Her deductible. She paid cash."

"Did you give her a receipt?"

"No."

She scowled. "That's because she didn't pay, did she?"

"She meant to. But she couldn't get out of here fast enough when she saw me. And Jim made sure she saw me, too."

Her shoulders drew up to her ears. "I don't know about that. Jim isn't one to play matchmaker."

"I don't know what game he was playing but I guarantee

you he called me over to her and introduced us like we had no idea who the other one was. Playacted really well, too. I'm surprised Lauren didn't remember how good of friends you both were with my parents."

"Hey hun." Jim strode into the shop, saw Luke, and flinched.

"What, you didn't think I was still here?" Luke's anger was revealed through his voice, but he respected Jim and Jim respected him. They would see this out.

"I guess I thought you were in the shop."

"Well, you can't avoid me forever."

"Wasn't trying to."

Sweat poured down Luke's back. His shoulders bunched. Even without being angry, the heat was intense, seeming to suck his bones dry. After living in the state penitentiary, he forgot the intensity of Texas summers.

"You said not to get involved with Lauren."

Jim nodded. "I did."

"And yet you call me over there to discuss her vehicle with her and go over the repairs."

"She saw you, Luke. And I thought it was best not to avoid any confrontation. I thought it was best she knows you handled the repairs so if anything arose, we already went over it."

"Did you know she had a daughter?" He swallowed at the halting screech of his words. He hadn't meant to sound so intense, so emotional. But how could anyone expect otherwise?

Jim nodded and grabbed a cup of coffee. "I don't know much about her daughter. Don't even know how old she is. I heard the father was some military guy she met when she lived in California and died overseas."

Luke's stomach dropped, rolled, burned. A likely story for a cover-up. Or wishful thinking?

"I'm sorry, man," Jim continued. "She saw you. Froze. I didn't think it was a good idea to pretend like you didn't exist. So yeah, I pretended like I had no idea of your past. Easier that way. Not the best option to ignore the fact you were the body tech who repaired her vehicle."

"I told you in the first place I thought it was a conflict for me to do it."

"And I told you you're the best body man I've got."

"She already asked me what I did to it. Like I would do something to make her wreck or something."

Jim cringed and set down his cup. "I doubt she meant it. Give Lauren some credit. She's a good person with a good heart who's been through hell. Learning the man she planned to marry didn't kill her sister after all had to have been a huge shock. She isn't going to accuse you of anything."

"Yeah. You're probably right," he said, swallowing his disagreement. No sense in continuing to argue. He'd go home and dive into the cold river water with an even colder beer to melt away his troubles. "Look, I'm putting up my tools and I'm gone for the day. See you guys tomorrow."

"Bye, Luke," Claire said.

"See you tomorrow," Jim said, but regret rolled through his voice. The back of Luke's neck tightened.

He walked out the door. He hadn't meant to stress his boss. Even though he didn't agree with Jim's decision, Jim thought he was doing the right thing. But none of this was right. Seeing Lauren, seeing the kid.

No sense in telling his boss the last time he saw Lauren, she was pointing a gun in his face.

Luke Twelve Years Ago

. . .

THE JUDGE READS THE SENTENCE, but all I hear is life in prison.

Life in prison.

I can't even fathom what that means.

They handcuff me. My body doesn't respond much. It's like I'm encased in a murky glass ball to prevent me from spreading germs to the rest of the world. You know, like murder germs or something. But finally, I have to react. The deputy yanks at my arm, so I have no choice but to follow.

My mother and sisters' wails jab a slight penetration into the haze of my mind, but not enough for me to focus. It's best this way.

I search for Lauren in the crowd. I long to see her, connect gazes with her, tell her I love her. The pain she is going through, the pain she thought I caused, is unbearable. I need to look into her eyes so she can see the truth.

Hungrily, I scour the room. The deputy leads me to the door. My steps falter when I spot her. Lauren huddles with her family. With Clint.

The real killer.

She's in danger.

"Lauren," I call.

The deputy squeezes my arm. "No," he says. I try to pull away, but I can't. The cuffs and his grip are too strong and I sense pandemonium. Eyes wide and teary, Lauren shoots her gaze my way for a split second. Her mouth opens, but no love shines in her eyes. She's heard enough testimony to believe me a killer.

"Lauren, please."

The deputy pulls me away and out the door and my muscles sag.

"Dad," I say, grabbing onto any life I have left. My mom and dad and two sisters huddle nearby, crying. Mom looks like she's about to collapse, and I shake myself out of my darkness enough so she doesn't panic.

I'm just as much to blame for Elizabeth's death. I ignored the signs of my friend's failing morality. My only goal was in being alone with Lauren. And my sister's alibi wasn't loud enough to hear over the fact Clint was the mayor's son.

Luke Present Day

Luke grabbed a beer and a float and jumped in the river. He wanted to forget about his day and the fact Lauren had a child. A child that could be his.

But he couldn't. He couldn't forget those eyes peering at him so curiously. The way Lauren shielded her body and the way Jim explained a rumor he himself didn't believe.

He drowned his beer and trotted up the hill to the house. He should have bought an ice chest full of the liquid to help him forget, if only for a time. He had to stop thinking about it, but he couldn't.

He had already lost too much.

He sent a message to his sister, Adrienne. His freedom was largely thanks to her. She had never given up on him. *Did you know Lauren had a daughter about the same age as when I went to prison?*

She didn't respond. She called him. He should have known.

"What the fudge are you talking about, Lucas?"

So she still didn't cuss and preferred to call him by his given name.

"I just found out," he said. "By accident. Rumor has it she got impregnated by some military dude who died overseas."

"Bullshit." Ahh, so there was that mouth he loved. "That's a crock of bull and you know it."

"I don't know much right now. I'm taking it slow and easy. I'll find out more."

"I'm coming home."

"No. No you aren't coming home. I'm happy with the way things are. You enjoy your time."

He should never have told her. She and her new husband, Zan, were off on a long vacation getaway in the mountains. They had already been through too much.

"Don't worry about it," he said when she didn't respond, and he was worried she was already packing her bags. Knowing his sister, she was. "Please."

She must have heard the urgency in his voice. "Fine. For now. But if anything happens. Anything at all—"

"Don't worry about it."

"Don't do anything stupid," she said.

"Well we've learned the hard way even smart decisions can give you a world of hurt."

The din of her silence clamored in his ears.

"Lucas…" she said, voice edged with concern.

His heart ached at the way she said his name. Antsy. Worried. Full of torment. "I'm not going to do anything stupid," he said. "Don't you dare come home. Besides, rumor is the girl's father was a military dude from California."

Ending the call, he strolled inside, fired up his computer, and spent the rest of the evening researching social media and anything on Lauren and her family. He wanted to see more pictures, study the girl and determine if she was his child.

But he felt it, deep inside his soul. He was a father. He knew it like he knew the sun rose in the east and set in the west, even if he barely had a chance to see it during the long years in prison.

His pulse grew hollow, a soft knocking in his throat as he bit back his grief. No time for bawling. No sense in letting tears free. They changed nothing. He hadn't cried in at least twelve years, not even the day he stepped outside of the prison gates and walked his way to freedom. He couldn't afford to cry, not caged with rabid men who'd rather stab you than look at you.

He scraped a hand over his face as emotions washed over him. Sadness, despair, regret. Then anger. Anger he had missed out on so much. He'd missed his daughter's birth. He'd missed his mother's funeral. Everything that had meant anything was now gone. His dad was still alive and touring the world with Charlotte, Luke's older sister, and he was able to live in the home he'd grown up in. But nothing was the same. Nothing would ever be the same.

Lauren should have believed in him. She should have told him the truth.

Jim's Auto Body had a file folder with her cell number. Luke had easily found her address. But calling was a lot easier than showing up on her doorstep and risking an arrest.

He shouldn't call her, but he ignored the reasoning ramble in his mind.

She answered on the second ring.

"Is she mine?"

She hesitated, her breath squelching in a release of air. His heart hammered against his ribcage, and he waited for her to speak.

He hadn't expected a response. Not a positive one, anyway.

"Lauren." His reedy voice made him cringe. He wished he could stay fierce and not resort to begging. But Lauren had always caused him to feel powerless over his emotions. "I deserve to know. I mean, did you have an affair with Clint?"

His voice hiccupped, a breathy rasp he couldn't control. He didn't believe his accusation, but the fact there was even a chance she developed a relationship with Clint tore him apart.

"What are you doing calling me?" she asked, but her voice was just as breathy, as if also having a hard time staying in control.

She still believed he killed Elizabeth. Did someone not tell her of the corruption that led to his imprisonment?

She had lived her life. Gotten over him, had a future. Until now, his only future had been a jail cell. And he never planned to go back to his past, to the woman he loved. He should leave things alone.

But he couldn't. Not yet. Not until she spoke the truth.

"Lauren," he said again, as if her name was all he could muster.

During his time in prison, he had written many letters to her and her parents. He had dreamt of the day he would one day see her, hold her, tell her of how many things had gone wrong. But he destroyed those letters. Never sent those outpourings of emotion. They were supposed to help him, but never, ever did.

"Don't call me again," Lauren said, her voice a live wire of fear and dread. "I'll have a restraining order on you so fast. Leave me and my family alone."

With that, she ended the call, leaving him completely bereft and debating what to do next.

CHAPTER SEVEN

LAUREN GROANED when the alarm rang way too early the next morning. She'd rather slide under the covers and never get out of bed.

Luke's phone call had left her sleepless. She was familiar with sleepless nights. The devastation of losing her sister and the man she thought she loved had hounded her for months and months after Luke's conviction. But Lauren had persevered, and she and Laramie had fallen into a reliable routine. With his return, everything was out of whack, especially her confused emotions.

She rose up in bed and planted her feet on the floor, guilt eating her. She'd been so cruel to Luke. Hatred for what he'd purportedly done had flamed out of her and at him. Maybe he was innocent, but at one time she thought he'd ruined her life. Now what? She had only her instincts to shove him away and protect Laramie.

She wasn't ready to share Laramie with him. She didn't want to break Laramie's trust in her. She wanted to continue her life in the bland and normal routine she'd clung to over the past few years.

Better to steer clear of heartbreak and remorse.

Maybe Laramie could handle it, but she was supposed to be enjoying her summer. Any excuse in the world for why she didn't tell her daughter the truth skated through her mind.

She had been so in love with Luke at one time. They had just graduated high school, ready to conquer the world, when she learned the boy she loved was a murderer. She was just a kid and then had one herself after losing her sister. It didn't seem fair, and it took every ounce of her willpower to pick herself up out of depression and move on with her life to make the best life she could for her child.

Driving to work, she passed the body shop, and it hit her she hadn't paid her deductible. Dread pulled at her, and she kept driving. A phone call should suffice. She didn't want to run into Luke again.

"We have you down as paid," Claire said. They didn't know each other well. Acquaintances, was all. "Five hundred dollars, cash. Did you not get a receipt?"

She closed her eyes and rested her head in her hands. She hadn't paid, and the last conversation she had with the owner was for her to go inside the office to settle payment there. But she forgot because she had fled.

Luke. Luke must have paid her bill. Fury burned her skin. She fidgeted, squeezing and releasing the office's phone cord.

He had called her last night. He obviously had her cell number, probably from the body shop. Should she tell them he was calling her and harassing her?

She bit down on a cold regret for thinking such thoughts. She had no right to destroy his life when he was trying to pick it up again.

"Oh, I, I guess I didn't. It happened so fast and I got confused. Can you tell me if the gentleman who worked on my vehicle, Mr. Fuller I believe? Is he working today?"

Claire had to know. She had to know who she was. But Lauren played dumb. She hadn't run in the same social circles as Jim and Claire. No reason to. Playing dumb was easy and her better choice.

"No, ma'am. He works part time. Generally only three days a week Monday through Wednesday unless there's a problem or if we get real busy he'll come in and help like he did when we had your vehicle. Was everything okay with your vehicle?"

"Yes. Yes, everything was good. Looks like I drove it out of the showroom. Thank you." Her words were true. Her vehicle hadn't been that clean in a while. The shop had given it immaculate care, but she wondered if the shop had given such careful attention, or Luke.

"Okay, ma'am. I can email you a receipt or hold one here for you to pick up."

"Would you mind emailing it?"

"Not at all," Claire said. "I'll get that emailed right away. Is there anything else I can help you with?"

"No. Thank you. I appreciate it. Have a good day." She hung up the phone and let out a whoosh of breath, then buried her head in her hands.

He had no right to pay her bill. Should she go see him again and pay him back? Or is that what he'd intended? She could mail it to him. She remembered his address like it was only yesterday since she'd been a part of his family.

They'd all been close at one time. His two sisters had been excited to help her plan their wedding and were helping them figure out what to do while they went to college. Then he dropped the bombshell of applying to Columbia University, and she hadn't had time to consider her options. She worried they had stressful times ahead, but they were in love and would do everything they could to make it work.

But they didn't. She'd stopped believing in him the moment of his arrest.

THE WEEKEND BEFORE THE CONFERENCE, Lauren took Laramie to her parents' where she would stay the week.

They stepped into a house filled with scents of apples, cinnamon, and vanilla. Laramie ran into her grandmother's arms, then straight into Grandpa's. He picked her up and twirled her around the living room, uttering wild promises of swimming, pizza, chocolate, and late-night movies.

"He's not a young man anymore," Lauren told her mom, hugging her and then releasing her purse on the table. "And she isn't a young child. He's going to hurt himself one day."

"He's as strong as ever. Constantly working and constantly moving. Sometimes I consider going back to work so I can have a vacation." She chuckled, but the smile on her face and the gleam in her eyes told Lauren she couldn't be happier.

Her parents had been lucky, and one reason she'd expected her relationship with Luke to work. They had married young, had two children, and stayed together even after one was murdered. They retired early and happy, and no doubt their love for life and each other kept their marriage alive, even after all their heartache.

At one point, Lauren considered their marriage inspirational, but she had lost her hope on a relationship like theirs a long time ago.

"Mom, I'm going swimming with Grandpa," Laramie said. "Be sure to come tell me bye before you leave."

"I will, love."

Her dad approached and gave her a bear hug, then a kiss. "How are you, darling?"

"Better now that I'm here, Dad."

He broke apart and regarded her at arm's length. "You know you're always welcome."

She nodded. "I know. I—"

"You've been busy. I know, I know. Well, once you get back from that conference of yours I expect you to come at least have dinner with us occasionally. Your mom misses you." He winked at his wife.

"Just mom?"

"Yep, just your mom." He chuckled and rubbed a knuckle under her chin as if she was still a child.

"I will, Dad." She had missed them. They lived twenty miles out of town, on the northeastern side and directly opposite from the westerly side where Luke lived. It wasn't hard to get to their twenty acres, which flourished under their care. She loved being here. Her dad reminded her of all the reasons she could trust a man, and he helped bring out the best in her, too.

Dad kissed her cheek. "I love you."

"I love you, too."

He kissed his wife, then waved. "Better get in that pool before Laramie does and splashes all the water out."

"Grandpa," Laramie teased.

Lauren's heart swelled. Despite her worries about going to this seminar, her daughter couldn't be in better hands.

"It smells delicious in here," she told her mom. Her dad and daughter strolled out the double glass doors and dove into the pool.

"Homemade apple and cinnamon ice cream."

She rubbed her tummy. "Oh, Mom. You're killing me."

"I want you to take some with you."

"I can't. I'm trying to lose all my weight after our last holidays."

"You don't need to lose any weight and you know it. You seem stressed, dear. Is everything okay?"

Lauren sank into a chair, instantly at home. The kitchen was farmhouse style with a massive farmhouse sink. Vases of flowers and bowls of produce enticed one to dig in. The walls were off-white, the windows were bright, and the light blue cabinets screamed creativity.

Despite the comfort, Laramie's stomach knotted. She debated on whether to tell them about Luke, but her mom's inquisitiveness burned her eyes. How could she not tell her?

"Here, let me fix you a glass of tea," Mom said.

"I'm fine."

"Look, I know everything with Clint has been crazy. But Laramie will be safe here."

Her sister hadn't been safe. Not that she would ever say that or blame her parents. She blamed herself more than anything. But was it possible to keep anyone safe?

"He asked me if she was his," she said, then shook her head. She hadn't meant to blurt it out like that.

Her mom set a glass of tea in front of her and frowned. "Who? Clint?"

"No. No. Luke. We saw Luke. At a body shop where he worked. He saw Laramie. And then later he called me and asked me if she was his."

"A body shop?"

She took a long drink of her tea. She needed to calm her nerves before she continued talking to her mother. Mom sat beside her.

"I had an accident." She held up her hand at her mom's growing concern. "I'm fine. My car needed minor repairs, and it turns out I take it to a body shop where Luke is working. He saw Laramie." Her voice cracked.

Her mom scanned her gaze outside the large double

windows at Laramie and Dad, then returned her attention to Lauren. "And? What did you tell him?"

"I denied it. And I told him to leave me and my family alone."

Her mom winced, disapproval lining her brow.

Her stomach curled. "You think I'm being harsh?"

"I think you need to let the past go. Realize he isn't the guilty one. Forgive him if you must, but most importantly forgive yourself."

Ice clinked as she lifted the glass to her lips, but she didn't take a drink. "Have you forgiven him?"

"I forgave him a long time ago. Before he was cleared. I had to or else I would have died of a broken heart."

"But…" Lauren's voice trailed, and she finally took that drink to clear the clog in her throat. Only it didn't help because she almost choked. She set the glass on the table and clenched her hands.

"I believe he's a good man," her mom said. "I've read about him. He was falsely accused, which is a travesty. We lost our little girl, but he lost his life, too. I feel terrible for him."

"So you think I should let him have a life with Laramie?"

"They should have a chance to know each other if they want. He's already been robbed of so much. And Laramie has been robbed of her father. You can't be her everything."

The back of her neck stiffened. "But how can I leave her alone with him?"

"You left her alone with Clint."

Lauren shivered and wrapped her arms around her shoulders. The heat of her mother's words pasted to her skin like goo, and still she shivered. A deep, penetrating tremor cutting her core.

Mom hadn't said it to be cruel. She was to the point, and full of love, and meant to reassure, encourage but also to get

Lauren out of the anguish in her head so she could think rationally.

She had left her alone with Clint. More than once. Clint had been part of her birthday, Halloween, Christmas. Why had she trusted him and yet turned her back on the man she was supposed to love?

Mom clutched her hand. "Tell her before you tell him. Let her decide."

"I don't know if I'm ready."

"You don't have to do it yet. Go to your conference. Don't worry about a thing here. Use your time away to think."

She didn't bother telling her Luke would be at the conference. Just because he was there didn't mean she would see him.

"I know, Mom. You're right. You won't say anything, will you?"

"Of course I won't, honey." She squeezed her hand then kissed her fingers.

"I know you won't." She didn't know why she asked. She trusted her mom like no other. But the fears kept pouring out of her, harvesting into doubt and confusion.

Mom dropped her hand. "Look. Life is a scary mess. You never know what's going to happen from one day to the next. But like I told you a long time ago, go after what you believe in with everything you've got. If it doesn't feel right to tell her, then don't. But don't refuse to tell her because you are afraid of change. Nothing can ever break your daughter's love for you and you for her."

Tears built in her eyes and she nodded. "But what about breaking her heart?"

CHAPTER EIGHT

Luke Twelve Years Ago

The eyes of twelve jurors scrutinize me, and sweat pours down my back. I thought I was prepared for the prosecutor's relentless questions, but he does a great job of creating doubt about my testimony.

"So you're saying you didn't kill Elizabeth Cooper?" Mr. Benoit asks.

"No. Yes, that's what I'm saying."

"But you saw her that morning?"

"I saw her. Playing out in the yard when I went to pick up Lauren. She came up and said hi."

"And you left her alone?"

"Yeah, but she stayed home alone all the time."

"And she was still at the curb waving when you turned the corner?"

"Yes."

"Was she worried? Frightened to be alone?"

"No. She didn't mind. And her mom was coming home soon."

"So you abandoned a little girl—"

"I didn't abandon her—"

"Because you wanted your adult time with Lauren."

I cringe. I never admitted to saying that, but Lauren had.

"You killed Lauren's little sister because she was an annoyance to you."

I shift in my seat. A drop of sweat lands on the table. Gross. "No. That's ridiculous."

Why had I decided to testify? Why did I think I could hold my own against this man who had years of experience badgering defendants? Clint testified I was a horrible person who liked to look at child porn. A disgusting life. Witnesses testified I was mean to Elizabeth. Witnesses had testified they saw me with Elizabeth before her murder. Another lie.

"Your cap was found near Elizabeth's body."

"I lost that cap."

Mr. Benoit's brows quirk, challenging and provoking me to lose my cool. Wayne had warned me these things would happen, but it's hard to stay focused. "Oh?"

"Yes. Clint killed Elizabeth." Whew, I had gotten that out. Finally. Too bad Lauren isn't in the courtroom to hear it.

"No evidence, no motivation, and nothing to point at what you claim. It sounds like you are saying whatever you can to direct your guilt another direction. Mr. Fuller, do you consider yourself a jealous person?"

"Not really, no."

"So you were never jealous of Elizabeth's affection with Lauren?"

One time, one time when Elizabeth had needled me enough I had reacted and said she was annoying and could she please shut up and leave us alone. My mind had been on a lot of things at the time, specifically how to tell Lauren I was applying to Columbia University. Her questions had been as relentless as Lauren's, only in a childlike annoying way. Elizabeth was a great kid, I loved her like a little sister, but the prosecutor had worsened every simple incident and made it seem I deserved the worst punishment even if the jury did find me not guilty.

"Mr. Fuller, are you going to reply to my question?"

"Objection, your honor." My attorney stands. "He's badgering the witness."

"Sustained. Mr. Benoit, if you have something to ask this defendant, do so, but stop the back and forth."

"Mr. Fuller. Your cap was found near Elizabeth's body after you mutilated her. Tucked under a tree as if you didn't realize you had dropped it."

"Why would it be tucked under a tree if I had dropped it? Sounds like a set-up to me."

"Your DNA was found on the cap."

"Of course it was. I wore that cap all the time and everybody knows it. But I lost the damn cap."

"Indeed, you did lose that cap. Near Elizabeth's body after you murdered her."

"I wasn't wearing my cap when I picked up Lauren that day."

"But Lauren says you were wearing your cap."

My throat clenches. "Memories are tricky. Lauren was used to seeing me in my cap. She's confused. The last thing on her mind was whether or not I wore my cap."

Mr. Benoit nodded, his eyes revealing another win for him. As if playing with my life was a game.

Not that it mattered. If I am found not guilty, Lauren and her family will hate me for the rest of their life.

"You prefer to look at naked pictures of young children."

"No. No." The thought sickens me, terrifies me. How could anyone believe that?

"Is that why you killed Elizabeth? Lauren turned you away and—"

"No!" I swipe a hand over my face and squirm. My veins bulge, a deep flush on my skin revealing inconsistencies in my words. But that's only fire and angry boiling my blood. To be accused of something like this is repulsive.

"Did you lose your knife too? The one found at the crime scene?"

I swallow. Apparently I had lost that knife and didn't realize it and the way he bounces his questions back and forth to rile me is working.

"Mr. Fuller? Do you plan to answer the question?"

"Someone stole it." It's the only answer I have.

"I pass the witness."

Wayne's turn comes to either save or destroy my life. He takes a minute to read something on his notepad. I draw in a breath and let it out slowly. Right now, my whole life depends on him.

"Mr. Fuller, you're saying someone else killed Elizabeth."

"I'm saying Clint killed Elizabeth."

"Objection," Mr. Benoit says. "Clint isn't on trial here."

"Sustained."

I sigh. Clint should be on trial here. If they let me speak instead of interrupting or objecting to everything I try to say, maybe I could get some words out. But right now, I look like an idiot. The jurors glare. They hate me. And I don't know how to make things right. I should have listened to Wayne's advice to not testify.

"The evening you found out Elizabeth was missing, you and Lauren had argued that day, is that correct?" Wayne asks.

"I wouldn't call it an argument. I had told her about my acceptance to Columbia and she was angry. She wanted to go home. I took her home."

"And what did you do after you took her home?"

"I went home."

"Did you hate Elizabeth?"

"No. I loved her like a little sister. And yes, like most little sisters, she annoyed me sometimes. But that doesn't mean I wanted her dead."

"Did you want her dead?"

"No, absolutely not."

"But you left her alone, standing at the curb waving bye."

"Because she said she was fine. She was just waving. She liked to do that." What was my attorney doing? Trying to make the jurors hate me more?

"So this wasn't her first time to be alone?" he asks.

"No. Not at all."

"And you were with Lauren most of the day."

"Until about six PM, yes."

"Doesn't give you much time to kill her sister then, huh?"

"No."

"Objection." Mr. Benoit stands. I have no idea what he's objecting to—he doesn't even say and probably doesn't know—but the judge sustains it. It's like he's a broken record with his sustains.

"When is the last time you remember wearing your cap?"

I have to think about the question a moment. The cap was special. Given to me by my father two years prior when he took me to my first—and my last—UT football game. He had taken me to tell me Mom was in full remission.

"The day before, I think."

"Do you remember what you were doing?"

"I had some friends over at my house and we barbecued and swam."

"So anybody could have taken that cap."

"Including Clint."

Mr. Benoit scowls. Another win for me, and it's sad I have to think of my life that way right now.

"I pass the witness."

Benoit leans forward. "Clint is your best friend, is he not?"

"He was."

"And yet you still try to pin this on him."

"He's the one who framed me."

"You've heard countless investigators on the stand. Even heard Clint testify himself. They did an extensive investigation. Interviewing witnesses. Taking in evidence. They covered all their bases."

"Objection," Wayne says. "this isn't time for closing arguments."

"Sustained. Ask a question or pass the witness, Mr. Benoit." The judge is starting to look bored. Too bad I don't have that luxury.

"You and Lauren argued a lot, didn't you?"

"No." My voice rises.

"You argued a lot about Elizabeth and how she annoyed you."

"Well, sometimes I got upset when Lauren let her tag along with us, but I can't say we argued about it."

"That's not what we've heard from others."

"Well, that's what you're hearing from me."

Mr. Benoit chuckles. The look on his face is like he made a score in his favor, and from there it only goes downhill.

Luke Present Day

Luke tossed and turned every night for the next week. He should leave things alone. Stop obsessing over whether the girl was his daughter. He had been robbed of the best years of his life. Why obsess over things he could never have?

No matter what, he would never get Lauren back. Her family would never be his. He had been exonerated. Cleared. But Lauren would always consider him guilty.

When the day came for him to pack and travel to Galveston, he actually looked forward to it. He hadn't been to the ocean since his release, and the DA was right that he could consider it a vacation. He arrived a day early to settle in and watched the sunset on the bay, a flaming orb dissolving into trickles of gold until every tincture disappeared into the water. He got up early and admired the sunrise while a soft breeze blew across his skin. The fingers of orange sparked from the edges of earth, blanketing the sky in color.

He didn't prepare his speech. The DA asked him to speak from the heart, so he would. It's not like he hadn't ever given a speech. He had been good at it in high school, had been top of his debate team, and he spoke a lot in prison to empower other inmates to overcome adversity, even if much of their adversity was psychological.

And if he fumbled, so be it. He didn't give things like that power over his life anymore.

When it came time for his speech, nerves didn't wrack him after his introduction and he stepped on stage, but he hesitated at the crowds of people. He hadn't expected many to attend, but then Brian said this conference was for all Texas prosecutors and their staffs.

He took a moment to breathe and nodded at their applause.

He waved, mostly to compose the crowd. "Good morning. I'm Luke Fuller. Most of you probably know me as The State of Texas vs. Lucas Donovan Fuller."

The crowd continued to cheer and ooh and aah and whistle as if he was some kind of celebrity. He glanced down, swiped his hands across his mouth, then looked up. The crowd calmed, and finally he spoke.

"The day started like any other. I'd barely graduated high school and was still planning my future. I thought I'd be a doctor, but I didn't quite know what I wanted. I only knew I wanted it to include the woman I loved.

"We fought that night. I told her I had been accepted into a college she didn't know I had applied for. We had been planning our college education for months, but living together was a different matter. It was definitely a stressful time. I would have had an alibi if we stayed together. My sister's alibi I had come home wasn't enough for the cops. Especially not when my sister claimed to have seen my good friend, Clint Merkel, with Elizabeth who was later found dead. You see, Clint was the mayor's son. And Elizabeth was my girlfriend's sister."

Lauren shifted in her seat, her pulse pounding in her ears. Luke scrubbed a hand over his face.

She took a breath and held it, releasing it slowly and straining to hear his words. His voice was loud, but the boom in her chest and the compression in her ears nearly had her passing out.

"I was with her when she learned about her sister," Luke continued. "My sister found the body. The cops thought I told her where to find her. My girlfriend crumbled into my arms and I held her as she cried. But later, I was arrested. They found my pocketknife near her body. They arrested me in front of my girlfriend, and I'll never forget the look of anguish on her face. She had indicted me the moment they put the cuffs on my hands."

Lauren held her breath again and scanned the audience.

He hadn't said her name, but she felt like a spotlight surged over her.

He didn't know she was in the crowd, and she shrank further in her seat. She didn't want him to know, didn't want him to lose his momentum. His speech held everyone captive.

When Elizabeth hadn't come home that night, they organized a frenzied search. Luke had come over to hold her in his arms.

"A friend of Elizabeth's and my sister had both seen Clint with Elizabeth, and other evidence clearly pointed to Clint. Never mind the fact I was home and grieving my fight with my girlfriend. Nobody listened to my sister. They withheld evidence of Clint's DNA.

"Meanwhile, evidence continued to pile against me as I sat in jail and awaited my trial. Friends who testified said I was violent, and that Elizabeth had a crush on me and I thought she was cute. My home was ransacked—in a legal way of course—but nobody found any evidence of anything in my home even though officers say they found evidence of child porn." He shut his eyes, opened them. "But I was found guilty the moment Clint and his father pointed their fingers my direction."

He paused. His shoulders dropped, his posture opening as each hand held the corner of the podium. He leaned closer to the crowd. Lauren's belly flopped.

"I was still a kid myself." His voice cracked. "But it didn't take me long to toughen up in prison. You know the rumors about how inmates don't like child killers, and I was accused of sexual assault as well." He visibly shivered and closed his eyes. "Well, part of that rumor is true. I was beaten to within an inch of my life, but gained respect when I stood up for myself. Inmates started listening to me, hearing my story, and those who claimed to be falsely accused came to me for advice. I couldn't judge them, for I had been falsely accused, too, and we started a support group. I survived largely in thanks to my cellmate who was a big tough guy and had taken me on like a brother. He believed my story. He was in prison for life for robbery and shooting someone—accidentally he said, but still he killed someone. He took me under his wings and helped me survive."

He snickered. "But nobody raped me, if that's what you're wondering. And I didn't rape anyone. Some fallacies of prison are just that. Fallacies. I didn't come out of there tainted and bruised."

He spoke briefly about his trial, about going to prison. Her body tensed as she listened, tried to absorb his words. He could have said so much more. From everything Brian had told her, Luke could have listed so much more of the corruption he'd faced.

But he played fair.

She relaxed in her seat but didn't want to bring attention to herself. The conference room was situated with tables and chairs, and her coworkers all sat at the same table. Everyone had turned their chair to face Luke, but from the corner of her eye she occasionally caught her boss glancing at her.

She ignored him, the throb in her ears thrumming louder.

"I could hold a lot of resentment for law enforcement and the criminal justice system. I don't. Well, sometimes I do a little."

The audience laughed. She wriggled, snorted, finally meeting her boss's eye and smiling a smile that didn't reach her heart.

He continued, "I only ask that, as prosecutors, you consider all evidence in a case, whether the suspect is your preacher's wife or the mayor's son or your biggest enemy. Hold everyone accountable for doing the best job they can do and make sure you are sending the right person to prison.

Now they have the Michael Morton Act, which means all evidence in a case must be submitted to defense and nothing can be suppressed. If only that had existed in my day. In many people's day.

"I know prosecutors have a lot on their plate, but I urge you not to automatically assume someone is guilty. If this case had been fully investigated and fully prosecuted, I wouldn't have missed my mother's funeral and I would have been able to tend to my dad when he needed help. But I've also learned a huge lesson in prison and upon my release. I've learned to take each day as it comes. I've learned to be grateful for every breath, every sunrise. A sunrise I thought never to see again." He waved his hand. "I've also learned not to think about what might have been. Thanks for allowing me to be a part of your conference. Thanks for listening to my speech. And thanks for inviting me. I wish you a very blessed rest of your convention."

He kept his hand up and backed away from the podium.

The crowd stood and erupted in applause. Her scalp prickled. She hesitated, but followed alongside the crowd, using their actions to guide her while her mind played catch-up.

Guilt consumed her. Guilt at all he faced and all he'd lost.

He had testified at his own trial. Had he been this believable? The jury hadn't thought so.

As everyone milled around and people approached him, she went for the door. The crowd of people impeded her movements, trapping her. Everyone wanted to go the opposite direction, moving toward him while she tried to flee.

Her skin burned the moment his eyes found hers, picking her out of the crowd. Her muscles tensed. Awareness tightened her blood. His forehead wrinkled. Their gazes were broken when someone slapped him on the back and people approached for handshakes.

She escaped out the door and barely made it into her room. She sank to the floor on her knees, a flood of tears weakening her and crumbling her bones.

This had been her fault. If nothing else, she had been partially responsible.

She'd turned him away that night, somewhat upset over their talk of the future. College was looming, taking precedence over their wedding. They had both been stressed. She was afraid they would break up, and she felt exhausted and afraid of the future.

If they'd stayed together, he would have had an alibi. Instead, already angry at him, she'd been distraught to learn her sister had been murdered, and he was the prime suspect. She had turned him away, and she believed he took that anger out on her sister.

As tears sobbed out of her, a silent solitude overtook her. What was done was done. The past was the past. Luke had survived, was well-adjusted, and he could start over.

She let the tears fall, a washing away of her guilt, then stood and stumbled to the bathroom to throw water on her face and freshen her makeup.

She would talk to Luke. Tell him she was sorry then move on with her life and let him move on with his.

But when she stepped into the reception hall, she didn't see him. Many people mingled and talked and ate, but no sign of Luke. She swam through the crowd, searching with no luck.

She wasn't ready to go back to her room, alone, but she wasn't ready to mingle amongst the crowd. She stepped outside and saw him sitting in the shadows, nursing a cocktail, and wondered how she could ever forget him or move on with her life.

What would have happened if their past hadn't turned out so horrific? Would they have married? Or would he have resented her for having a baby and changing his life's plans? Or would they have grown together as a family and had more children?

She'd never know.

He would have made a good father. The Luke she had known before would have done anything in his power to make things work, to give a good life to his children. He came from a good family. His father had turned to one too many drinks, but only after his wife had died. Luke's sister had moved back to take care of things.

Because that's what his family did. Take care of things and take care of each other.

She exhaled her regret and squared her shoulders, then approached him.

She intended to tell him about Laramie. She couldn't take anymore away from him, and no matter how much it hurt, she would tell him. Her mother's advice about telling Laramie first was spot-on, but she ignored it. As the father, he deserved to know.

He'd found a quiet corner away from the lights and the crowds. A sultry breeze blew off the coast, the waves whooshing to shore, only a sound and a feeling in the depths of night. The heat was suffocating, smothering her. Or at least that's what she blamed on her inability to breathe.

He hid in the shadows and sipped his drink, but acknowledged her with a wary nod. She pulled out a chair and sat without asking for permission.

"Your speech was..." How to describe it?

He cocked his head, his gaze watching, waiting. Despite the heat and humidity, shivers crawled over her skin. Pinpricks, piercing open her soul. She hesitated.

"I've been bombarded with people stopping to tell me how great it was. Thanks for sharing. Blah blah blah."

"It was," she said. "Great." She tapped her fingers on the

table, wishing she grabbed a drink from the bar before venturing out here. "Everyone's been gushing about you. You're lucky to have found this private spot."

He only nodded.

"I do appreciate you sharing your story, and I hope it helps people. I-I'm so sorry. Sorry I didn't listen." He'd tried to call her from jail to plead with her until her parents put a stop to it. His sister had approached to talk, until they'd stopped that, too.

"What's done is done," he said, the exact words she'd thought earlier. They'd always been on the same wavelength until that night when everything changed.

"True enough," she said. "But it doesn't make me any less regretful."

He took a pull from his drink. She licked her lips. Her throat was raw and parched, the words she meant to say worsening the scorch.

"What are you doing here?" he asked.

"I'm the victim coordinator for the District Attorney's Office. I'm actually teaching a class tomorrow."

His eyes squinted at her. "Was it your idea to invite me to speak?"

She sneered. "Absolutely not. I was furious at my boss when he told me he'd asked you."

"So your boss knows about us?"

"About our past. Yes. But only he does. Unless any of my coworkers put it together after your speech."

He chewed on his lip.

"I'm glad he did ask you, though. At first yes, I was furious. But I enjoyed hearing you speak, and I think it helped people. Newbie prosecutors and even the older ones. And it gave me good ideas on things to talk about tomorrow in my class."

He tilted his head and studied her. "What's your class about?"

"Helping victims. Tips and techniques. Things I've learned over the years. But we also need to remember that the families of the accused are victims. Even though we don't deal with them, we should stay compassionate and attuned to them. So many times in trial, I see people laughing and joking during breaks while the jury is out, but the defendant is still there. I might have done it myself a time or two. And the majority of those times, the defendant deserves no compassion. But they have families."

Her voice softened. Unshed tears rubbed her throat raw yet again. Would she ever be done with those tears?

"It sounds like you love your job."

She nodded and drummed her fingers on the table. "I do. I really, really do. Mostly, I love helping the victims get through the trial and take their next step toward their new life. Sometimes it isn't easy, and sometimes I have those victims who aren't able to deal with what happened to them. But I do love my job. I have a good boss and I work with a bunch of great people."

She clenched her mouth shut, already revealing too much. Why was she talking to him like he was an old friend?

"That's good. It seems like you're good at it."

"I feel like I am, most of the time. But there are times I'm not so good. There are never any winners in my line of work. Someone always suffers. But as you can see, I do okay for myself. And I do okay, and yet you paid my five-hundred dollar deductible. You shouldn't have done that."

"It was nothing. Your wreck was my fault."

"How do you figure? I'm the one who drove out there."

His eyes twinkled, and for a moment she almost felt like he was her old friend, her lover.

"Anyway, I won't keep gushing, but I apologize for being

so rude. Accusing you of doing something to my car." She snickered and waved her hand through the air. "That was ridiculous. And I'm sorry. Just sorry. I'm sorry I didn't believe you."

"Sorry you threatened my life?" His eyes gleamed, and his lilting smile told her he wasn't angry. But he should be angry. He had every right to be angry.

Stiffening her shoulders, she leaned forward and planted her palms on the table, prepared to tell him exactly what she'd planned to tell him when she searched for him.

She couldn't allow room for friendship or attachment. Might as well blurt it all out. Plenty of time for regrets later. What was one more regret to deal with, anyway?

"She's your daughter."

Saying it hadn't released the pressure inside. If anything, it built into an inferno. Her head spun as if she'd been drinking. And oh how she wished she had been.

His eyes bulged, then squeezed shut. He pinched the bridge of his nose. Electricity zinged through the air, shocking her skin over and over.

Now he knew. No turning back.

LUKE WAS USED TO LOSING. Once out of prison, he was grateful for a new life and never expected anything else. The speech was a good catharsis and would help him move forward in writing his book, but how could he move forward, knowing he had a child?

His skin tightened, burned, his body ripped apart, piece by piece. The jagged hole in his gut grew wider. Heat swelled behind his eyes. He chugged a breath. Another. Then hollowness took over.

He had lost everything. Everything. And he had fought for years to maintain his dignity. What was the point?

He lifted his head and squinted at Lauren. He didn't fault her for her decisions, even the decision to doubt him. "She's mine?" His voice crackled, as if bees attacked and stung at his defenses.

"Who else's would she be?"

He hung his head and let the tears fall. He hadn't cried in so long, couldn't afford to cry. His body ached. His breath stalled. He planted his elbows on the table and rested his head in his hands. His shoulders shook, a map revealing every ounce of his grief. Spasms racked his body. His bones almost snapped.

She didn't touch him, only sat nearby in silence. He didn't want her to touch him, didn't want her sympathy. But damn, a little compassion wouldn't be so bad.

"Her name is Laramie Elizabeth Cooper," she finally said. "Named after my sister Elizabeth."

Cooper. Not Fuller. It should have been Fuller, named after Luke. Luke should have had that right. Should have had the right to know his daughter.

His tears dried, but his sorrow grew louder, escalating into scorn. Bitterness. Something he had fought against to keep his sanity.

The tide swelled and the waves crashed a distinct sound in the darkness. He held on to that. The waves rolling, the earth rotating, and everything continuing as it should, despite the unfairness of things.

"Why don't we go to my room where there's some privacy and talk about this," she said.

He lifted his head gave her a slow blink. "What's there to talk about?"

"I told you about Laramie, but she doesn't know. I don't want her to know."

"Of course you don't," he said, defeated. His breath wheezed, a choking, escaping, dying of his dreams.

They'd talked of having children, dreamed and planned of a bright future, but that future was snatched from him the moment the cops placed those cuffs on his wrists.

He had changed in prison. He'd been forced to be hardcore to keep away from those who would do him harm, but deep inside he was still the boy who had fallen in love with the woman who sat before him now.

"Clint was her godparent." Her voice cracked. "She thinks her dad died at war."

"How honorable." Sarcasm dripped from his voice.

"More so than letting her know her father was in prison for murder."

Her words stung, but he was accustomed to the pinch in his heart. "So you'll continue to lie?"

"I don't know yet. But I appreciate it if you keep this to yourself until I decide."

He stood and saluted her as a harsh cold conviction slapped his face. He had no plans to pick things up where they left off. He hadn't even had plans to see Lauren or her family, and wouldn't have if she hadn't come to his home. He should never have come home. How could he start over in the one place that destroyed him?

No sense in dwelling on impossibilities, but he could damn sure pack up and move. Both his sisters had. His father had. Why not him?

"I don't plan on telling her anything, or getting within a hundred feet of you two. Great to see you though. Have a good life."

With that, he walked away.

CHAPTER NINE

Luke Twelve Years Ago

By the time the judge sentences me to life in prison, I'm too numb to care. Wayne asks if I want something to calm my nerves, but I refuse.

The judge asks if the victims have an impact statement they want to read. Wayne had warned me about this part. The victims—Elizabeth's family—can get up there and read an impact statement which goes to the prison system with the rest of my paperwork. Lauren's mother steps on the stand.

The paper shakes in her hand. I'm not even sure how she can read. I don't want to listen, but neither do I try to reach out anymore. She lost her daughter, but everything has been ripped from me. I will never have a daughter, a son, or a family.

"Luke," she says, her voice wobbly. But she gains strength as she glares at me. Hatred fuels her. "You took away our daughter. You took away everything. We trusted you. You lied, over and over and over. I'm supposed to forgive, but life in prison doesn't make up for the life you took from us. So brutally. Lisa was so young. She had so much potential. A bright, beautiful child full of love and laughter. I can't imagine her fear when the man she trusted with all her heart robbed her of everything."

She breaks down and weeps. My throat gurgles, but I can no longer cry. She probably thinks I have no feeling, no reaction, no care in the world. I've given up.

Mr. Cooper speaks next, but Lauren refuses. Still, she sits in the courtroom, her sniffles loud and booming to my core. I wish she would speak, though I won't have a chance to. I wish she would sit up on that stand and look at me and tell me she's one-hundred percent convinced I'm guilty. I want to look into her eyes, breathe with her again, and connect our souls.

But I can't. And I never will again. The rest of my hopes die.

"Luke," her father says. "A man who was like a son to me. A man I took hunting and fishing. A man I thought would be my son one day. Your father is a good man, but I tried to be a mentor as well. I've seen you grow over the years and was excited for your future. You were going to be a doctor. But deep inside, everything you showed us was a lie. You were living another life, a deviant life. Your greed, envy and lust got the better of you. A man I thought would give me grandchildren. A man who took my child's life in a brutal and unimaginable way. Maybe one day I'll forgive you, but I hope you can never forgive yourself."

———

Luke Present Day

. . .

Luke drove home, his body in a furious knot. His eyes focused on the road while the havoc in his mind continued to rage.

He had a daughter. A daughter with the woman he once loved.

After his release, he planned to live a simple life. He loved working with cars, but only did it part time for something to do. Otherwise, he might become a hermit and it was hard enough going back to the real world. Despite his innocence, his punishment lingered. People still wondered. He didn't want to be tied down to a job when he'd already missed out on life, and the compensation he received for his wrongful conviction was enough to live on.

He'd fish, hunt, make jerky, grow a garden, and live a simple life. Finish the book he was writing, even if it killed him to rehash the past.

Lauren complicated his plans the moment she stepped on his back porch. He never expected to experience such emotions when he saw her, no matter how often he'd visualized a meeting. And then to learn he had a child.

Protective instincts burned his skin. Such a vulnerable age for a young girl. She had no father, no father figure. Clint had been a part of her life, even a godparent.

He pulled off to the side of the road and cried.

Everything he'd lost. Everything he'd missed. It all tore out of him in large, gulping tears. Since his release, this was only the second time he cried. The anger and grief culminated into a screaming rage in his body.

He wouldn't let it defeat him or turn to bitter resentment. He had a new life, new opportunities, and he refused to imprison his mind. He had to get it together, and he had to keep it together.

One thing prison taught him was resilience. Many dark days impossible to end. He'd learned to clear his mind and meditate, and it brought him a deep sense of clarity and control. He focused on that now while the Jeep idled and cars whooshed by.

If he completed his story now, Lauren would be hurt in the process. So would Laramie.

His daughter.

As if that wasn't bad enough, a letter from Lauren's parents was in his mailbox when he arrived home. He hesitated on opening it, unsure if he wanted to know what it said. Her mother had been like his second mother. She had doted on him. He'd respected the hell out of her father and remembered the harsh words they spoke from the victim impact statement during the punishment phase of his trial. He'd cried that day, alone and in the transport car back to county jail before his transport to prison. But they had been the last tears he shed until now.

He tore open the envelope, his heart crashing against his ribs. He read the words and focused on breathing to avoid passing out.

Dear Luke,

We're so sorry for everything you've been through and for not trusting in you. Despite our grief and the words spoken at your trial, we forgave you long before we knew the truth. We hope you will find it in your hearts to forgive us, as well. You were a victim in all of this, too. Life is full of grace and hardships. Sometimes more hardship than grace. We hope you will find the grace through the hardships you faced, as we have. We hope you take the opportunity for this second chance at life and live it to the fullest, and we offer many prayers for you. We have many good memories with you, despite the bad. Maybe one day we'll see you again, maybe we won't, but please know you will always hold a special place in our hearts.

With love,
Joe and Beth Cooper

Tears bled through the written words on the page by the time he reached the end. Hands shaking, he gripped the paper. He sniffled and read it again and again until tears blurred the words.

The fact they forgave him before they ever believed in his innocence was confirmation of the good-hearted people they were. He wondered if he should read between the lines when the letter said *second chance at life and live it to the fullest* if they hoped he pursued their daughter.

No way in hell. They would never hint at such a thing, and Lauren would be furious if they had. Still, it stoked the fires within him and gave him hope.

He wanted to see their daughter. He wanted to see his daughter and have a chance to know her. Even if she didn't know him and only thought of him as a family friend, that was enough for him.

Everything in his body settled as determination grounded any other plans. He wanted to see Lauren again, too, and hoped like hell she agreed. Because he had been falsely imprisoned and had a child out there, she had no choice but to agree.

Lauren left the conference a day early, concerned about Luke but also concerned about Laramie. Now that he knew the truth, would he do something stupid? Approach her and belt out the truth, demand a chance to know her? Laramie would learn about how her mother had lied. But Luke had suffered as well.

She didn't tell her mom about seeing Luke at the conference, and gave a lot of false smiles until she was on the road with Laramie.

She was glad to be home, ready for her own bed and to

have an extra-long weekend. She dreaded going back to work. Although she couldn't imagine Brian saying anything to anyone, just one word, one hint, could spread rumors. Brian kept the file in his office, but did that mean no one else made copies for him or read the contents? And with everything going digital, someone would eventually scan it into their system.

Her main goal was to protect Laramie, but she wasn't sure continuing to lie was considered protection.

Brian was out most of the next week, and no one acted strange or said anything except for a few comments on how well Luke's speech went, how sorry they felt for him, and the girls commenting on how hot he was. By the end of the week, her stomach finally relaxed.

Until Luke called her on Thursday morning.

"What are you doing calling me at work?" She rose and shut the door.

"I gave them a fake name."

"Most everyone here heard your speech. They might recognize your voice."

"Highly unlikely. But if someone does, what difference does it make?"

What difference did it make? Would it matter if her coworkers knew her sister was murdered? She considered herself lucky they didn't already know. She was the only local Bryan had hired when he brought on a new team, and back then social media hadn't been big. Her aunt, who owned the local paper, had safeguarded the family. The townspeople had protected them and their town. Lauren stayed out of the spotlight and now nobody could search for Lauren Cooper and learn anything except for a talented musician with the same name.

Even national news glossed over the fact yet another man had been exonerated because of a dirty politician.

She returned to her desk and bunched her fist in her hair. "Okay, well what can I help you with?"

"I've had a lot of time to think."

Chills crawled under her skin, into her spine. "About what?"

"I'd like a chance to get to know Laramie."

Her throat constricted, pain radiating from her neck and twisting in her spine.

When she didn't speak, he continued in his long Texas drawl. "Not to tell her or anything like that. Just one day to spend with her, as if we were friends or something. Y'all can come to my place and swim and go boating and we can grill something. One day. That's all I ask."

"One day?" she finally managed.

"One day. Would that be so bad?"

"She's a smart girl."

"I imagine she is."

"She's already questioned me."

"Okay. So you think spending a day with me will make her question you more."

She twirled the phone cord around her hand, then released it along with her breath. "Let me think about it," she said.

"We can plan this weekend or the next," he offered.

"I'll let you know."

She had already decided to see Luke again and talk to him about Laramie, but not with Laramie. She wanted to apologize and get the rest of their feelings out in the open. He deserved to see his daughter. He'd already been robbed of way too much.

Despite all the emotions he wrought in her, she had missed him over the years. Things had been abruptly taken from her. Her sister, her boyfriend, her hopes and dreams.

She loved her life now, she did, and she'd choose the mundane over any other of life's surprises.

But she'd barely dated. Because of Laramie, she hadn't planned to date until her daughter graduated. No sense in putting her through that chop-chop of courtship. She wanted to be a good influence on her, show her relationships were meant for eternity. Maybe refusing to date didn't help, but Laramie came first. Her career came second. A personal life was low on the list.

She'd never found another man to stir such intensity in her as Luke had. She thought she'd never love again. If she saw him, talked with him in the present tense instead of the past, could she get over her feelings? Get closure and get on with her life?

Studying the phone as if it held all the answers, she brainstormed a resolution. Spend the day with Luke and Laramie and watch how they acted around each other. Then she would decide if she would tell Laramie the truth. If she hated him, why bother telling her? Right? Not such a bad idea.

She picked up the phone to call Brian.

"I've decided to hold a meeting to let our team know I'm the sister of the child killed."

His intake of breath was palpable through the phone. "That's great."

"On one condition."

"Absolutely."

"I won't go into any sordid details. They'll obviously figure out we dated. That's a given because he said so in his speech. But it stops there. As far as I'm concerned, it stays within the office as any case does."

"That's a high condition. In this day and age, I can't guarantee it won't hit social media within minutes."

"It's the only way I will agree."

"Okay. I'll send a memo to set up a meeting tomorrow

morning."

The next morning, Lauren second-guessed her decision to tell her coworkers about her history. Keeping it secret hadn't been difficult, so why admit it now?

Everyone grumbled about the meeting. Attorneys with tired faces and administrators eager to get back to their work—or at least get out of the conference room and off the hard, inflexible chairs.

Brian talked about cases and things—he often rambled to hear his own voice. But when he handed it over to her, her words stumbled over her breath.

Situated at the end of the table, she cleared her throat and leaned forward. She'd have to speak loudly to reach all seventeen employees throughout the room, and no way would her wobbly legs hold her if she stood.

"Many of you heard Luke Fuller's speech last week."

There were nods, peaks of interests, and some eye rolls.

She continued, "I thought it was only fair to let everyone know the child who was killed was my sister."

Gasps. Heads turning, eyes wide. Everyone's attention was on her now.

She shrugged and held up her arms. "I don't know why, I um, wanted to expel any rumors before they started. My sister was the one killed, and his sister is the one who found her."

People mumbled, asked questions, but Brian hushed them.

"His speech really hit home with me," she continued. "After working here, I see there were a lot of flaws in the way the investigation was handled. But we're a better team, and we won't stand for those mistakes.

"Luke and I were friends in school. His release was hard on me. But I'm better now, and he deserves a chance to have a successful life. I thought it only fair to let everyone know, so no questions or rumors arose later. We both want to be left out of the news and out of the spotlight."

She clasped her hands together and nodded, finished with her admission. Everyone wore sympathy, some even cried, and her heart swelled. Her job and coworkers sometimes irritated her, but they all cared for and supported each other. Brian was a good boss who produced a good sense of office morale.

"We don't work on revenge and sovereignty," Brian interjected. "We work on justice. And justice means not only putting the bad guys behind bars, but making sure the innocent ones are exonerated, and never brought to that point. We must remember everyone is innocent until proven guilty, and we should study each case with meticulous care. If you have any doubts, talk it out with our team. And remember, we all support each other. Out of respect for Lauren, this office isn't to talk about our opinions or make judgments on this case. When we find Clint Merkel, we will prosecute to the fullest extent of the law."

People hugged her or patted her on the back then filed out of the conference room. Tamra approached and clutched her hands. "Let me know if you ever need to talk."

"I will, I will."

Closing her office door, she exhaled, calm overtaking one of her biggest fears. Her coworkers knew she was the victim of a horrendous case. She could be back in the spotlight, pitied, criticized, or gossiped about. *Poor Lauren. What she's been through.* She didn't want to go through that talk again, having suffered plenty after the murder.

She picked up her pen and checked the first thing off her to-do list, then picked up the phone to call her next victim. Time to put it behind her and get back to work. Time to face the day and the next case.

She'd decide what to do about Laramie later.

CHAPTER TEN

That evening, Lauren cooked tacos for dinner. She spoke to Laramie as she helped with the food. "Luke invited us to his house to go fishing and swimming."

Laramie stopped peeling the cheese and crinkled her nose. "But we have a pool."

"A community pool full of kids. And you can't fish in it. Don't you want to go out to the river?"

Her chin jutted. "With Luke? I thought you hated him."

Lauren shrugged and reeled her attention away from the stove to chop tomatoes. She didn't want to push her daughter to agree, but after deciding to see Luke, she was ready.

She tilted her head and returned her attention to the cheese grater. "I have Jana's birthday party, remember?"

"Oh, that's right. That's fine. I'll tell him no."

"It doesn't start until six. We can go out for the day and I can come in for the party. I'm staying overnight, remember?"

She turned back to the stove and stirred the beef as it popped. She clicked the temperature down to low and wiped her hands. "Yes, I remember. I'll tell him we have other plans."

Was that nonchalant enough?

Laramie pushed the bowl of shredded cheese aside and grabbed the bag of lettuce. "No, Mom. It'll be fun. He probably wants to make amends. Unless he's going to kill us both."

Lauren snapped her gaze to Laramie, who wriggled her eyebrows and snuffed back a giggle. "I'm kidding, Mom."

They ate dinner and watched movies, but Lauren's stomach churned all night. She wrestled with telling Laramie, but telling her now would make her want to avoid going out there. She would be angry, probably for a while. Why not get to know Luke first?

She texted Luke her decision and warned him not to say anything, touched by his reply. *I understand. That's your decision and you can tell her when you're ready. Thanks for giving me the chance to get to know her. I look forward to seeing y'all tomorrow.*

And tomorrow came way too soon for Lauren's liking. She was a basket case and almost canceled several times. If not for Lauren rushing her to get there and have time to swim before the birthday party, she might have canceled.

She turned the vehicle into Luke's driveway, and tires crunched the gravel. Laramie sat up straighter in her seat to peer out the windshield.

"Cool place." She unbuckled her seatbelt. The vehicle stopped, and she opened the door and jumped out.

The sky was a perfect blue concoction of fluffy clouds and sunshine. Like all Texas summers, the heat and mugginess snatched her breath. She longed for the river.

Luke strolled up to greet them. Lauren fought the urge to admire his body, the bulge in his legs under his swim trunks and the frame of his upper body in a wife-beater tee. His biceps bulged larger than they had at eighteen, but initiated the same reaction. Dry mouth, body burning, mind hesitating to react.

Luke offered Laramie a handshake, and Lauren held her breath. They hadn't officially met, and he promised he wouldn't say anything. But would Laramie sense it?

"Hi Laramie. I'm Luke. Nice to meet you."

Laramie nodded and shook his hand. "Thanks for the invitation to your house. It's beautiful out here."

"Welcome. You wanna check out the river?"

Laramie swirled her head to find her mom, eyes wide. "Can we?"

"Sure. Whenever you're ready."

"Do you need to change into anything?" Luke asked.

"No," Laramie said. "We've got our swim suits on under our clothes, but I need to grab my bag with sunscreen."

"I've got an ice chest full of snacks, sodas, and water, and I've got sunscreen and anything else you could think of."

"Oh. Okay."

"Hop in the Jeep. We'll drive down."

"Cool."

The Jeep's tops and doors were all off, so they literally hopped in. They drove down a hill about a hundred feet, then he stopped and they walked through an outcropping of rock to get to the water.

"Be sure to watch for snakes around here," Luke warned.

"Yes, father," Laramie joked, then giggled when she stepped around a rock. "Sorry."

His head snapped around, his gaze finding Lauren's. Eyes wide, she shook her head. No, no, no, Laramie was joking. Ironic, yes, but a joke. Like all parents warning a child to watch for snakes. His eyes narrowed, then he focused back on the jaunt to the river.

The trip wasn't far. They stopped on a smooth boulder

with a belly full of sand and slopes of water. Laramie tore off her sandals and cover-up then dipped her toe in.

"Nice," she said.

"Wait. Don't forget the sunscreen," Lauren said.

"I will later. I put some on before we got here."

"Well, do a little more."

Laramie rolled her eyes but sprayed sunscreen around her body and face, then slid into the water.

"Wait for us," Lauren warned.

"It doesn't get deep until further out," Luke said. "This is a great swimming hole. The bottom is nothing but soft sand."

"I don't want Laramie traipsing off by herself and finding trouble. The river can be a dangerous place." She removed her shorts and t-shirt to reveal her one-piece and ignored Luke's lingering gaze as she sprayed on sunscreen.

The water was soothing, cooling her skin. She sank in all her body and let out an "ah". No jumping in. Too much rock outcroppings and shallow water.

The river's coolness sizzled as soon as Luke took off his shirt and submerged his body. She imagined the entire water boiling under the heat of him. He was cut, ripped and smooth in all the right places. Apparently, prison had kept him lean and mean.

She shook that thought aside and dove underwater. A good way to cool off.

They had fun swimming. Laramie chattered about school and set the tone for the day and mentioned how, no matter how much she enjoyed learning, she enjoyed summers better and wished she never had to go back.

"What grade are you in?" Luke asked.

"I'm starting seventh."

"Seventh. Wow."

"Yeah." She swam away, then back. Luke winked at Lauren. His eyes were soft, filled with an inner glow that bespoke of his appreciation for this moment. Lauren's heart pattered.

"What's your favorite subject?" he asked.

"I love music and I kind of like math."

"Oh, so you're in band?"

"Yes. I play the flute."

"That's cool. Are you any good at math?"

"Better than my mom," she said, then laughed and dove underwater. She continued to chatter and swim, swimming away and coming back, then swimming away again.

"This sure beats the community pool at home," she said.

Luke beamed. "Does anyone want a float?" he asked.

"I'm good," Laramie said.

"Me, too," Lauren said. "Although I should work on my tan."

Laramie swam away. Luke sidled closer to Lauren and whispered in her ear, "You have a beautiful body."

Heat dipped into her pelvic area. The pressure in her body intensified, and the flame he built within her ignited to a solid state of arousal.

Smiling, she splashed away, keeping her distance from him so her daughter didn't notice her attraction. This day wasn't about her, or about them. It was about Laramie. Even though she didn't know Luke was her dad, it gave them an opportunity to spend time together and get to know each other.

Why had she agreed to this? The feelings he stirred in her were dangerous. She couldn't afford to fall for him. Her life had no room for a man, especially one who exhilarated her.

They ate lunch, sandwiches Luke had already prepared, then he took them canoeing in his small metal boat. Laramie never squirmed when he brought out the worms and handed her a pole.

"I'm impressed," he noted.

"I grew up around the river," Laramie said. "I learned to hook worms when I was like three."

He gawked at Lauren, and she smiled and nodded at her daughter's admission. He didn't need to know Clint had taken her a time or two, an attempt to give her a normal life. Overcompensation, or so Lauren thought. On thinking it over, she recognized it as grooming, and her throat stung with nausea.

"What time is it?" Laramie asked at one point.

Luke peeked at his watch. "Almost four," he said. "Why? Are you ready to leave?"

"No, but I've got a birthday party at six and I need a little time to get ready."

"Oh." His face fell, and he scowled out the water. "I have some hot dogs to grill."

"Sorry. The party was already planned. Can we do it another time?" her daughter asked.

"Sure." He paddled the boat back to the shore. "If you're like most girls, you probably need more than a little time to get ready, so I'll get you back to shore."

"Thanks." She gave her mom a cringing smile.

They loaded in the Escape, and Laramie gushed about how much fun she had and thanked him for the invitation. Luke nodded a thank you, but his smile didn't reach his eyes. He stood at the driveway and watched them leave, his lips pressed tight and face slack.

"That was fun," Laramie said on the drive home.

"It was," Lauren agreed.

"I felt bad. He looked so disappointed."

"I should have warned him ahead of time. I honestly never thought we'd stay that long."

"He's a nice guy."

"He is." He had always been a nice guy. Charming, caring, and always putting other people's comfort before his own.

Even at the rough age of eighteen, he had been selfless. Why had she believed he could take another's life so brutally?

As Laramie took a shower and got ready for the birthday party, Luke texted her. *Thanks for coming out. Any chance you could come back after Laramie goes to her party? I still have hot dogs to cook.*

She considered her response. Her decision could be disastrous without child supervision, but she wanted to so much.

It's just hot dogs. And maybe a beer or two he texted after she hadn't responded.

Sounds fun, she replied. *I'll be there soon after six.*

She showered and changed into shorts and a shirt, but took her swimsuit in case they went out on the river again. Laramie's birthday party was overnight, so she wouldn't be home until sometime late tomorrow, but Lauren would be home way before. She wasn't about to tell her daughter her plans to go back out to Luke's. No sense in stirring up curiosity.

Hot dogs and a beer or two. How much trouble could she get into?

With Luke, she could get into a lot of trouble. On the drive to his house, she repeated an affirmation. "I am a strong, capable woman. I can resist my attraction to Luke. I am willing to get to know him again, but I refuse to fall into bed with him."

He greeted her with a beer, twisting the top off only after she'd seen him. In another life, he wouldn't have questioned giving her an open beer, and she hated it was mostly her fault.

"Hey there." She nodded her thanks and accepted the beer. The affirmations she told herself on the drive crumbled. She wanted to touch him, taste him, explore every inch of him.

"Thanks for coming back," he said.

"Thanks for inviting me."

"I've got margaritas if you prefer."

"Oh, goodness. As good as that sounds, I have to dive home tonight." Although she wasn't sure she wanted to.

He nodded. "I can start the hot dogs as soon as you are ready."

"I don't mind waiting a while if you don't."

"Perfect. I'm not hungry yet."

"I'd love another swim, actually," she said.

"Well, come on."

They hopped into the Jeep and drove down to the river. Jumping out, he grabbed the ice chest. She reached over to nab a handle. "Let me help."

"I've got it."

"Okay. I'll just admire your muscles."

His smile pinpointed the heat in her pelvis. She cocked her head, then dipped her gaze and sauntered forward. She hadn't meant to flirt.

Or had she? His muscles were lean and chiseled, expanding every inch of his body. She assumed he performed hardcore workouts in prison, but didn't ask. He wore sunshades and a cap, so it was impossible to see his beautiful green eyes.

She was so confused about her feelings for him. One minute she wanted to hate him, the next…

He set the ice chest on a rock. She tore off her shirt and regretted her diminutive bikini top. She slipped off her sandals and dipped her toe in the water. "Damn, this feels good."

He pulled off his shirt and tossed it near the ice chest. "There's nothing better. But I'm putting in more than a toe." His smile curled the heat already scorching her body, and he dove in. She doffed her shorts to reveal the rest of her bikini before he sprung out of the water. He swam forward to seize his cap and shades and for a moment, she thought he was swimming toward her. Every inch of her body tingled.

What had she been thinking coming back here? Wearing a bikini? Flirting?

She nabbed two beers and floated toward him, handed him his, and moved a few feet away. Not too close. "Lounging in the river with a beer. Nothing better. I haven't done this in so long."

"I try to do it every day." He settled into a spot near a rock, the water rippling over him. "Well, usually with a glass of water and not beer. We forgot towels."

"That's okay. Laramie had fun today."

His face gleamed. Her heart dipped. She wanted to tell him so many things, like how sorry she was for not trusting him.

"Good, good. I'm glad to hear that. I did, too. I hope y'all will be back."

"It's hard to keep her away from the water."

"Me, too," he said, his shoulders hunched. She sensed he wanted to talk about it—the fact he had a daughter who shared some of his traits—but she didn't want to ruin a good moment with such a sensitive subject.

She let it go and sipped on her beer. "It's amazing out here. I'd be out in this water every chance I got."

"You and Laramie are welcome anytime. Open invitation."

She nodded and took another sip. "If I did it too much, I'd get fat on beer."

"I usually have tea or water. I've got some in the ice chest."

She giggled and leaned her head back to float on the water. "No, no. This is perfect."

They continued to sit in silence until their beers were empty. A slight breeze lapped against the water. Birds chirped. A distant rooster crowed. Such peace.

"I'm about to grab a cup of margaritas," Luke said. "You want one?"

"Are you trying to get me drunk?"

"Not intentionally, no. I promise I didn't make it too strong."

"Well, I would love one."

He grabbed her empty beer bottle, swam back to the ice chest, and poured them both a drink in a red Solo cup. He swam back and gave her the drink, then held up a spray bottle. "You're a little pink."

"I should probably put on a little more sunscreen before the sun goes down."

"I'll spray some on your back and shoulders if you don't mind."

She presented her back to him. "Thank you." She winced when the cold spray hit her shoulders.

"Sorry." His warm hands rubbed her skin. Her resolve shattered.

The awkward phase of first dates, first kisses, first attraction. Not a first for them, but first for today. She erased thoughts of what could have been to enjoy the moment. Counselors told her so, even if she hadn't seen one in years.

She faced him. He tossed the spray bottle on the nearby rock. She took a sip of her drink before lifting his shades off his face and onto his cap. Their gazes locked.

"That's better," she said.

He licked his lips. "Why is that?"

"Because I can see your beautiful eyes."

His breath whooshed out of him in a sound that unraveled the rest of her. He traced her collarbone, then hooked his hands into her hair and planted his mouth along her neck to suckle her skin. She cambered her head back and let him savor her.

"I taste like sunscreen," she said.

He inched away until he rested against the rock, a fight against attraction, the water creating a current against his movement. "I've never tasted anything sweeter."

She drained the margarita in her cup, stole his and gulped the rest, then leaned over to set the cups on the rock behind him. "Don't let me forget those."

"Okay," he said, his voice a low gurgle.

She pressed closer, and he had nowhere to go. "Is that a rock I feel or are you happy to see me?" Her hands trailed along his body.

Groaning, he took her mouth. "I've never been happier." His tongue delved into her mouth, taking, nourishing, combining into a feverish intensity. Her mind spun, darkness and light crafting buoyancy with the water.

His knees dug into the sand, the water not too deep, and she sat on his lap cradling both legs on each side of him. Her hands skated across his body, down to his shorts. She pulled them aside, her fingers curling around his cock.

Her pulse danced a desperate rhythm, and she took over. Kissing him, touching him, savoring him. He unclasped her top and cupped her breasts, and she sank down into him and slid him into the sweet warmth of her body.

Their bodies moved together, water slapping against their skin. He clamped his hands on each side of her waist and pumped into her. She tightened and released around him, and they surged together, came together, exploded together. After the longest, hottest release of her life, she collapsed against him in shuddering gasps of completion.

She stayed a moment to let her breath and thoughts subside. Hating him proved safer. But she couldn't. She had once loved him. Even if it was only sex now, she couldn't deny their connection. She hated herself for believing the worst.

Water lapped against the rocks, the sound a soothing

calm after a stormy crescendo. She didn't regret their lovemaking, but she couldn't fall into this secure state.

Luke Twelve Years Ago

The bulge in my pocket burns my skin. I can't stop thinking about the ring or where the best place will be for my proposal. My parents are out all evening, and I consider the big oak tree. But here at the water's edge might be best.

We swim, the ring safely secured in my shoe. Now isn't the time. I don't want to drop it in the water, and I'm fumbling everything I touch. Lauren looks too hot in her bikini to resist, so I swim over to the shore and sit on my favorite rock.

She cocks her head my direction and smiles. "What are you doing all the way over there?"

Chills thrum my achy body. I don't know why I'm feeling so shy. I want to get out of the water and propose. I don't want to touch her until she says yes.

Not that we haven't made love plenty of times before. But today is different.

We've already discussed our plans and dreams, and marriage seemed like a given to most people. But nothing had been finalized. I've heard all kinds of talk from family about how our names and relationship was like a couple on a soap opera. That makes me laugh.

All signs pointing in the right direction.

"Luke?" she says again.

"I don't know. I'm kind of hungry. You wanna grill some hot dogs?"

"No. I want to swim."

I drink a soda while I watch her dive in and out of the water. She's beautiful, inside and out, the most beautiful woman in the world. The sun descends, sprinkling gold across the water. Last night, I sat on this same rock with my mom watching the sunset and telling her about my proposal. And doubting how I can provide. We're only eighteen. We both have to get through college and getting my medical degree won't be easy. My mom's advice: *the key to staying together is growing together. You'll have your differences, and you'll each have your own interests, but be sure to share interests. Listen and grow together, not apart.*

That sounds easy enough.

I guess Lauren tires of waiting on me to come into the water, because she steps out and struts toward me, water dripping from her body. She folds her arms over her waist. I stand with a towel and swathe her once she reaches me.

"Brr."

"It's a hundred degrees outside," I say. "How can you be cold?"

She shimmies her shoulders and draws the towel closer. "It's cold when the sun goes down."

I kiss her, and she returns the kiss. My body erupts. Every nerve ending tingles in desire. She presses her pelvis against mine and groans.

I pull away and clasp her hand. "Come on." I bend down, retrieve the ring from my shoe, and slip it into my pocket before I slip on my shoes.

Now might be the perfect time, but I don't want her shivering on the shore.

"Why are you in such a hurry?" she asks as we stroll back up to the house. I should have driven the Jeep down. We'd get home quicker.

Once we make it to the large oak tree, I grab her and twirl her around. Lights are shimmering. My mom loves the glittering white lights in the summer, and it casts an ambient glow even though the sun hasn't completely descended. I press Lauren against the tree bark and kiss her again. The ache in my loins is almost too much, but I release her and drop to my knee. I reach into my pocket and pull out the ring.

"The reason I've been in a hurry is because I've been trying to find the perfect time to propose. Lauren, I love you with all my heart and soul. No time is more perfect than the present. Lauren, will you marry me?"

Her smile spreads wide across her face. She giggles and pants, then drops to her knee beside me. I clasp her around the waist and stand.

"Yes. Yes, I will marry you."

I grasp her hand, and the ring glides smoothly, fits perfectly on her finger.

I kiss her, and my mom's other piece of advice flickers through my head. *You'll face some dark times. There might be moments she wants to leave you or you want to leave her. There might be times your marriage feels like a prison sentence. But never let go. Never give up.*

LUKE PRESENT DAY

LUKE'S HEARTBEAT SLOWED. Lauren was close enough her pulse thumped against his chest as if their heartbeats melded together.

He was surprised she came back. Watching her and Laramie leave ripped grooves into his soul as if he was watching them walk out of his life for good. His heart ached.

It was silly, and he shouldn't get so attached, but he couldn't control the emotion.

He'd had a blast today, and they seemed happy, too. He might have imagined a future like this at one time, but he couldn't afford such fantasies now.

She pulled away. He patted her leg. "Are you okay?"

"I'm okay." The sun slipped behind the horizon, leaving a golden dusk trail.

"We should get out of the water before we can't find our way," Luke said. He guided her to the shore. She shivered. Sundown cooled the air to a brisk chill.

"I'm sorry I forgot towels," he said.

"I'll be okay. It feels good." Her teeth chattered.

He laughed. "You're just trying to make me feel better."

He grabbed the ice chest, and they hopped in the Jeep. He blasted the warm air, but it didn't get warm enough until they got to the house.

She jumped out of the Jeep and spread out her arms. "See. I'm already dry." He grabbed towels from the house. She showered while he built a small fire in the pit on the ground next to the deck. Then he stood and studied the darkened sky, the last vestiges of purple disappearing beyond the horizon. The half-moon offered a soft glow, the stars gleaming bright in the countryside.

Adapting to the openness had taken awhile. In prison, he'd been alone, despite the crowd. But here, he was out in the boondocks with the crickets croaking and the coyotes yapping, echoing and prolonging the eerie silence afterward.

He loved it. But after his release, he dreaded every moment. The silence. Feeling incredibly alone. He'd considered a pet, but the upkeep was more than he was willing to handle at the moment.

He jumped when the door slammed and Lauren waltzed out.

"I love jalapeno poppers," she said. "Can't remember the last time I've grilled some of those."

"I've got the makings if you want to do it."

She clapped her hands together. "Yes, let's do that."

"I picked enough jalapenos this morning, but we can always grab more from the garden if you want."

"Too dark and I'm afraid of snakes. I'm sure you have plenty."

She prepped the poppers and he prepped the fire, and they drank another margarita while the food cooked. They sat around the fire under the stars instead of the deck, near a large oak tree that had been the focal point of many parties with friends and family. They chatted about the weather, the river and the current news. Once the poppers were done, they ate a few and chatted more, but nothing too serious.

"You wanna just eat jalapeno poppers and margaritas tonight?" he asked, never wanting this night to end.

"Sounds wonderful."

He grabbed a stick and thrust a wiener on it. "How about we at least roast wieners?"

Laughing, she seized the stick and jabbed it in the fire. "I thought I had already roasted yours."

His loins jumped. "That you did."

She removed the burning wiener from the fire and blew on it. As she took it from the stick she muttered. "Hot, hot, hot."

He grabbed a paper plate and placed it under the wiener, where she let it fall. "Of course, it's hot silly. It just came from the fire."

She set the plate on the table and blurted, "I'm sorry I didn't trust you."

"You didn't trust that the hot dog was hot?" He took his from the fire and blew, but laid it across the plate before sliding it from the stick.

"No." She swept her hand through the air. "About everything else. For years I thought you had slaughtered my sister. How can I step away from that and remember what things were like before?"

Shadows skimmed Lauren's body. The dim light from the fire and from the deck's lighting flickered around her, enough to discern most of her features. He leaned closer and brushed a finger across her cheek. "Knowing me the way you did, how could you even think I would do something like that?"

Lauren shrugged. "Maybe I had a few doubts, but I called it wishful thinking. Then I went through such pain and heartache I didn't have room for doubts. Everyone convinced me. Your cap. Your knife. Your motive. Clint..." Her voice bubbled, a tenuous thread of something he couldn't name. Regret? Remorse? Confusion?

Luke jerked away. His muscles tensed, gut twitched.

"We became friends. Not like you and I were, but he was there for me—"

"Of course he was." His voice was harsh, hot like the fire steaming from his pit.

"As Laramie grew up, he became her godfather. But she didn't like him and never wanted to be alone with him. She never accused him of anything, but she steered clear of him. Even her instincts were right and I couldn't see through my pain."

He stood. Yes, they should have this conversation. They needed to have this conversation at one point. And now was as good a time as any. But it was too hard to sit. Too hard to face the demons that Lauren's mistrust in him had stirred.

"If I had doubts, I...I—"

"You had too many people lying to you."

She stood and planted her palms on his chest. "But you never lied, did you? You were the only person who didn't."

His skin itched, hot from the nearby fire and from her touch. Hot from irritation. "I'm writing a memoir," he blurted. What better time to tell her than now?

The crease between her brows tightened. "You what?"

"Got offered a lucrative deal, and my sister Charlotte will be here soon to help with marketing once it's complete. A memoir of my life. Of my prison sentence. Of everything."

"Of me and Laramie?"

"I don't know yet. It isn't finished."

She dropped her hands but didn't turn away.

"This is the same oak tree where I proposed to you."

She nodded but remained quiet.

"I'd never publish it without your approval. Without you reading it first."

"It's okay," she said. "I can't control what you do and I wouldn't want to. You deserve to share your story. People need to hear your story."

"I don't want you to remember what things were like before. I don't want you to remember me as I was. I want you to get to know me for the person I am today."

She slid closer and wrapped her arms around his neck. "Okay, then let me get to know you for the man you are today." She tippy-toed up and speared her hands into his hair, pulling his head down to hers where she plundered his mouth. He returned the kiss, and her groan undulated deep to his core.

He cupped her ass in his hands and lifted her. She wrapped her legs around his waist and he walked with her up the steps to the porch, toward the door, and inside.

"The hot dogs probably won't be there when we come back," he said. "Coons will get them."

"The only hot dog wiener I'm interested in right now is yours," she said.

He shut the door behind them and carried her to his

room. It was the first time they'd been in a bed, together, making love, in twelve years. They didn't rush. He explored her body, and she explored his. He cherished every inch of her, raining kisses across her body and promising forever with each nip of his tongue. The tapestry of their lives stitched into something he obtained if only a little while.

The sheets tangled around them. He kicked them off. The cage of his resistance disintegrated with each breath, each moan, each pulse of his climax. They came together, then he gathered her in his arms and held her while they slept.

CHAPTER ELEVEN

THE BUZZ on her phone woke Lauren. She stirred and took a moment to remember where she was. Luke's bed. She stretched her arms overhead. Luke was already up. The smell of bacon drifted to the bedroom.

She reached for her phone to check the message, then scrambled upright. The message from Clint chilled her. *Keep Laramie safe. She's in danger.*

Her hands shook. She pulled on her clothes and rushed outside with her purse to Luke.

"Good morning," he said. His lips flattened in a thin line, the furrow in his brow shooting aches through her body.

She held up her phone. "Clint texted me. 'Keep Laramie safe. She's in danger.'"

He dropped the tomato. It rolled over the table and splattered to the ground. He set the knife on the table and turned off the grill.

"I'll drive you to town."

"No. No. I can't leave my car."

"I'll follow you to town."

"I'll be fine, Luke."

"No."

"Yes. I have a gun. I know how to use it. I practice at the gun range believe it or not. I'll be fine. You stay here."

"She's my daughter too." His voice wrenched her soul apart. His jaw tightened as he glared at her.

"I know. But…"

He held up his hand to stop her, although she had no idea what to say.

"I'm sorry I can't stay for breakfast."

"Text me when you get home."

She nodded. Her only concern was getting to Laramie. Did Clint mean his text as a threat or a warning? Was he trying to dissuade her from seeing Luke? If so, how would he know she was with Luke? Any message from Clint was a threat.

She called Laramie on her drive to Tiffany's house, but she didn't answer. Probably still asleep. Her daughter was never up before nine during the summer, and it wasn't even eight yet. Lauren hadn't had coffee or showered, and her clothes were rumpled. But she didn't care.

Her phone buzzed. The speakers in the Ford read out the text from Clint. *Didn't mean to scare you. Just want you to be wary of Luke. He isn't innocent.*

Her stomach clenched. Was he watching her? Did he know she had been at Luke's and now she was running to Laramie? She studied the road and each car that passed, but nobody followed her. The crime she dealt with in her job made her paranoid. It was easy for criminals to hide. But hopefully, eventually, they got caught.

She pulled her car in front of Tiffany's and parked, urgency cramping her stomach. Was Susan awake? She unbuckled her seatbelt and sent a quick text. Susan was a stay-at-home mom who doted on her children. Tall and fit with sunny blonde hair and beautiful brown eyes, Susan and her husband were a power couple. Retired military, he was a commercial airline pilot and loved his job, but not more than his wife and kids. They had two other children besides Tiffany, ages eight and four. Lauren had always liked Susan, and their children had been friends since second grade.

While she waited for Susan to reply, she debated on whether to respond to Clint. Deep inside, she knew she should ignore him, but her motherly instincts were too strong. Clint was a danger. He hadn't reached out until now. She should call her boss or call the police first. But they would tell her not to respond. They would want to take her phone, change her number, or something to protect her. She no longer trusted Clint. She feared him. But she had to believe he had cared about them at one time.

Clint, where are you? And what do you mean she's in danger? Please tell me where you are. Turn yourself in.

She hit send, her mind reeling over what she had just done. Her phone buzzed, and she jerked, but it was Susan texting to say she was awake and would be happy for company.

Lauren didn't hesitate. Susan opened the door and waved at her approach.

"Hey. I'm so sorry to come so early."

Susan wore chic yoga pants and a long flowing shirt, her hair in a ponytail. She clutched a cup of coffee, the steam rising. "No problem. Sorry I didn't respond earlier. I was doing my yoga and didn't have my phone. Is everything okay?"

She hesitated. Not because she was afraid to talk to her friend, but because she was afraid to make it reality. "Um, not really. Do you have a minute to talk?"

Susan shuffled aside. "Absolutely. You want a cup of coffee?"

"Would love one."

They walked inside, and Susan shut the door behind them. Lauren felt tacky in her shorts and flip flops from last night, her hair ratty from swimming. She hadn't planned on staying at Luke's and hadn't packed anything extra. Clint's text had left her no time but to react.

Susan opened a cupboard and pulled out a cup, then pointed at the creamer and sweetener on the counter. "Help yourself."

"Thank you." She fixed herself a cup and sat on a stool near the kitchen island. "I'm so sorry to bombard you so early."

"It's fine. Really. But I sense there's a reason for your early morning visit."

Might as well lay it all out on the line. Susan had always been a good friend but wasn't afraid to tell it like it is. "I got a message from Clint. Said to keep Laramie safe. And it freaked me out."

Susan didn't balk. "Laramie's safe."

"Are you sure? Have you checked?" She bolted up. Where did Laramie sleep?

"I'm positive. Checking on my kids is the first thing I do every morning. But come on, I'll show you." She waved, bidding her to follow.

She let out a sigh of relief. Laramie was asleep on the floor in her friend's room, piled high with blankets and sleeping bags. Her friend slept beside her, the bed empty.

She followed Susan back to the kitchen, chuckling out a jittery laugh. "They don't believe in beds?"

"I don't know what it I about those two girls but no, they prefer the floor when Laramie stays overnight."

She sat at the island and swiped a hand over her face. "Until Clint is caught, I can't leave Laramie alone for a second. I'll have to take her to work with me."

"She can stay with us until summer camp. Then we go on

our annual road trip in a few weeks. Why don't you let her come with us then too?"

"No. I appreciate the offer but I've got my parents." She could never relax if Laramie wasn't nearby, within eyesight. Susan's annual road trips put them in different states for days.

"We're not leaving until after camp. So let her stay until then."

"No. No, I can't put that burden on you."

"It's no burden. Don't forget my dad is the next street over. And he's more paranoid than any of us put together."

Susan's dad was retired military and had taught Susan survival skills at a young age. She could handle herself. She and Lauren had gone shooting together many times. Still, it was hard to trust anyone with Laramie's safety.

"I'll consider it. For now, I'll take Laramie home."

Lauren stayed for a while and watched her daughter swim while she sat with Susan under the covered porch. She sent a quick text to Luke to let them know they were fine and to have a good day, refusing to tell him how much she already missed him. And she jumped at every buzz of her phone, wondering if Clint would ever reply.

When they were about to leave, Susan once again offered to have Laramie stay with them. "You can stay with us too," she said. "That way you don't have to be alone. This house has plenty of room."

She almost considered the offer. Almost considered going back to Luke's or even asking him if he wanted to stay with them. But she was a strong single mother and didn't want to let fear run her life.

"I appreciate everything, Susan. I'll let you know if we need anything."

Laramie wasn't happy about leaving, and she sulked when she had to get up early and go to work with her the next morning. She dragged out of bed, whining the entire time, but perked up when she saw Tamra.

"Hey, Laramie. Glad you got to come today. Lauren, Brian is in his office and wants to see you immediately."

Her shoulders drooped. She expected an easy day. "Why?"

Tamra shrugged. "I don't know, but he's in a lousy mood. Laramie can stay up front with me."

"Thanks. I'll be back, Lare."

She tapped on Brian's door before peeking in. He didn't stand, but waved her in. His head was bent over a mess of files.

Great. Was she about to lose her job? Be written up? Should she have checked the papers and social media this morning to make sure nothing was amiss?

She should have told him about Clint's text.

She hadn't even stopped in her office to put down her purse and it hit her that she forgot to clock in. She dropped it to the floor and settled into the chair. "Everything okay?"

He barely glimpsed up from his file, his forehead bunched in a strong frown. "Is everything okay?" she asked again. Her pulse wavered and her distress grew. She didn't like the almost imperceptible way he bit his lip and refused to look up at her. She couldn't tell what was in the file and didn't bother moving to look.

Probably the file on Roland Tucker. He'd been accused of sexually assaulting his stepdaughter, and while she handled many similar cases throughout her career, this time she had a problem with believing the victim. The wife was divorcing the husband and making a huge outcry in the middle of it all. She called at least once a week belting out threats and had been caught in several lies. The proof was his word against hers and even the prosecutor was thinking of rejecting the case. The mother didn't understand what was taking so long, and Lauren stopped returning her calls. Had she called to complain to Brian?

She straightened her spine against the low back chair and rested her forearms against the armrest. If so, she had plenty of defenses.

But instead of talking to him about the case, she decided to come clean about the text. "Clint texted me yesterday."

His head lifted, glasses drifting down his nose. "He what?"

"He said keep Laramie safe. I was going to let you know, but it was Sunday. And I decided to ignore it. But only... I didn't ignore it. I messaged him back. I know I shouldn't have. But his message scared me. Then it pissed me off." She took a breath. She was speaking way too fast, fumbling for control.

Brian's face paled. "What did you text him?"

She leaned over and dug in her purse for her phone, then straightened and read the text. "Clint, where are you? And what do you mean she's in danger? Please tell me where you are. Turn yourself in."

Brian pulled off his glasses, then shut the file and folded his hands, glaring at her. His pen remained clasped between his fingers.

"When was this?"

"Yesterday morning. Seven AM."

He dropped his pen, the sound a mellow cling against his desk. He looked serious, but firing her was a serious circumstance. "Did he reply?"

She dropped her phone back in her purse and avoided his glower. "No."

He made a steeple of his fingers and planted them under his chin. "I need you to listen very carefully to me."

Her mouth grew dry, whole body tingling. "Okay."

"If he messages you again, let me know immediately.

We're tracking his phone but it's taking time. As you know it isn't always as quick or easy as the movies say it is."

"Right. Okay. I know."

"Don't try to play bait. Don't try to outsmart him. Don't try to appeal to any emotion you think he might have for you or your daughter."

Her face grew hot. She swallowed the shame in her throat, but it burned her belly. "I know."

"If he wants to meet you, call me or the chief right away. Don't ever agree to meet him. Don't ever try to make him think you are on his side."

She rubbed her palm behind her neck. "You're scaring me."

"You should be scared. I have even worse news."

Her blood ran cold. She shifted in her seat and dropped her hands. "Okay. What's worse?" Her voice came out in a breathy wisp. She'd seen him angry plenty of times, but she'd never seen him so resigned. As if fate had already been determined.

"There's been a homicide."

She took a deep breath and held it, already imagining the worst. Her daughter was safe, but what about her parents? Luke? She hadn't talked to them this morning.

"In Cedar Falls. Very similar circumstances to your sister's death."

She struggled to breathe. Her ears flamed, aching into a deep cavernous void as if she was being plugged up from the inside. She blinked, bottling her emotions.

"Anyone I know?" Her voice sounded distant, underwater. Cedar Falls was only forty-five miles away, a growing city she often visited for shopping and eating and getting away. A city not in their jurisdiction.

"I don't think so. But…"

"But what?"

He opened the file and pulled out a picture with a grim twist to his mouth. "This is the girl."

The picture was a school photo. A beautiful young girl smiling into the camera. She didn't recognize her, but the similarity to Elizabeth, even to Laramie, unnerved her. Dirty blonde hair flowing past her shoulders. Light brown eyes sparkling in mischief. She smiled at the camera in a way she would never smile again. Spots flashed in Lauren's vision, and she tore her gaze away. She hunched over and rocked back and forth in the chair, pressing a hand into her stomach to keep her emotions in check.

He slid another picture over. "We spotted Clint on a security camera at a convenience store."

She cried out, then closed off her throat to muffle the grief. Her hands shook too much to grip the picture. That dark cavernous drum in her ears deepened, widened, pressing into her skull and compressing her chest as if she were being buried alive.

He tapped the file folder. "There are gruesome pictures in here of the crime scene. You don't have to look at them if you don't want to, but if you want to see the similarities."

She stood, almost knocking over the wooden elephant on Brian's desk. "No. No, I don't need to see them. I need to… to…"

"It could be coincidental," he said.

"It's not."

"Of course, it's not. But we know where he is now, and we will find him."

She nodded, but her legs were too weak to move. "When did this happen? Was it after… after he texted me?" Her words came out garbled and stuttered.

"She was discovered late last night. It could have been before. It could have been after. There's no way to know. The child was reported missing on Saturday."

She collapsed back into her chair and buried her face in her hands.

"We'll have police patrol your neighborhood." He stood and walked around the desk, planting his hand on his shoulder. "Go on home. We'll handle things here. We will get him, Lauren. And he'll never hurt another soul."

―――

Laramie's eyes squished together when Lauren burst into the reception area. "We're going home."

Laramie jumped up.

"Everything okay?" Tamra asked, studying her.

She shook her head, her throat on fire with grief for the family who suffered exactly what Lauren's family had so long ago. "Not feeling well. I'll talk to you tomorrow."

Lauren drove home in a haze. She turned into the drive, shifted into park and clutched the steering wheel. The idling vehicle droned in her stomach.

"Mom?" Laramie asked. "Okay, now you're scaring me. Did you get fired or something?"

"I wish it was as simple as that." She brushed a hand over her face. "A child was found murdered last night."

Laramie's mouth dropped open. "What?"

"Clint was spotted in the same town. It's still under investigation but they're trying to find him."

Laramie's chin trembled. "Where?"

"Cedar Falls."

"Oh. That's…"

"Yes, that's close."

"That's so terrible for the girl's family," she said.

"Yes. Yes, it is."

Laramie flung herself into Lauren's arms and let her hold her for a while. They cried together, and Lauren brushed her fingers through her hair. But her daughter wasn't one to stay down for long. She pushed away and sat upright, her chin jutting in determination. "You need to tell Luke."

Cold swarmed Lauren's body at the thought of telling Luke. She nodded. "Yeah. Yeah, I do."

"Tiffany is home. I talked to her earlier. I'm sure it's okay if I stay with her."

Lauren narrowed her eyes at her daughter. "What are you doing?"

Laramie shrugged. "I'm not playing matchmaker, if that's what you think. That's just weird. But he deserves to be told in person that the man who was his best friend and framed him for murder has murdered another child."

Lauren planted her hand on Laramie's forehead. "Are you sure you're only twelve years old? You are way too smart and mature for such a young age."

"What can I say? I have the best mom on the planet."

"Uh, huh. And now you're trying to bribe me. Because you want to go back to Tiffany's?"

"No. But I don't think I should be there when you tell Luke."

Lauren let out a loud sigh. "Okay. I'll call Susan. But I don't want you girls outside alone. Don't walk around the neighborhood. Don't do anything if Tiffany's parents aren't nearby."

"Okay, Mom."

Within minutes, Lauren was dropping Laramie off with assurance from Susan she would be safe. She dreaded the visit with Luke and didn't bother warning him she was coming out. He might already know about the child. The police might have already notified him, but Lauren had to make sure.

He was sitting outside on the porch fooling with a fishing pole when she approached.

Her stomach flipped when he smiled and waved. Judging by his demeanor, he didn't have a clue.

"Hey," she said, stopping beside him.

"I'm glad you stopped by. You want a drink?"

"This isn't a social call."

His eyes darkened, body slumping. Not her best way to handle this situation.

"Okay." He set his pole aside.

Throughout the entire drive here, she'd weighed how best to tell him. And she could think of no other way to tell him than to blurt it out. "They spotted Clint."

His gaze popped back to meet hers. He straightened in his chair. She sat beside him, knowing if she didn't, her knees would buckle.

"He's on a security camera at a convenience store in Cedar Falls. The same town where a brutally murdered twelve-year-old child was discovered late last night."

He shot up from his chair. "Fuck." He slammed his fist into a deck pole. "Fuck!" His face contorted, then hardened. His eyes filled with tears. He turned away from her and continued to curse and swear.

She went toward him and put her hands on his back. "Luke." She'd had time to process things. Luke hadn't. She was amazed at her composure.

"This should never have happened." His forehead touched the deck pole and he held on as if it was the only thing keeping him upright. His nose flared and eyes remained closed.

"I'm partially responsible," she said, the heavy weight of grief numbing her.

He reeled to face her, his forehead bunched in a scowl. Sweat rolled down his taut jawline. "How is that?"

"I let you go to prison. I didn't listen to your sister. I

didn't fight for you. We let a terrible man go free to continue committing murders."

He stepped away from the railing and away from her touch. "The cops are responsible. The cops and the former DA for withholding evidence." He swiped a hand over his face. "He'll probably try to frame me again."

"Maybe so. But things are different now."

"Maybe. Maybe not. But I know how quickly things can take a turn for the worse."

He clenched and unclenched his fist until she clasped his hand and rubbed it between hers, also checking to make sure he hadn't injured himself when he hit the decking.

"They're going to find Clint," she said.

His mouth constricted, and he nodded, his eyes furiously blinking. She planted her hand behind his head and brought his forehead to hers.

"They're going to find him," she said again, with more force as if she actually believed it. Because she had to believe it. She had no other choice but to believe it. They couldn't *not* find Clint. He couldn't be allowed to roam free and continue to kill innocent children.

"Sure," Luke said, his voice dark and weighty. "They'll find him. He'll have an alibi. I won't."

"You have an alibi with me."

"Not every single night."

"Things are different now, Luke."

He pulled away from her, his gaze unfocused as he turned away to stare out at the horizon. He chewed on his lip and shook his head.

Her heart ached for him and all he had suffered. The entire Clint matter had never been handled properly. They should have had him in custody before news of Luke had ever been released. Supposedly they had enough evidence to exonerate Luke, but Clint fled before they locked him up. She didn't understand.

She stood with Luke for a while but left him alone to stare out on the horizon. Here for him if he needed companionship but remaining silent. She shouldn't have been so harsh in her narrative, but she had a feeling it wouldn't matter how she said what she had to say. The news would have shocked him regardless of her method.

Luke's gaze remained unfocused as he spent this time grieving, thinking, wondering, and feeling guilty as hell. Another family had lost their child in the most brutal of ways, and all because of a sick bastard he once considered a friend. A sick bastard who had framed him. He had been Clint's best friend at one time.

Once he was in prison, he and his sister spent hours researching ways to appeal his conviction and talking to different attorneys who specialized in those fields. But things moved too slowly in his world, and Adrienne had her own life to live. He begged her to get on with it.

And he worried about her. If she got too close, Clint could silence her.

Time stood still in prison. Twelve years was like an eternity, except for those on the outside who continued to fight for his freedom. Day turned to months. Months turned to years. Each moment in their life was fleeting, and something they took for granted. It could take months to hear back on the appeal or the writs or the numerous other requests. Months to get an answer on anything. Nothing was ever rushed on the outside. To most people who had never experienced it, one more day in prison was nothing but a penance the inmates probably deserved.

He was acutely aware of Lauren behind him. She remained close, silent and observing in case of another breakdown. He had to pull it together, compartmentalize his feelings into little nuggets until they became powerless.

Plenty of time for breaking down later. He wanted her here, but he wanted to be alone. She'd probably think he was crazy if he plopped down on the deck and meditated.

He shuffled his feet, afraid to look at her in case his control shattered and he started crying like a baby. He'd already cried in her arms, and once was more than enough.

"Where's Laramie?" he finally asked, his voice garbled.

"She's with a friend."

"Is she safe?"

"Yes, she's safe."

"How can we ever be sure?" The pressure rose in him again, fracturing his control.

"I guess we can't ever be sure about anything, can we?" Lauren asked. "But when I told Laramie about Clint she asked if she's supposed to just hide away in the house forever?"

"It's better than the alternative."

"My mom and dad suffered great loss with Elizabeth's death. I can't even imagine." Her voice cracked with tears, but she kept going. He watched her, the way her blue eyes watered and turned into a churning ocean full of torment. "To make matters worse, we thought she had died at the hands of someone we trusted. And she did. Everyone in town trusted Clint. He came from a good family. Everyone in town trusted you, too. But nobody knows when their last breath will be. Nobody. And I don't want Laramie to grow up fearful of living. We are careful, but I can't keep her locked up in a pris—"

She stopped, her lips pressing closed.

His chest clenched. "It's okay. You can say it. You can say prison. I'm used to the word by now."

Afraid they were taking too many steps backward, he pulled her into his arms and rested his chin on her head. Things might never work out, but he didn't want to lose their fragile hold. He was desperate for the chance to get to know Laramie, but for now he would do it on Lauren's terms. He had a daughter now, and his protective instincts could overtake their common ground.

No doubt Clint would come back. Clint would try to hurt them. And Luke had to be ready.

CHAPTER TWELVE

LAUREN JUMPED every time her phone sounded. She kept it on vibrate during the day, but turned it on at night so she would recognize each ring tone.

Clint hadn't responded, and she never tried sending him a message again.

She and Luke texted every evening. A quick hello, how was your day, or something similar. During a moment of weakness, she sent him a text about telling Laramie the truth. *I want to tell Laramie about you soon. I just don't think it is great timing with everything going on with Clint. Too much stress and I don't know how she will take more bad news. Do you mind waiting a little longer?*

His reply made her feel even guiltier. *I've waited this long. Guess I can keep waiting until you feel the time is right.*

She triple-checked the doors and windows every night, and was comforted to see the patrol car parked outside. Brian had pulled some strings and assured her they would protect her home and keep them safe. Because of her relationship with Clint and his past history, they suspected he would show himself one day, so an officer watched her house at night.

It chilled her to think of all the times she willingly let Clint inside her home. They had only been friends. She refused to acknowledge anything other than friendship or even allow him to consider it.

"It's a little eerie, isn't it?" Laramie asked one night when Lauren dropped the curtain and stepped away from the window.

She sat on the couch and patted the seat next to her. Laramie slid in beside her, and they cuddled together. "It is definitely eerie," she admitted. Laramie's hair tickled her cheek, and she flicked it away. "And I'm sorry you have to go through this."

Laramie pulled away and blinked at her. "What in the world, Mom. It isn't your fault."

"Maybe we should move."

"Clint could follow us anywhere we go if he really wanted to."

"We could move in with Grammy and Granpa."

Her nose scrunched. "Mom."

"Susan offered us to let her stay with us."

"Eh. That's okay." She narrowed her eyes. "Are you scared?"

She toyed with her daughter's bangs. "Not really. I know the officers who patrol, and the ones who stay nearby at night while we sleep. I just don't want you to be scared."

"We can't live in fear our whole lives."

Lauren cocked her head at her daughter. "But we gotta be careful until Clint is caught."

"Well, there's always staying at Luke's."

"Laramie!" She reached for her daughter and tickled her.

Laramie giggled. "Okay, stop, stop, stop. I surrender."

They both froze and looked at each other. Clint had

tickled Laramie several times until she said those words. Lauren had asked him to stop because Laramie hated it so much, and Lauren rarely tickled her because of it.

Tears filled her eyes. "I'm sorry."

Laramie brushed her soft knuckle over Lauren's cheek. "It's okay, Mom. It's okay."

By Friday, Laramie was growing antsy about going to work with Lauren. On their way home, she groaned about their weekend plans.

"Let's invite Luke over for dinner," she said, surprising Lauren. "I could make him our famous spaghetti."

Her breath tingled. "That sounds fun. What gave you that idea?"

Laramie shrugged. "He seems like a good guy. You want me to call him and ask?"

"Sure. I'm sure he'd be thrilled."

Lauren didn't tell her daughter why he would be thrilled.

"Hey Luke," her daughter said. "It's Laramie." She paused, indicating he spoke, but Lauren couldn't hear his words.

"Mom and I were wondering if you wanna come over for dinner tonight." She smiled, ogled Lauren, and nodded. "Great. We're heading home now. Probably will stop at the store first. No, no, you don't have to bring anything. Come on over when you're ready. Okay, see you then." She ended the call. "Okay, he'll be on his way soon."

Lauren's stomach wrapped into all sorts of knots. She turned into the parking lot of the store. "Okay, let's grab what we need."

It didn't take them long to go through the store and get home. Lauren took a quick shower to freshen up, then found a cute t-shirt dress and sandals to wear. Nothing too fancy, but something comfortable like she'd wear at home on a Friday evening or any day of the week. She touched up her hair and makeup, keeping it casual, and sprayed a hint of perfume on her wrists. She kept her diamond studs in her ears, then walked out the door.

"Just in time, Mom. He just drove up." She gave her a once-over. "You look very nice."

"Thanks. Not too nice I hope."

Her daughter rolled her eyes. Her belly fluttered. This wasn't a date. They weren't dating. Not really. He had every right to be with another woman if he wanted. They'd never talked exclusivity. But this felt like a date. It felt like the rest of her life.

And it felt like Laramie was trying to set them up.

He knocked on the door, and she let Laramie answer. "Hey, Luke. Glad you could make it."

Her twelve-year-old daughter, so adult like.

Luke swooped in with flowers for Laramie and a bottle of wine for Lauren. Laramie grabbed a vase, filled it with water, and set the flowers on the table. "These are lovely. If you want to open that bottle of wine, I'm about to get dinner started."

Luke winked. Lauren handed him the bottle opener, and he complied.

"It's still early to eat, though, don't you think?" Laramie asked. "We could sit outside. Or chitchat on the couch or sit here at the table."

Luke scooted out a chair and sat. "That works for me."

"What have you been up to?" Laramie sat beside him. Lauren wondered what she was up to. Was she matchmaking? Or did she have suspicions and want to get down to the nitty-gritty?

"Mostly I've been working on the house. Giving it fresh paint in the living room. And I've worked some at the body shop, but that's only a few hours a week. What about you?"

"Mostly I've been swimming all summer. And hanging

out with friends. Until I had to spend my days at mom's work. But next week I'm going to a summer camp."

"Oh?"

"Yes, it's a camp I've gone to since… well ever since I can remember. It's a lot of fun. Then school will start. And we'll go school clothes shopping."

"Laramie," Lauren said, her voice a warning. Maybe she shouldn't say anything right now and break the mood, but she thought Laramie knew. She was sure they had already discussed this.

She turned to look at her mom. "Yes?"

"You might not be going to summer camp this year. Remember?"

She jumped from her seat. "What?"

The chair stumbled, almost fell. Luke reached over and grabbed it to keep it steady, then stood also, staying in the corner.

"I don't know if it's a good idea right now. We'll discuss it later."

"Mom, you have to let me go! This isn't fair!"

"Stop throwing your fit, Laramie. I haven't decided yet."

Laramie glared at her mother, lower lip trembling and thrust out into a pout. Her eyes watered. "Yes, you have."

"No, I haven't. I'm still thinking about it. But—"

"But I might get kidnapped or run over or killed or something horrendously terrible might happen, Mother. I know!" Her voice was loud and multilayered as if she'd heard these things her entire life.

But Lauren hadn't always been too overprotective. Not like this. Laramie had to understand things were different right now.

Her daughter stormed to her room and slammed the door. Lauren flinched but didn't go after her.

She turned to Luke. He stood in the corner, keeping quiet and out of family business. Although she appreciated him not getting involved, she wondered what would happen if he felt like part of the family. To have a partner by her side, helping her with her child and helping make these important decisions.

Now wasn't the time to tell Laramie, not with her so upset, but one day soon.

"I'm sorry you had to see that," she told him.

"Sounds like she's upset about this event."

"It's a weeklong all girls extravaganza. She's been going since she was five. Her and several of her friends."

"So it's like a school thing?"

"No. Girls from all over the state go to this summer camp. They teach them skills and let them play and have fun."

"Sounds like it's secure."

Luke and his calm wisdom. How exasperating. She walked to the table and sat, planted her elbows and dropped her head in her hands.

"It is secure. But is it secure enough? With Clint still out there? He's already murdered another child."

He approached and rubbed her shoulders. Irritation prickled, but it wasn't at him. It was at herself, for needing and enjoying this so much. For worrying too much about Laramie and being tempted to prevent Laramie from having a life.

He sat beside her, their knees touching, her face planted in her hands as if the darkness gave her more insight to help her decision.

"It's not my say," Luke said, "But you should let her go. Help her develop her skills and become the strong woman you are."

She lifted her head. "It should be your say."

He shrugged. "Well, until you make that decision…" His voice trailed, but she sensed the anticipation in his tone.

"I don't feel like a strong woman," she said.

He flicked hair away from her face. "You are way stronger than you realize. Let her go. Take time off for yourself if you have any vacation days. We can do our own form of camping."

"Oh. So you want me all to yourself?"

"For a week? Absolutely." He paused, then continued. "I worry like hell for her. But you can't stop her from having fun by over-worrying and over-protecting."

"I know. I know." She squeezed her eyes shut for a moment.

The chair scooched backward, and he stood.

"Luke," she called, before he put too much distance between them.

"I'm going home now. You need your mother-daughter time. You can talk and plan or whatever it is you need to do."

"No. She'll be disappointed. She wanted to cook for you." Lauren bolted upright and walked toward him. Her heart hurt. She wasn't ready for him to leave. "I'll go tell her she can go. That'll perk her right up and if you're not here, she'll have another reason to hate me."

"She doesn't hate you."

"She's a tween. Of course she hates me. And Luke?"

"Yeah?"

"I'll tell her the day she comes home from summer camp."

LUKE WATCHED Lauren walk to Laramie's room, his heart hurtling into unknown territory.

He'd grown familiar with numbness, and the sensations he encountered since his release were as if experiencing them for the first time.

He'd wanted to give Lauren her space and let her make

the decision on when to tell Laramie. As much as he longed to tell her, now was too much. She should go to her camp and not worry or think about anything other than having fun with her friends.

Anticipation buzzed his veins. Soon, she would know. But how would she react? How would she feel about having a former prison inmate as a father?

She skipped out of her room, nearly barreling him over with a hug. "Luke. I'm glad you're still here!"

For a moment, he thought Lauren had told her, and she was going to say she was glad he was her dad. But she stepped away and opened the fridge. "I'd be disappointed if you didn't stay for my spaghetti, garlic bread, and Caesar salad."

His stomach grumbled. He had been about to throw a steak on the grill, but he was elated when she called and invited him to dinner. "Is it the same one your grandma used to make?"

She pulled things out of the fridge. "Yup. Passed down for generations. Mom's been teaching me since I could barely stand."

"I can't wait to have it."

"I can't promise it will be as good as Grammy's, but I don't do too bad."

"I'm sure it's just as excellent."

"Well, like Grammy always says, get out of the kitchen and let this woman cook."

He laughed, saluted, and strolled past Lauren, who stood in between the kitchen and living room.

"Grab yourself a glass of wine. Or there's beer in the fridge." Lauren retrieved two glasses from the cabinet and sat them on the counter. "We have a nice place to sit outside. I'll join you in a few once I help Laramie get started."

"Will do."

He poured a glass of wine, kissed Laramie on the head and Lauren on the cheek, then strolled out the back door.

This was heaven. This was family. No amount of badness could overtake this good, and he was determined to enjoy every moment.

CHAPTER THIRTEEN

Luke's stomach churned when Laramie bounced to her friends and leave to summer camp. She pivoted to toss a quick wave before diving into the van. He gripped Lauren's hand, and she turned to him and gave him a trembly smile.

"A week will fly by," she said.

"It's hard to watch her leave." Luke's voice cracked. He didn't want to rob Laramie of her independence, but Clint was still out there. A danger. He had killed another child. How many had he killed and gotten away with since Luke's imprisonment?

"She'll be fine. Everyone knows to watch out for Clint. And it's a secure area. One mother is an off-duty officer, and the police will remain close at all times."

Luke squeezed her hand, dropped it, and turned to the car. "Then I suppose we best get on our way."

"Where are you taking me?"

"I can't tell you. It's a surprise."

She followed him to the Jeep, the tops and doors all off. Luke had planned the day, secret plans, like the old days when they had enjoyed surprising each other. He was pleased she agreed when he'd asked her to spend her vacation days with him. They texted every single night, sometimes falling asleep between sends. Flirtatious texts that developed into something more, and now they were spending time together while Laramie was at summer camp.

He drove back to his home. He stopped and shut off the Jeep, then slipped out and went around assisting her to slide down the massively high seat.

"Is this where we're going?" she asked, her entire face scrunching.

"Would you be disappointed if I said yes?"

"Not at all."

He took her hand and walked her to his motorbike. "We're going on a bike ride."

"Okay."

He handed her a helmet. "Put this on."

Her nose crinkled. "No way."

"Yes way."

"Are we going on the highway?"

"Just the country road."

"And how fast could you possibly be going on this country road? If it's anything like the old days, not fast. I prefer to enjoy the view. Besides, how can I enjoy resting my face against your back if I'm wearing a helmet?"

Heat coursed through his veins. He hung the helmet back in the shed. "Fine. You win. But that means I'll only go slower."

He fired up the bike. She sat and wrapped her arms around him, and he drove away. Hot wind whipped across his face, his body tingling when she planted her head against his back. He stopped under a tree near the slab road where the river roared under the concrete. He kicked his stand into the dirt and stood, then helped Lauren off.

"I remember this place," she said. "It's been a while since I've been here."

Luke pulled her into his arms and kissed her. He rested one hand on her lower back, the other along her neck, and cradled her. Water babbled over rocks, the sound a gentle lull as his tongue delved into her mouth, a slight touch of discovery.

He pulled away before it proved too difficult. She blinked, smiled, her lips parting.

"I remember being here, too," he said. They'd snuck away for alone time, away from parents, friends and prying eyes. They enjoyed trekking over rocks to the nearby sandbar, and he had folded out a blanket for them to lie under the stars for hours.

Her face beamed, her words bringing him back to the present. "Are we going to make out under the stars?"

"No. But I wanted to bring you here again. Come on, hop on. We've got more to see."

They drove through the countryside. The county road followed the river and was mostly all dirt, with occasional paved portions. Ranch land bordered both sides, with homes spread sporadically along the river. He stopped on the edge of a rock and parked the bike, and they strolled hand in hand along the riverbank near the craggy slab road that connected both sides.

"This road is a mess," Lauren said. "Last year's flood tore it up even more than it already was."

"I see they repaired one side since last I remember, but it's as rough as it's always been. I thought we'd drive to Castle Springs and rent a kayak."

She halted, hesitating. "Oh. I'm not sure I have what I need to go kayaking."

"I have a backpack of water and necessities. Remember,

today and tomorrow is my day to surprise. Then it's yours. But only if you're up for it."

She nodded. "Okay, let's do it."

They drove to Castle Springs, a tiny town flourishing along the riverbanks, and rented a two-person kayak. The town's general store had a bar inside, and served food all day, but it hadn't been here when they were young. They stopped for a sandwich and chips before heading out. He helped her slather on sunscreen and placed a hat atop her head.

The river flowed well after the previous rains, with many sections they didn't have to paddle. He enjoyed the view, especially of Lauren's backside as she sat in front of him. Her hair was tied in a ponytail and the feminine muscles in her back contracted. Water rippled over rocks, hills rose around them and crested in greenery. Some trees perished on the banks, knocked down from the last flood. They stopped near a boulder and stashed the kayak in a clump of trees where it couldn't float away, and sat on the bank to rest and drink water.

"It's crazy how much the river has changed," he said.

"Have you come out since your release?"

He shook his head. "Only at my house."

"I haven't either," she said.

"Since my release?"

"No. Since your incarceration." She stuck out her tongue, swallowed a gulp of water, then screwed the lid back on and dropped it in her lap. "And for the record, it's barely rained during your incarceration." She waved out her arms. "You get released, then it floods."

He lifted his brows. She teased, and he teased back. "Really? As if the world was grieving me and waited in anticipated breath for my release? Then cried tears of happiness."

She tilted her head, a cocky smile stretching her face. "You really are a writer, aren't you?"

He tugged her in for a kiss. "Come on. We're only halfway to my house and it'll take an hour or more to get there. But you need more sunscreen."

"Only if you plan to slather it all over me."

"Hmm." He grabbed the bottle, this time it wasn't a spray bottle, and poured lotion in his hands. He had no intention of having his way with her, but he rubbed his hands all over her body to give her a taste of what he planned later. He capped the bottle and stood, ignoring the throbbing pain in his lower extremities.

"Come on."

"That's not nice," she said.

"You asked me to put sunscreen on you and I did."

"Harrumph," she enunciated, all smiles.

His shoulders muscles burned by the time they got home. They loaded the kayak on top of the Jeep and returned it. He would drive the motorcycle home while she followed in the Jeep.

They made it to the general store by almost six that evening and sat on the deck and drank iced tea, listening to live music played by a local band. Folk-rock eased his soul. The sun was high in the sky, but people leaving from their workday stopped to enjoy nature's beauty. They ordered burgers and sat a while longer before heading home.

Dusk settled in once they got to Luke's.

"Why don't you get a shower and slip into something comfortable?" Luke asked.

She faced him and grabbed his hands. "You're not showering with me?"

"I've got a few things to take care of."

Her shoulders shimmied. "Oooh, I see. Okay. Should I take my sweet time?"

"Twenty minutes or so. Whatever feels right."

She bumped her nose on his. A thrill shot through him.

She dropped his hands, grabbed her suitcase, and disappeared into the house.

He took a quick outdoor shower and pulled on a fresh pair of jeans, boots and a tee. He activated the glimmering white lights on the porch and tree, then set flowers on the tables—the one on the porch and under the tree—and switched on soft classic rock.

Dusk settled into evening, the sun too far gone to offer any sustenance. But that's exactly how he liked it when she stepped out of the house. The lights illuminated around her. He drew in a quick breath and halted his stride up the steps, admiring her beauty. She wore a white cotton dress with dark brown cowboy boots. Her hair flowed down her shoulders and back. He strolled up the porch and took her hand.

She gasped. "This is beautiful."

"You're beautiful." He led her to the tree. It offered massive shade in the daytime, but the limbs offered relief in the hot summer nights. The dirt was like a makeshift dance floor. He spun her around, drew her close to his body, and wrapped his hands behind her waist.

"Aren't you going to shower?" she asked.

"You don't like my dirty, sweaty body?"

Her hands skated up his chest. "I love your dirty, sweaty body. But I thought you might want to cool off. It felt amazing."

"I had a quickie outdoor shower."

"No fair."

"We can have one together later. I needed the time for the setup."

"Well, it looks amazing."

"You look amazing."

He whirled her around the dirt, under the lights, dipping her as if they were in a fairy tale. Their bodies swayed together. His body ached. Their gazes drowned into each other. They danced for hours, but he wasn't ready for the night to end. His calves and hamstrings burned, but they didn't stop until he lowered his head and kissed her. Then he lifted her in his arms, carried her to bed, and they made slow, sweet love.

He recognized this was temporary. Everything happening now was temporary. He made no plans. Couldn't afford to make plans. But he appreciated the moment.

He woke with the sunrise and cooked breakfast on the grill. He set out two canvases and a table full of paints along the edge of the deck. The echo of her footfalls jolted him to finish his tasks. He poured water in the cup near the paints and topped off his coffee.

She stepped outside. His skin fluttered, a light breathy wisp of air that deepened in his stomach. On that first day she had come to his house—to kill him—she admitted she hadn't painted in years. He hoped this wasn't too much.

He saluted with his coffee mug. "Good morning."

"Good morning," she replied. "What's this?"

"I thought it'd be fun if we painted together. You know, like one of those painting parties where you paint and sip wine? Only we will sip mimosas under the morning sunrise."

Her chin trembled. "Sounds amazing," she said. "Not sure how well I'll do since it's been so long."

"None of that matters. Have fun and enjoy the process of creativity."

He flipped a pancake off the grill and into a plate. She shuffled to him and wrapped her arms around his waist, snuggling her face in his chest. "Thank you," she said.

His pulse soared. He had never stopped loving Lauren. Never. Whatever happened, he would always love her. But he wouldn't come on too strong. *Enjoy the moment.* His new mantra. He hugged her back, then grabbed the bottle of champagne. "Let's get started on those mimosas."

CHAPTER FOURTEEN

Lauren ate a light breakfast, too excited to eat. Sipping the mimosa, she dipped her brush in the paint and wondered why she hadn't painted with Laramie. Why hadn't she shown Laramie how important it was to embrace your creativity? Life shouldn't revolve around work. Going to school, going to work, going home and forgetting your dreams. Dreams could live in the real world. She could work a full-time job and still make time for aspirations and creativity.

Her brush swept across the page. She painted a tree shrouded in lights, similar to the tree on Luke's property. A woman wore a delicate white dress that swayed as she danced under a bright moonlight. Then animals popped out under the moonlight. Birds, bunnies, foxes and frogs.

Everything she had felt—the difficulties, fear, hopelessness and everything she'd been tempering for the last decade—flowed from her paintbrush.

"Amazing." Luke's voice stroked her ear, sending fire down her spine.

She sneered at his and chuckled. He'd never been a painter, but it was good. He used every color palette, a mix of circular patterns, boxes and triangles melding to make one shape. "Thank you. Yours is too."

"No, it's not."

"It is." She set down her brush and took a drink. Her shoulders ached, her lower spine tightening. She got up and stretched. "It's unique. That's what painting is all about. Make it yours."

"Why did you laugh?"

She tweaked his nose and smiled. "Because. It's cute."

"I blobbed paint on the brush and went with it. But mainly, I was too busy watching you."

"Mine isn't finished."

"Take as long as you need."

She slanted her ear to her shoulder and took a breath. "I need to take a break before my body breaks apart. Too much sitting." Then she switched sides and slanted her other ear to the other shoulder.

"I know the perfect way to take a break."

She pitched her head back and opened her mouth, stretching the back of her neck, throat, and chin.

"If you want to hold that mouth position and kneel on your knees, that's a great break."

She lurched upright and smacked him, laughing the entire time. He fixed his hand around her waist and pulled her forward, his mouth lowering to hers. Her body responded. She couldn't get enough of him, and they spent the rest of the day in bed.

The next morning, she slipped out of bed before Luke. Today was her day to surprise him, and she couldn't wait to get started. They'd have to stop at her house to grab backpacking gear, then to the store and grab snacks and water, but that wouldn't take long. She wanted to get an early start.

She kissed him awake, and her phone sounded her boss's notification tone.

"What in the world?" Luke grumbled at the R2D2 tone.

She rolled away from him to view her phone. "My boss. I wonder what he wants."

"Doesn't he know you're on vacation?"

"He never cares. Besides, he has no idea I'm with you." She glared at her phone and let out a curse when she saw his text.

Where are you? I need you here ASAP.

She sent a reply. *I'm on vacation. About to be out of service for a while. Backpacking.*

His reply came less than a minute later. *Cancel. I need you here now.*

She messaged Tamra to find out what was going on, but Tamra told her she didn't know. *I'm sorry. Probably best to get here.*

She called the office to speak with Brian, but he ignored her calls and text. She threw her phone across the bed as Luke nuzzled her neck. "Not fair," she said.

"What's wrong?" he asked.

"Brian wants me to come in ASAP. He needs me now." She finger-quoted her mocking tone.

"I need you now, too," he said, but pulled away from her and off the bed. "But you better go. Something might be wrong. Maybe they arrested Clint or something."

She let out a long, wallowing sigh. "Doubtful. But it's not common for him to do this, so I guess I better go see what's wrong." She grabbed her phone and texted. *I've got to run back home and put on work clothes. I'll be there soon.*

He instantly replied. *Come as you are. It'll be fine.*

"Is he seriously kidding me?" she said. She had jeans and a t-shirt with sandals, so it's not like she would look completely disheveled, but his replies flustered her.

"Do you want me to come with you in case something is wrong?" Luke pulled on jeans.

"No. I'll be fine. I'll call you as soon as I'm out."

She scrambled to brush her teeth and throw on makeup then kissed her goodbyes to Luke. "I'll call you soon."

Over an hour later, she stepped into the office in a hurried frenzy. She didn't bother clocking in. She went directly to Brian's open door and tapped before entering.

He glanced up from his file and nodded his head toward the door to suggest she close it. Her gait was slow toward the chair, a hesitation to learn what was so terribly wrong. And something was terribly, terribly wrong.

Did something happen to Laramie? No. Surely, they would send someone to tell her.

"I'm sorry I called you in on your vacation. You know how I feel about phone calls."

Indeed, nothing could be wrong and Brian considered it urgent. He hated the telephone and preferred face-to-face. She tied and untied her fingers together and sank to the chair. He didn't remove his glasses. They were low enough on his head he could study her and the file at the same time.

"Another child has gone missing in Cedar Falls," he said.

She closed her eyes and summoned a deep breath, a deep courage. But her breath didn't cooperate. Her lungs burned, air fluting through her in an avalanche of terror. She opened her mouth to pull in more air and reached her gaze skyward.

"Her name is Marci Kay Thomas. She's twelve."

She cried out. Despair gnawed her insides.

"And Clint?" she finally managed.

"He's nearby."

―――

Luke waited hours to hear from Lauren. He sent a few texts asking if everything was okay, but he didn't want to appear too frantic when she didn't respond. He took care of the garden and other household chores, mostly roaming. Usually, fishing and swimming took his mind off his troubles, but not today. Heaving out a breath, he considered running to town and check on her. If something had happened to Laramie, no one would call him, and Lauren would be too distraught.

The past couple of days had been amazing. He was skeptic enough to believe it was temporary, the veil of their relationship would crumble and she'd run as far away from him as possible. For him, this was the real thing. He loved her. He'd never stopped loving her, but the past love was nothing compared to this. He strived to be patient with her. He feared she'd run if she knew he wanted to spend forever with her.

Finally, a text from her said she'd be here soon. His muscles, weak from the stress and anxiety of worry, sagged. He fell into his outdoor chair and waited, freeing his jumbled thoughts.

The rumble of her car when she pulled into the driveway relieved him. He examined the security camera and tried to read her body language. Her shoulders were slumped, head lowered, and she shuffled her feet. He stood and met her at the steps of the porch. She dropped her purse and rushed into his arms.

"What happened?" His voice was gruff, thick with the glue of foreboding.

"Another child has gone missing. Clint was seen on a security camera in the same store."

He pulled away but kept his hands on her, holding her at arm's length. Tears shone in her eyes, her chin trembled.

"Where?" he asked, trying to stay calm.

"Cedar Falls. Same town as last time." Her voice was slow and filled with dejection.

Sharp pain rattled in his chest. His throat bottled up tears he didn't have time to release. That restraint made it hard to breathe. Grief radiated through him, breaking his reserves apart limb by limb.

"Is Laramie okay?"

She nodded, large tears spilling from her eyes and down her cheek. "I plan to pick her up today. She needs to be home with us."

Us. She'd said the words as if they were normal. His heart pinged a warning. She was distraught. He couldn't have too much hope they would be a real family.

"What about the girl? I mean, shouldn't we help in her search?"

"Brian doesn't want me to. He says they have enough help." She shook her head and looked away from him. He finally dropped his hold on her and they walked up the rest of the stairs. She didn't sit, only stood beside the deck rail and scanned the horizon. Birds chirped, the river flowed, and ducks quacked.

"The reality is they can never have enough help." She said it, soft and resigned, as if she knew the child's fate.

"Where are they searching?"

"Everywhere, I suppose. They've gone to his house. His grandparents' house. He owns their property, so they're searching everywhere."

"The basement?" he asked.

"Yes."

"The storm cellar?"

She turned, her eyes shining with emotion. "Yes. I remembered the cellar. The only sign the cellar had been used was a picture of Laramie. Last year's school picture, the one he held in his wallet. It was on the floor, scuffed. Otherwise, there's been no sign of him. They're searching for other properties he or his family might have. His dad was rich, left it all to him, so he's not hurting for money. He could have all kinds of properties. But for whatever reason, he chose to stay close and take children from only a few miles away." She turned away, her lip quivering. "Children who have the same dirty blonde hair as our daughter."

"Because he wants us to know." Luke's statement was in its purest and rawest form. He didn't have time to think about it or shave off his reaction. Clint wanted them to know he was close. He wanted them to know they'd made a mistake. And he wanted them to know he was coming for Laramie next.

"We need to get Laramie," he said. "Keep her home. Take her to work with you. Or hell, let her hang out with me during the rest of the summer."

Keep her safe. Because Luke had no doubt she was Clint's next target.

———

Lauren rushed to her car. Luke followed, his footsteps crisping through the grass in a frenzy that put her on edge.

She took a deep breath, her pulse a staccato rhythm in her ribcage. Luke wanted to help, but she was determined to remain in control. She didn't want to tell him it wasn't his place. It should have been his place. But she had every intention of bringing her daughter home safe. Without Luke's involvement.

"Lauren." He clasped her elbow as she climbed into her SUV. She slid into the seat and turned to him. He'd fussed as soon as she told him she was going alone to pick up Laramie from camp.

She fired up the engine. "I'll be fine. Besides." She buckled into the SUV and puckered her lips, trying to make light of the situation. "No men are allowed."

He stood at the door and scowled. "Is that even legal anymore?"

She reached over to grab the door and crinkled her nose. "Well, I'm certainly not going to fight the camp director over it."

He leaned in and cradled her chin in his hand, holding her gaze. Chills swarmed across her arms. Clint had kidnapped another child. She wanted to rush to her daughter, but she never wanted to leave Luke again.

"Be safe," he said, pulling away. "Text me when you get there. Text me when you get home."

"I will." She shut the door, waved, and drove away. "Bye."

Her stomach clenched in a slurry of fear, panic, and dread. Part of that dread was because Laramie would not be happy about leaving. The rest of that fear was based solely on worrying for the missing child.

They had to find Clint before he killed again.

On the drive there, she called the camp director. Although she didn't go into details, she wanted Nancy to know how vitally important it was not to let Laramie out of their site.

"She's perfectly safe here," Nancy said. "We've got a lot of activities she won't be happy about missing."

"I know camp is safe, but we're dealing with a monster unlike anything you or anyone else have ever dealt with. She needs to come home. Will you have her ready to go?"

Nancy agreed and after hanging up the phone, she pulled over and texted Clint. No way could she drive the way her entire body quaked.

She knew she shouldn't contact him. Brian had warned her, and Lauren wasn't naïve enough to believe she could change Clint's evil intentions. But if she could pretend and bring him out of hiding, she would do anything to keep her daughter safe. And any other child Clint targeted.

Every text came back undeliverable. Her hands shook as she dialed the number. What would she say to him if he answered?

It came back with a message. Disconnected.

"Dammit!" Her eyes burned, throat cramping, all the dread she had bottled thinking about speaking to him emerging in a roar. She beat the steering wheel in frustration and defeat.

Until Clint was caught, they were completely at his mercy.

She squared her shoulders and blinked away tears. Laramie was her priority, and she needed to get herself under control.

She gripped the sweaty leather steering wheel cover and drove the rest of the way repeating a prayer. "Please, please let this child be found safe. Please, please, let Clint be caught and this child be found safe."

When she made it into camp, she drove up to the main building and parked. Her legs were weak and rubbery as she walked to the door. Laramie was waiting for her in the lobby, sulking in the background, chin puckered in defiance.

Lauren greeted the camp director. Nancy once again spoke about how safe things were here, but Lauren only let out a brittle smile. "It's time for us to leave."

Nancy nodded and quickly disappeared.

They had no idea what a kind of person they were dealing with. Lauren barely knew, and she had known Clint since grade school.

Laramie jumped up from her corner and wailed. "Mom, you can't make me go home. The swimming race is tomorrow and we only have two more nights."

Lauren's heart sank. She knew how much Laramie looked forward to her swim meet and the last night of camp. "You need to be safe. Don't fight me on this."

Her face fell and she fluttered out her arms. "But I am safe. I'm surrounded by people. Brenna is a police officer."

Lauren picked up her daughter's backpack, eager to get home before dark. "Come on, get your things."

Laramie stomped her foot and crossed her arms over her chest. "No. Either tell me what's going on, or I'm not leaving."

She looked at the ceiling, searching for an answer, then studied her daughter's sullen expression as if that would give her an answer.

Laramie deserved to know. Lauren needed her with her to watch over her and make sure nothing happened, but she didn't want to scare her daughter.

She sat on the bench in the empty lobby and folded her hands in her lap. "Another child has gone missing where Clint was spotted nearby."

Laramie's face paled. Her mouth opened, closed, her chin trembling. Lauren reached for her hands and pulled her close. A clump of tears fell down Laramie's cheek.

Her ribs tightened, entire body clawing for breath. It felt as if someone was squeezing her tightly, hollowing her out, and she would soon disintegrate. She fought for words. "Now do you see? Clint is out there. He's dangerous."

Laramie threw out her hands, but they weakened to her sides. "Can't you stay here with me? Like you used to? We're as safe here as home. Probably safer."

Lauren considered her options. She had attended with Laramie the first few years, then gave her independence this one week out of the year. Plus, she had been so busy with work she had stopped taking this week-long vacation for summer camp.

Why not stay with her? Let her finish camp. It would give them a new opportunity to bond, and Lauren could find a way to tell her about Luke.

"Please, Mom." Laramie's eyes grew eyes wide and pleading. Refusing was impossible.

She tried anyway. "I don't have any clothes here."

"You have time to run home."

She let out a sigh and ran her hand over her face. "I don't know if it's a good idea."

"Why not?" Her voice was steady, low-pitched as she studied Lauren with questioning eyes.

Lauren shrugged. "I probably have spare clothes in the car." She didn't dare tell her it was because she had spent the past few days with Luke.

Laramie ran into her arms and hugged her. "Thank you, thank you, thank you. This will be awesome. Thank you."

Every doubt fled at her daughter's enthusiasm.

She texted Luke the news. He quickly responded. *I don't like the thought, but I understand. Please be safe, and have fun. And text me occasionally?*

I'll text you every night, she typed and hit send.

Even better, he replied.

She settled into camp. They ate dinner and afterwards, the kids teamed up against the adults against a game of charades. Lauren found herself mimicking a person on a bike. She stomped her feet and tightened her elbows close to her body, circled her forearms and inching forward until someone called out, "riding a bicycle!"

She wiggled her finger at her teammate. "Yes." Then bent over with her hands on her knees from laughing so hard.

The next morning, Lauren's tiredness was fulfilling rather than exhausting. She stayed awake longer than she should have texting Luke, then got up early for a picnic breakfast with their daughter. Then came the swim meet. Lauren jumped up, cheering for the kids but especially for Laramie. Her lungs swelled in pride. Her muscles relaxed and for a moment, she had to sit back and take a deep breath at the overwhelming pleasure pooling inside her.

She hadn't done so badly as a single mom. Laramie was well put together, hardly a child anymore, and she had a good head on her shoulders. A pang shot through her. Luke had missed out on so much.

Clint was a killer. Although he was never a father, he tried to be a father figure. More a friend and supporter, but he had always been around to help when she needed someone or when her own father wasn't available.

His actions were the worst form of betrayal. From the time Laramie was little, he had hung around, and he was the only friend who knew Luke was the father. He had protected them from the beginning.

A sharp pain hit her chest. She now recognized his actions as grooming, and remembered one time he had waltzed into their home with a package when Laramie was five.

"Hey, doll." Beaming, he ruffled Laramie's hair and kept the pretty package close to his torso.

"What's that?" Laramie asked, bouncing on her feet.

"Yes. What is that?" Lauren asked. Clint was always doing good things for them, but Laramie remained shy of him. Today, her eyes were wide as she shuffled closer to him.

"I don't know. Why don't we take a peek?" He handed the package over to Laramie, who squealed.

"May I open?"

"It's okay by me." Clint pointed at Lauren. "If your mom approves."

"Sure, Lare. Go ahead and open."

She ripped the package open and pulled out the exact doll she had been eyeing since before Christmas when all the promises of being good and getting toys blasted on TV.

Lauren hadn't been able to afford to buy it for her, and she had refused offers from Clint.

Laramie ran into his arms. "Thank you, thank you, thank you."

He patted her back and winked up at Lauren. "You're welcome."

Laramie sang and carried the doll into the living room. Clint followed Lauren into the kitchen.

"You've got to stop spoiling her," she said.

"I'm not spoiling her. Besides, I have to bribe her to like me."

"That's not true at all."

"It is true. Besides, it's the least I can do."

She waved her hand. "Oh, stop it. You do more than enough. More than I deserve. I appreciate you coming over to help with my plumbing. With Laramie starting school this year, I can't afford to hire a plumber."

"It's not a problem. I'm happy to help."

Clint was always helping. Changing the oil in her car, helping with home maintenance, driving Laramie to school when Lauren had to be at work early. Even taking her fishing.

Laramie splashed out of the water, and Lauren shot up, too, shaking away the images of her old life. Clint would be found, he'd go to prison, and pay for the lives he had taken. Including her sister's and including Luke's.

She ate a picnic lunch with Laramie, and afterward they sat at a table and crafted jewelry. Laramie created a bracelet, and Lauren a matching necklace. She refused to give Clint or their past anymore of her attention.

Laramie wrapped the finished bracelet around her wrist and reviewed her creation. "I'm glad you're here, Mom."

Lauren tugged her daughter's ear, but avoided too much

affection because of the nearby girls. She didn't want to embarrass her tween. "I'm glad I am, too."

Laramie snatched a pendant from the pile. "But you should use this on the necklace instead of that rock thing."

"Hey, this stone is nice." A mix of turquoise and deep blue. She took the piece Laramie handed her. "What is this?"

"A floating charm." She nabbed a few small trinkets including a cross, a star, a fish, a crescent moon, and a few colored rocks. "See, you add these to the locket charm."

Lauren opened the locket and let Laramie add them. "I see. That is pretty." This time, she couldn't resist showing her affection. She ruffled Laramie's hair and bent to kiss her on the cheek.

That night, they held an award ceremony. Photos flashed on the screen, showing the week's events. A lump grew in Lauren's throat at the earlier days she had missed. She treasured her relationship with her daughter and never wanted their closeness to end, but Laramie deserved the truth. Summer camp ended tomorrow, and they'd pack up and head home. Then, she planned to tell Laramie about Luke. A lot of things could change once Lauren's secret was out. Telling Laramie who her father was might not only change the family dynamics, it might change the dynamics of her friendships. Having a father who was in prison for the past twelve years—even if he was innocent—could cause tongue wagging. The press could have a field day with their story. Or they might remain silent. Laramie might peacefully accept it and nothing else would be disrupted.

But Lauren's instinct was to prepare for the worst.

CHAPTER FIFTEEN

Luke Twelve Years Ago

THE FIRST DAY OF PRISON, my gut churns bile. I've been clenching my teeth so hard the past few days that my jaw hurts. I force myself to relax.

There's a long check-in process. I'm ready to just get it over with already. After a few holding cells, I'm marching to what will be my home until it gets disrupted again. Here, I'm a nobody. Just a number, a face. Nothing about my previous life matters anymore except what everyone thinks I did. Even if many of them don't know yet, they will soon enough.

Anxiety rushes through my body. I have no idea what to expect. My mouth is dry and every part of my body tingles in fear. I try not to expect the worst, but I do. I usually never have trouble getting along with people, but how can I fit in when everyone thinks I'm a child killer?

Everybody stares at me, but it's more hushed than I expect. My pulse drums in my ear. I keep my chin up but gaze down. I figure it is better this way. Don't want to appear too cocky.

Some of the guys I met in the county jail who had already served time gave me a few pointers. Learn cards, find some tables, initiate conversation but don't be too overbearing. But there's no time for that now. They lead me to my cell. My feet feel like I'm wearing shoes wrapped in concrete.

My heart stops when I see my cellmate. He's massive. Not old, but older than me. His wrinkles look wise, as if every layer reveals a persona, a clue, a story of who he is and who he might have been before whatever crime brought him here.

I decide I might as well get it over with. I face him and offer my hand. "My name is Lucas, but my friends call me Luke."

He inspects me a moment, then grips my hand. I almost cringe at his strength. "May I call you Luke, then?"

I nod then swallow the lump in my throat. "I hope you will."

"Luke, I'm Jonathan." He drops my hand but doesn't step away. "What are you in for?"

My chest squeezes, lungs pulling in harsh air in order to breathe. I feel my face blanch. "I'm sure you've heard it before, but man, I am completely innocent."

"Aren't we all?"

"They say I killed my fiancé's sister." My voice warbles, my throat aches. My limbs go numb and I wonder which bed I get because I seriously would like to lie down. I sit on the bottom. At least it's better than collapsing.

"But you say you didn't?"

"I know I didn't." The strength behind my words must have convinced him.

"Then who did?"

And so I tell him my story.

We become friends. Man, this guy, Jonathan, he becomes my savior. The first time I'm beaten in prison, Jonathan struts up to them and demands they stop and they do. I hurt for a few days, but Jonathan teaches me to take up for myself. And I might have already believed in taking up for myself in my past life, but doing so in prison requires a whole new skill set.

I'm alone the next time I'm beaten. The punch to my face takes me down. They strike my stomach several times, keep hitting, calling vile names that I start to believe. They don't let up until a guard came. I sulk back to my cell and Jonathan says something I'll never forget.

"Are you truly innocent?"

I cock my head. I've made many bad mistakes, but I'm not guilty of the charges if that's what he means.

"If you are innocent," he continues, his voice all boomy, "then you must stand your ground. Believe in yourself. Fight back until no one is willing to challenge you."

I press the napkin against my bleeding nose and duck my head. "Is that what you do?" Jonathan was serving time for robbery and although he admitted he was guilty, his biggest mistake was following his friends. So long ago, such a young life wasted.

"Damn right that's what I do," he said.

And so I did.

The next time a group tries to attack me, I hold my ground. I've been working out with Jonathan. He's not here with me, which is even better because I don't need anyone thinking he's my savior. Still, six guys against one can be damn intimidating. My knees shake, but I don't buckle. The first guy hits me square on the chin backs up when I don't fall. I hit him back. I'm willing to hit them all back until they stop.

"You're a dirty child killer."

"I didn't do it. I was framed. My best friend framed me." I keep hitting. Dammit, I keep hitting until everyone retreats.

For a while, the pain is unbearable. The fear is worse than any fear I could ever imagine. The truth of that fear far outweighs my expectations. If not for Jonathan and his wisdom, I might have died.

But I won't lie. I keep fighting for a while. The anger stage of my grief is easily recognizable. I'm angry at the world, angry at the people who put me here, but most of all angry at Lauren for not trusting me.

I get in fights now. A lot. Usually I'm the one seeking them out. I'm not the scared little eighteen-year-old I once was. I came here strong but stupid. I might still be a bit stupid, but I'm getting stronger every day.

Mostly the guys I like to fight are the bullies, the ones who like to pick on others, especially the ones who pick on the younger guys who come here for the first time. Like they did me. I'm the one who takes up for the others when necessary.

Ramone is a big guy, almost forty years old. He's been in here since he was twenty-three. Robbed a convenience store and shot the cashier, who later died at the hospital. His biceps bulge and his bulky shoulders almost reach his ears.

But I'm faster.

He's cocky, but I'm a sonofabitch. I don't cower to him, not anymore. People look up to me now. And I like to think of myself as an inspiration.

Ramone and Johnathan have such similar stories. Both robbed a convenience store, and both with a gun. Johnathan was following his friends and didn't kill anyone. Made a huge mistake, but grew up in prison. He's a big guy too, but he's a softie and he cares about people. Ramone just wants to strut around and try to prove himself. Probably to himself more than anyone else.

I'm in my cell when I hear about Ramone's death. He got himself into a fight he couldn't get out of. What should have been a simple fist fight turned deadly with a shank. I feel sorry for the guy who killed him. He was only trying to protect himself, and he was scared. But one thing I can say about Ramone is he did fight fair and would never have manufactured or used a weapon. His only weapon was his fists. Even after using a weapon in his robbery, I've never known him to use one in his fights now.

I'm so over the fighting. I'm ready to settle down, learn, grow, and help others. Like my cellie does.

Other men like Ramone are out there, and others will emerge. It's the nature of prison. But I know now that getting into fights daily with a guy I detest isn't going to earn me any points, and I need all the good behavior credits I can get.

My anger toward Lauren is waning. She lost her sister and was lied to. I worry about her. Adrienne still comes to see me at least once a month, but I beg her not to. She needs to get on with her life. I don't ask her about Lauren anymore. Lauren moved off and refuses to talk to my sister. And I don't blame her.

Maybe I've grown up. This is my life now.

Luke Present Day

MORNING CRESTED ALONG THE RIVERBANKS, an eruption of pink and gold. Luke strolled downhill, savoring the coolness of morning before the summer heat struck. He searched the ground for snakes and stepped over the path leading to the river.

He had stressed about Lauren and Laramie being gone. Two days had passed quickly enough, but he missed them both and feared for their safety. Lauren had texted this morning they'd be home soon.

I plan to tell her today, she texted earlier. *Will let you know how things go.*

His gut knotted, tension coiling his spine. He practiced patience—one benefit of his prison sentence was learning how to let go of things you couldn't control. He would give Lauren time, but after Laramie found out he was her father, she might never want to see him again. He wished he could be there, but it was best if Lauren told her alone.

He sat on a rock jutting out of the river and closed his eyes, savoring the morning sunshine on his face. The flowing water offered its own form of meditation. Water trickling over rocks, birds singing and chirping today's praise, and…

The stench jolted him back to the present.

His eyes flew open. Buzzards swarmed behind and to the left of him. Had they been there before? His heart pounded.

Probably a wild animal. Deer or coyote. But he had to know for sure.

He stood on the rock and noticed the body sprawled in a large thicket of grass.

"Fuck." His heart tripped, and he stumbled over his own two feet. Once he reached shore, his movements were quicker and smoother than he'd expected, but his insides quivered. He grabbed his phone. No mistaking the fact she couldn't be saved.

His mind raged over what to do as he waited a heartbeat for the operator to answer. He'd likely be arrested, no questions asked. Did he have anything in the home to take care of before his life was abruptly taken from him again?

He scurried to the house and spoke to 9-1-1, then sat on

the porch and waited. It took thirty minutes for police to arrive. Which was quick, all things considered.

He recognized the district attorney. He'd met him at the conference where he spoke. Brian wore a suit and tie, way too hot for this Texas summer.

Should he have called Lauren? Did she know?

Luke pointed to the river. "I walked there this morning for a swim and saw the body."

"Can you show us?"

"Sure."

Half a dozen men followed Luke along the path.

"See, from this angle, you can't see anything but the river," he explained. He pointed to the rock. "Once I got on that rock, I noticed the smell."

Three men walked over while the DA stood next to Luke. The officers who stood nearby had their hands perched near their guns, ready to shoot Luke at any wrong move.

The men immediately reacted when they noticed the body and before long, police swarmed with more vehicles and crime scene investigators. They took photos, and Luke handed over the card in his game cameras without checking to see what might be on them. Maybe, hopefully, whoever did this had been caught on them.

Clint had done this. No doubt in Luke's mind.

His one and only hope was Clint's discovery. For without that brutal piece of evidence, accusing eyes would once again turn to Luke.

CHAPTER SIXTEEN

LAUREN GOT the text notification the moment she was going to tell Laramie the truth about Luke. Since it was an unknown number, Lauren hit play from the car.

I miss you and Laramie. I hope to see you soon. XOXO, Clint.

Laramie's face paled, and the hitch in her throat came out as a breathy gasp. Lauren's stomach lurched. She reached for her phone in the console and yanked the wheel, the car swerving into oncoming traffic.

"Mom!"

She got back in her lane as a rush of adrenaline surged through her. Luckily, no cars had been coming, but she should have been paying attention.

Tears welled in Laramie's eyes.

"It's okay," she said. She unlocked her phone and took it off Bluetooth, then called Luke. He didn't answer. Neither did Brian. A text from Clint didn't constitute a police emergency, so she left a message for Brian and continued driving home.

It was still early in the day, so she could have called the office, but Brian always had his cell phone with him when he wasn't busy. No point in calling the office if he wasn't answering his cell. She trusted he would call back as soon as he could.

"It's okay," she told Laramie again, who sat like a statue beside her. Luke didn't always have great service, and maybe he was down at the river, but she hated that he didn't answer.

Laramie's chin trembled, her head shaking, fingers clenched in her lap. "I don't want to go home tonight."

Her pulse tilted. "Neither do I. We'll go to Grammy and Granpa's house tonight. I've got to swing by ours first and get a few things." Now was definitely no time to tell her about Luke. Too many emotions skyrocketing all over the place, and she was way too vulnerable after hearing that message from Clint.

"I just don't want to go home alone, even right now," Laramie said.

"I know, baby. How about I call Susan and see if she can meet us?" She trusted Susan to handle herself in an emergency. Better than calling someone at work. She didn't need the drama or the gossip.

Laramie's posture straightened and her mouth relaxed. "Okay."

She called Susan and explained the situation. "I hate to involve you," she added, "but I don't want to call the cops right now. I mean, nothing actually happened. It's just a text message, right? But we don't want to go home alone, and my boss won't answer his phone."

"Of course I'll meet you there. You know you and Laramie are always welcome to stay at our house."

"I know. And I appreciate that. But for now, we'll go to my parents."

Susan and her daughter were waiting for them when they arrived home. Laramie bounced out of the car to hug Tiffany, and they walked hand in hand to the house.

"I'm so sorry," Lauren told Susan.

Susan looped her arm through hers. "Don't you dare apologize. We'll stay as long as you need us."

As they walked into the house, her cell rang her office's ringtone. "Oh, I better get this. Hello?"

"Have you heard the latest?" Tamra asked, her high-pitched voice jolting Lauren's spine.

"Oh, God," she muttered. She wasn't sure she could take any more bad news. "What's up now?"

"A body was found down by the river at that man's property." Lauren heard the pounding of Tamra's hand on her desk, which Tamra did often for dramatic effect. "Dammit, what's his name? The one released from prison."

Her stomach plummeted. "Luke."

"That's it."

Lauren dropped her purse, tongue bitter, mind reeling. Susan stood beside her, studying her. Her legs wobbled. She gave up on regaining her composure.

"Where's Brian?" she asked.

"He's gone out to the property. I'm so sorry. I forgot about your sister. Forgot that was the man accused—"

"It's okay." Lauren didn't brush her off. She didn't want to be rude, and Tamra was a friend. "Let me know if you hear anything new, okay? Text might work best."

"Okay. See you Monday."

She ended the call, stooping to pick up her purse and drop in her phone. Her knees nearly buckled.

Susan rubbed her back. "Everything okay?"

She swiped a hand over her face. "Where are the girls?"

"They went into Laramie's room."

She collapsed into a chair and told Susan the story.

"Oh, dear."

She buried her head in her hands, then straightened. "I need…"

"I'll take Laramie and Tiffany home so you can take care of what you need to take care of. They'll be safe. I promise. Tom is home now. My dad is just down the street. And we have a security system that would blow your mind."

She let out a trembly smile. "I know. I trust you with everything. But…"

Susan held up a hand. "No buts."

"I don't want to ruin your trip."

"The offer still stands for Laramie to come with us."

"No. No way. I… just can't. With everything going on, I need her here with me."

Susan rubbed her shoulder. "We don't leave for a couple of days. Take care of what you need and we'll be in touch later."

The girls were happy to be spending more time together, and soon she was on her way to Luke's.

The drive was hellish, her thoughts a tumultuous path of destruction. What if Luke was put behind bars again? What if Clint was never caught? Her job as a victim coordinator was to assist victims, and victims were involved in this case. Although it wasn't ever her duty to attend a crime scene, she wasn't about to sit around and wait.

Cop cars surrounded the house when she pulled into the driveway. She walked around the corner and found Luke on the porch. His elbows were perched on his knees and he leaned forward. He grimaced when she stepped on the porch, his face pale.

A cop stood on the deck, gripping the rail and watching the property. She nodded a greeting and continued her way to Luke.

"What happened?"

"I… I…"

She kneeled to her knees and took his hands.

No way in hell would she do what she did twelve years ago and turn her back on him. He hadn't done this.

"What happened?" she asked again, a soft caress of words.

He squeezed her hands. "I found a body. A... a child."

"This morning?"

"Down by the river."

"Oh, God." She was aware a body had been found on his property, but hearing his words made it all too real. Chills swam down her arms. The memories of finding out about her sister nearly consumed her, but this was the present and another family was about to experience a world of hurt.

She squeezed her eyes closed to wash away the dizziness, but her stomach lurched and her eyes flew open to ground herself. He pulled his hands away and buried his face in them.

His shoulders didn't shake. Tears didn't fall. He pressed his fingers into his eyes then dropped his hands and sat upright, maintaining control. His eyes were waxy, forlorn, a new crease forming between his brows. She brushed her thumb across his cheek.

"Are you okay?"

His jaw clenched. His mouth was a thin line, but she he continued to clench his teeth. He dipped his head and nodded.

She stood before her back and knees gave out on her and sat on a chair beside him. "Do you need something to drink?" she asked him. "Water? Tea?"

"I should be asking you."

"It's fine. I can get you something."

"I'm good. But if you need something."

"I'm fine."

She wondered where Brian was. A crowd circulated down by the river, but she sat beside Luke and waited. Finally, her boss walked up to the house. It would look odd she was here. He had no idea of any kind of relationship between her and Luke. The slight dip in his brows gave away his curiosity.

He stepped up on the deck. "Hey, Lauren. What are you doing here?"

He was never known for being subtle.

This was no time to explain exactly *what* she was doing here. Her job description didn't include attending crime scenes, but she didn't care. Today was still a vacation day, and she worried Luke was on the edge of a breakdown.

"I came to check on things," she said. Might as well keep it simple.

"They're working on the crime scene. I'm heading back to the office."

"Is Luke allowed to leave?"

"I'm not going anywhere," Luke said.

"I thought I'd get you out of here and take you to lunch or something."

Luke shook his head no, a clear indication of his intentions.

"I'll find out," Brian said, then strolled away.

"I need to go get Laramie from her friend's house," she told Luke, figuring she'd use Laramie as an excuse. It might persuade him, and it was true. Every moment away from her daughter carved a hole of dread in her chest. Her breath hurt.

Brian came back and nodded. "The sheriff said it's fine for you to go have lunch. Of course, don't leave town or anything."

"Of course," Luke said, his voice drab.

Lauren stood and nodded at Brian. She owed him an explanation, and she deserved to know where the investigation stood, but right now her only goal was to get Luke out of here.

Brian said goodbye and turned to leave.

"Oh, Brian?" When he stopped and burned, she continued. "On the way home from camp, Clint messaged me again."

"Sonofabitch," Luke muttered.

"Same as before when the first child was found," Brian said.

"Yes. Said he missed us and hoped to see us soon."

Luke jumped out of the chair, hairs balled into fists. She palmed his chest to keep him calm. Nothing he could do about the situation now, and he must have realized it because he took a deep breath and let it out, his chest rising and lowering.

She dropped her hand. "I left you a message earlier with the number he texted from. I didn't recognize it."

Brian nodded and grabbed his phone. "Okay. Thanks. I'll see what we can do. Y'all can go on now." He walked back down to the river, his phone to his ear.

"I'd like to change out of my swim trunks and tee," Luke said. "Pull on some jeans. But I'll take my own car so you won't have to come back out."

"You're in no shape to drive."

He cut her a look that could have knocked down the strongest of men. It didn't work on her determination.

"I'll bring you back later," she demanded.

His sigh was more of a weighted and soundless reaction. His shoulders dipped.

"I'll wait while you get changed."

Luke was back and ready to go in less than five minutes. He'd changed into jeans, sneakers, and a vintage rock tee. They didn't speak on the drive to town, and the first thing she did was go to Susan's.

She parked the car. "Got to run in and pick up Laramie." When she didn't move, Luke patted her arm. Panic clumped in her stomach. "I didn't have a chance to tell her about you."

His lips pressed together and he hung his head. "I won't say a word," he said.

His forlorn look almost did her in. She let out a long sigh and opened the door. *Here I go.* She dreaded telling her daughter the truth about everything. Her legs trembled as she walked to the door.

Susan invited her in, but Lauren declined. "I've got a friend waiting. We wanted to let Laramie know what's going on."

"No problem. I'll go get her."

Laramie came out, her feet dragging. "That was quick. Can't I stay here with Tiff?"

"No, darling. We need to go."

They said their goodbyes, but Laramie cheered up when she found Luke in the passenger seat. "Hey, Luke. What are you doing here?"

Luke shrugged. "Your mom invited me to lunch."

Laramie shut the door. "Cool."

They stopped at a café and ate lunch. The adults didn't have to talk because of Laramie's chatter, but Luke laughed, his eyes sparkling in ease. They went home and started a game of Monopoly. Lauren couldn't remember the last time she and Laramie had played, but Luke had perked up.

"This is kind of strange," Laramie said.

"What's that?" Luke asked.

"Me, enjoying playing Monopoly with you guys more than being at my friend's."

Lauren's phone buzzed. *Are you home now?* Brian asked.
Yes.
Is Luke with you?
Yes.
Can I swing by to talk to you both?
Laramie is here.
It took a moment for him to respond.

"Mom, it's your turn."

"Oh. Sorry." She dropped her phone to the table and rolled the dice. Her phone buzzed, but she moved her game piece before picking it back up.

This is important, Brian texted.

Come on by, she replied.

"Are you going to play with us or play on your phone?" Laramie asked.

"I'm talking to my boss."

Laramie narrowed her gaze at her mom. "You mentioned an emergency at work. And now y'all are acting strange. Don't you think I should know what's up?"

Lauren folded her hands together and rested them on the table. She glanced at Luke, and he nodded.

"Yes, you deserve to know," she said.

Laramie straightened her shoulders and pulled away from the table, resting against the chair. "Good."

"This morning, while Luke was walking out to the river, he came upon a dead body."

Laramie's eyes rounded and she leaned forward, resting her forearms on the table. "What?"

"The police are investigating. We think it could be the same child who went missing in Cedar Falls and Clint was seen in that vicinity."

Laramie slapped her hands over her face. "Oh, God." She lowered them and rested them on Luke's shoulder. "Are you okay?"

Tears welled in his eyes, and he nodded. Lauren's heart swelled. Her daughter was concerned for Luke and all he had been through this morning. She memorized the look of Luke and his daughter, the angles of their faces and grip of their hands.

Maybe one day, she'd paint the image.

"Brian is on his way here," she said. "He has something important to tell us."

Luke nodded. Laramie released her hold and stood. "How about I search the house for some dinner?"

"You're already thinking of food again?" Luke teased.

"I'm a growing woman," she teased back, patting her stomach. "Besides, Brian might want a snack."

By the time Brian arrived, Laramie had put together a plate of cheese, crackers, cookies and a pitcher of tea.

"Hey little squirt," Brian greeted.

She curled her nose at him, smiling the entire time. He'd always called her little squirt.

"Watch it or I won't give you a snack," she quipped.

He reached forward and nabbed a cookie. "Are these homemade?"

"Yep. Fresh out of the oven. Would you like a glass of tea?"

"Sure, thank you. Unsweet, please."

She sat the plate on the coffee table and beamed, arms outstretched. "Anyone else?"

"No, thank you," Luke said as Lauren shook her head.

When she disappeared into the kitchen, Brian shot her a questioning look.

"I'll send her to her room in a minute," Lauren said. Laramie was enjoying serving her guest, and Lauren didn't mind prolonging any more bad news.

Ice clinked in the glass as she brought him a glass and held one of her own. He grabbed cheese and crackers and asked her questions about school. Every time Lauren opened her mouth to tell her daughter to go to her room, Brian said something else. Was she excited for school starting? What were her favorite subjects? Lauren appreciated his effort to include her daughter, but now wasn't the time.

"Laramie," she finally interrupted. "Will you go to your room for a bit? I'm sure you've got things you can do."

"Actually, I don't."

She pointed to her room. "Go to your room."

"Moooo-ooooom." The one syllable word was drawn into four.

"Make your shopping list for school clothes so we can do that this weekend. But right now we have some things to discuss."

"About the girl who was found on Luke's property?"

Lauren narrowed her eyes. "Laramie." Her voice was a warning signal, and Laramie reacted by jumping up and huffing.

"Fine," she said.

"Great to see you again, Miss Laramie. Thanks for the snacks and chatting with me," Brian said.

"Great to see you, too, Brian," she said, and waved.

Lauren appreciated Brian's handling of her child. The door didn't slam. He'd always insist she call him Brian instead of Mister anything.

"I'm sorry," Lauren said. "I do appreciate the way you handled her, but I know you don't have time to chit-chat."

"No, it was a nice diversion." He leaned forward on the couch and grabbed a cracker but kept it in his hands. "Things are under investigation and I may have no right to tell you this, but as your boss, you have the right to know." He nodded at Luke but didn't include him as having any rights.

"Okay," Lauren said, dreading the news.

"Your game cameras came in very handy. Good job on hiding them so nobody could see them." He opened his briefcase and pulled out a file folder.

Brian and his pictures. He always thought pictures told more than words in their cases, and they usually did.

He handed it to Luke. Luke gasped. Lauren slid beside him and skimmed over his shoulder.

The picture was of a man carrying a large trash bag. The

image was impossible to determine who the man was. It could even be Luke. Too many shades and shadows, and the angles were wrong to catch his face.

"Here are a few more."

Brian handed them the pictures, always knowing exactly what order to do things for the biggest effect. The picture was a clear shot of Clint.

Several good shots of Clint.

Her body collapsed into the back of the couch cushion. She slapped the back of her hand over her clammy forehead. Heat traversed from her head, tricking down her arms and flaring into her toes. She opened her mouth, but her throat was too closed to absorb air.

"Oh, God." Her voice cracked. She knew, she knew all along and had no doubts, but seeing it like this punched her in the gut as a roller coaster of emotions slammed into her.

He had held her while she cried after Luke's imprisonment. Celebrated birthdays with her. Helped her paint her living room and took her mom to the hospital once when she couldn't drive herself after eye surgery. He'd visited her sister's grave with her on the anniversary of her death. Sometimes she had to tell him he was being too domineering, and he would pull back. But he always acted like a friend and never pushed himself further than that.

He came to visit her after Laramie's birth. Had waited in the waiting room with her father. People had even wondered at one time if he was the father. Never, never had he shown a violent side.

But then, neither had Luke, and she'd believed he was capable of killing.

"I'll make sure there is constant surveillance on your house and at school once it starts next week. He's targeted you once, Luke. Looks like he wants to target you again and make it look like you are the one who did this. He's always wanted to be Laramie's father, so you've got something he wants."

Lauren opened her mouth to say something, but Brian shushed her with an open palm.

"It doesn't take a rocket scientist to figure it out," Brian said. "Seeing Luke and Laramie together confirmed my suspicions. It's none of my business."

A sheen of sweat clung to Luke's brow. Lauren swallowed hard at a tangle of words stuck in her throat.

"She doesn't know," she said, her voice pitching into a category of dread.

"Well, she's a bright young woman. We'll make sure she's safe." Brian stood and gathered the photos, sticking them back in the file.

Luke stood and shook Brian's hand. "Thanks for coming. For telling us all this."

"No problem. Obviously, your property is now a crime scene, so be careful and don't disturb the area."

"Of course."

"Call the cops if there's anything you can think of. Or if you have any suspicion of lurkers."

"Will do."

Lauren hugged her boss. "Thank you."

"You, too. Be sure to call if anything happens. Anything at all."

"I will." She walked him to the door and watched him leave, then stared at the door once she closed it.

What now?

PLAYING Monopoly with his daughter had calmed him. Life, laughter, light. *Love*. It had erased the violent images in his mind.

The DA's news didn't surprise him or relieve him. No question now Luke hadn't done this, but in that short time span between finding the body and Brian's visit, he had resigned himself to the fact he could be going back to prison.

That's how little he trusted the criminal justice system.

Relief didn't come easy, even with a cleared name. Not when a young child had been murdered, her parents devastated. She'd never grow to have her own children, life, family, college.

If Clint had been the one behind bars twelve years ago…

What was done was done. Luke had to face it, live with it, get over it. Or else he'd go crazy.

Even after the DA left, Luke fought the demons of blackness overcrowding his mind. He remembered being segregated from the rest of humanity. The way he'd felt blinded over the past few years, recalling the person he'd always been. He recalled the isolation, the deep hopelessness, and the way he'd learned to meditate, so he took a deep breath and faced Lauren.

"We have to tell her."

"Tell her what?" Lauren asked, although she had to know what he was talking about.

"That I'm her father. Before others figure it out like Brian did, and she hears a bunch of rumors. She deserves to know and hear it from us."

"She deserves to hear it from me when I'm ready."

"You promised you would tell her when you got back from camp."

"Things have changed. It's not good timing. Not after everything else."

"Will it ever be?" He paced across the floor, his hands bunched in his hair. "No, we tell her together. Now. We've developed a bond, and I don't want to lose that trust."

"She's already been through too much."

"She needs a father more than ever now. She needs me."

"She has you."

"She needs to know. When she finds out, she won't trust me anymore."

"Well I won't trust you if you tell her. You can blame me. It's my fault."

The door to Laramie's room crashed open. Lauren turned to her, eyes wide, blood draining from her face. Before either of them could react, Laramie stormed in, her face contorted in fury only a young woman could display.

"I knew it. I knew it." She pointed her figure at Lauren. "You lied to me. But I knew you were lying. I knew all along. But you." She aimed her finger at Luke. "I didn't expect that from you. I thought maybe you didn't know. But you did know." Her voice cracked. Her eyes closed briefly, her mouth thinning into a line. When she opened them, they were blank and steely.

"Laramie, wait!" they both called, but she was out the door and down the street faster than they could react.

CHAPTER SEVENTEEN

LAUREN GRABBED HER SHOES, but Luke was already racing toward the door, his heart pounding in his throat.

"Give me your keys." He stopped at the door and held out his hand, but she fumbled around in her purse way too long. Anticipation itched through him and he finally shot out the door. "Never mind. Catch up with us," he said before taking off running.

"She's probably at the pool," Lauren called behind him.

He'd hesitated too long, and Laramie had been quick. She already had a two-block head start.

He had no idea where the community pool was, but he ran her direction. She'd disappeared down the block, but he ran and ran and ran until a little old lady scrambled out onto the sidewalk. He had to stop before he bulldozed over her. She held a cane and pointed it at his chest.

"What are you doing, young man?" she grumbled.

"I'm trying to get to my daughter." He pointed to the lone figure, but she was disappearing between homes again.

"Looks like you're chasing after a young woman to me. I'm calling the cops."

"Please do," he said. He could easily knock this woman aside, but he worried she'd trip and fall. She looked like she was barely standing.

"Do I need to go after my shotgun?" she asked, her sharp-eyed gaze sliding over him.

He imagined her wielding a shotgun at him, but he'd be gone by the time she grabbed it.

"Ma'am, I'm not a sex offender. That's my daughter, and she just found out I'm her father, so she's a bit upset about it."

"Sounds like a lie to me."

He considered knocking the old woman aside and take off running when Lauren pulled up in the car, her windows already rolled down.

"Hello, Mrs. Sanderson. We've got to get going, but I'll stop by and see you soon."

Her hesitation gave him enough time to safely escape her cane without knocking her over. She lowered it and nodded. Luke jumped into the vehicle, sweating and cursing, and Lauren pulled away.

"Crazy old woman."

"She's a sweet little thing."

"Yeah, seems so," he muttered. "Laramie went that way." He pointed in the direction he'd last seen his daughter disappearing in an alley between two homes.

"That isn't the way to the pool."

"Maybe she isn't going to the pool. Does she have friends around here?"

"Not in this neighborhood."

"A park?"

"It's on the opposite side."

"Maybe she's just running and taking a circuitous route."

He caught a glimpse of her in the alley and didn't wait for the car to stop before he bolted out. "There she is."

She had disappeared again by the time he made it through

the alley. Lauren met him on the other side, and he was panting by the time he climbed back in the car.

"We jog through this neighborhood all the time," Lauren said. "She'll cool down in a minute."

"Where do you jog? Take that path."

"She's already gotten way off it. We normally jog the opposite direction, to the park and around. She's heading the direction to town."

Sirens wailed, and soon a cop car was flying down the street.

"Guess that old lady called the cops after all."

Lauren followed the police who had stopped on the other side of the street near her and the sweet little lady now known to Luke as Mrs. Sanderson's house.

"I know this officer." She slammed the car in park, then stepped out and talked to the officer while Luke remained seated, antsy and worried about his daughter. He considered sliding into the passenger seat and fleeing, but for now he played by the rules.

———

THEY SENT OUT A SEARCH PARTY. Lauren called all of Laramie's friends and checked her favorite hangouts. She checked her phone for anything out of sorts and wondered if some of her friends lied for her.

The police got involved with the suspicious friends, but because she hadn't been abducted, they didn't file an Amber Alert, even after Lauren's begging and pleading with them to do so.

"Clint is out there. She could be abducted."

"She's probably gone to a friend's house. Let's give it a little more time," the sheriff said.

One benefit of working for the DA's office was she had

friends in high places. They all assured her they would find Laramie soon, and although she had to wait for a missing person's report, she still got fast help.

Her stomach twisted in knots. Laramie hadn't taken her phone, which was unusual. She hated being away from her phone, but it was a good way to track where she was. What if she had gotten lost? Or picked up by some stranger? What if Clint had found her?

She got the phone call at close to midnight.

"I'm at a friend's house."

Relief washed through her at her daughter's voice, but anger quickly replaced relief.

"I saw it all over Facebook my family is looking for me," she continued. "Some people even say I'm a runaway. How embarrassing."

"You did run away."

"Can I stay here tonight?"

"Absolutely not. Where are you? I'm coming to pick you up."

Luke stood beside her, his face twisted as he listened to her side of the conversation. He planted his arm on her lower back, but her legs almost gave out.

Her daughter's sigh was long and heavy, slicing through the phone. Although Lauren didn't recognize the number she was calling from, she could find out easily enough if Laramie didn't admit where she was.

"I'm at Tiffany's," she said, then hung up.

Lauren raced to her vehicle, Luke right behind her. "Call Brian and the sheriff and let them know I'm going to pick up Laramie," she told him.

He opened the passenger door. "Okay. I'll do it on our way there."

"No. I'm picking her up. Alone. We need time to talk, and if she decides she wants to see you, then I'll call you."

Luke shut the door. "Okay. But don't forget you drove me to town, so I don't have a way home."

She hesitated. "Okay. Just… wait here if you don't mind. I'll be back soon."

Lauren drove to Tiffany's house, her mind a screaming mess of rage and relief. How dare Laramie do this when Clint was out there and a child had been murdered! No, two children had been murdered, and she continued to wait on edge wondering when Clint would come after them.

And she was sure he'd come after them. Why go to the trouble of dumping the body on Luke's property if he intended to leave them alone? Was he aware they had renewed their relationship? Is that why he did this?

No answers to her unending questions. She gripped the steering wheel and surveyed the dark night. Every shadow was a threat. Her nerves tingled. He could be out there now, watching them. The darkness hitched her imagination into overdrive, and she had to force herself into calm.

Nobody was following her, and Clint wasn't some ghoul who could roam the streets without cover. Even if, at this moment, he appeared to be unstoppable.

He would be caught. And stopped.

She parked at the curb to Tiffany's house, shut off the ignition, and jumped out of the vehicle, locking it behind her. She'd rather play it safe than sorry and didn't want to come back out with Clint waiting for her in the backseat.

All the lights to the house, including the porch light, blared as she walked to the door. She hoped the police put a scare on Tiffany, who denied seeing Laramie. Susan walked out the door with both girls. She wore long pajama pants and a t-shirt with a short bathrobe and slippers.

Susan took her in a hug. "I'm so sorry. I had no idea." She patted her on the back before pulling away.

"It's okay. I'm glad she's safe."

"Tiffany has a few things to answer for. She's in a world of trouble."

Lauren nodded. "So is Laramie."

Laramie huffed off to the Escape, and Lauren said her goodbyes. Laramie stopped at the door and glared at her mother when she couldn't open it. Lauren grabbed the key fob to click unlock, and Lauren slid into the seat and let out a big dramatic sigh.

"You locked the door?"

"I didn't know how long I'd be in the house, if I had gone in the house. Let's not forget there's a man out there who wants to kill us. And he's already killed two people."

Maybe it was a bit extreme and overdramatic, but her daughter was way too naïve to take it seriously.

She drove away, toward their home, thinking about Luke. He was still there, unable to get home unless he called someone, and there wasn't anyone to call. Her friends were coworkers and she wasn't going to involve them. His family didn't live nearby, her parents lived too far out in the country, and his house was too far to walk.

So, despite the lateness, they'd have to have this confrontation tonight.

She parked in the driveway, but before Laramie opened the door, she grabbed her hand. Laramie turned to her, glaring, but didn't move.

"I'm sorry for keeping the truth from you. You have to understand why I did it."

"Well, I don't understand."

"Your father was in prison. When he was released, I... I just wasn't ready."

"I knew you were lying. All along I knew. But for Luke to lie to me—" Her voice cracked, her lower lip quivering, but she didn't cry.

Just like her momma, she had learned to keep her tears at bay.

She smoothed her hand over Laramie's hair. "He did it because I asked him to. He didn't want to betray my confidence."

"So instead he betrayed mine."

"It wasn't like that."

"Yes, it was."

"He didn't have a choice in the matter."

"He had every choice."

"No, Laramie Elizabeth. He didn't. If he had told you, I never would have had a relationship with him. And I never would have allowed you to have one with him."

"Really? You're going to those extremes now? Call me out by my middle name and say we could never have a relationship?"

Elizabeth. She'd been named after Lauren's sister who had died, and the name slipped so easily when she was angry and frustrated. As she was now. But her daughter was too close minded to open her views. She'd been hurt, and justifiably so, but Lauren had to make her see it wasn't Luke's fault.

"That's what trust is all about. If I couldn't trust him to let me tell you on my terms, then how could I ever trust him about anything else?"

She folded her hands over her chest. "Okay. Well, how can I trust him now?"

"Laramie." Her voice erupted as a warning, and they both paused.

"What, no middle name now?"

Another pause, this one long and awkward.

"Can we not go inside?" Laramie asked.

"Luke is here."

She threw up her hands. "Why is Luke still here?"

"Because he came into town with me and doesn't have a

ride home. He wants to see you. He's very hurt. But it's your decision. We can wait until tomorrow."

"I thought we were going school clothes shopping tomorrow."

"Not if you're still angry."

Laramie leaned her head back on the rest and blinked. "I- I don't know if I'm ready to see him."

"That's fine. You can go to your room. Get yourself a shower and get to bed."

"Do you have to take him home tonight?"

"I don't want to leave you alone. I can let him take my car and bring it back early in the morning or he can get a hotel. We'll figure something out."

"Okay."

They opened the door and jumped out. Insects buzzed, creating an eerie hum in the night. Lauren regretted not having a garage as she and Lauren rushed to the door.

Luke wasn't in the living room when she opened the door, and Laramie bolted to her room. Lauren roamed the house, but Luke was nowhere to be seen. Her belly clenched, and worry escalated into fear.

No sign of a disturbance, and Luke could have left on his own terms, but what if something had happened?

She turned on the porch light and found him sitting outside, in the dark. Relief whooshed out of her in a sizzling sigh, and she switched the light back off and stepped outside.

She should have known. He loved the outdoors, and the night was thick enough to blend into the shadows.

"What are you doing out here?"

"Giving you both space."

She sat beside him. "Laramie is in the shower and getting ready for bed."

He only nodded. His mood was pensive, as thick as the darkness. Crickets chirped. The window blinds were all closed, so barely any light slipped through from the inside. She listened for the shower running but couldn't hear anything. She didn't want Laramie coming out and finding them gone.

"I'm sorry, Luke. So very, very sorry. I should have done things differently. Handled things better. I'm sorry I hurt you. Sorry I hurt you both."

Luke didn't say anything, but he finally did reach his hand out to hers. They clasped hands, he squeezed hers, and then looked at her and nodded.

"It's okay. You weren't ready. And I understand."

She shook her head. "No, you don't."

"Yes."

The outside light came on, and Lauren wrenched around, but there was no way to see inside the house. It went back off, and Laramie opened the door and poked her head out.

Lauren dropped her hand and stood, waving for her daughter to come out. "Hey, Laramie. You want to sit with us a minute before you go to bed?"

She walked outside and shut the door. "Okay."

"I'm going to grab us some tea, if that's okay."

Laramie nodded and sat in the chair where Lauren had been.

"Chamomile for everyone?"

"Sure," Laramie said. Luke had turned away, but she saw his shoulders shaking. She quickly escaped inside, hoping to give the two loves of her life this moment to reconcile.

Because she did love Luke. She would always love Luke, and she hoped they'd survive their history. She regretted stealing the time she had stolen from Luke and Laramie. They deserved a chance to know each other, and she had been selfish in her decision.

Selfish, and fueled by fear. An emotion she couldn't allow

herself any longer. She steeped the tea and watched the time, giving them at least fifteen minutes.

And resolved to never again let fear rule.

———

As soon as Laramie walked out the door, Luke cried. He didn't take her in his arms, didn't whisper sweet sorrows, but when he finally did speak, it was only two words.

"I'm sorry."

Laramie scooted close and patted his shoulder. "It's not your fault."

"Your mom was only trying to protect you."

"I can't figure out what she thought she was protecting me from."

He raised his head, dumbstruck at how much she resembled him and Lauren. A beautiful replica of love.

He chuckled, but not a real laugh. A laugh full of sorrow and regret. "The fear that your father was a murderer."

"But you were released from prison. Exonerated."

"Doesn't mean she didn't still have fears."

Laramie released her hold on his shoulder and grabbed his hands. He squeezed hers, then lifted them to his mouth and kissed her knuckles.

"Look, she had her reasons," he said. "And I uh, I…"

"Didn't want to betray her confidence. I know."

He studied her, amazed at her wisdom. Lauren had done a fabulous job as a parent, a single mother raising her daughter alone. And, he'd told himself the day he was released from prison, he couldn't afford to let regret keep him from enjoying the rest of his life.

He was proud of her. Proud of both mother and daughter.

"I'm sorry I broke your confidence," he said. "Your mom had her reasons, and I respect the hell out of her."

"You more than respect her, I'm thinking."

Their eyes met, and he smiled.

"I'm glad you're my dad."

His heart filled to the point he was afraid of it bursting open, yet again. He'd missed out on so much, but he'd do it all over again if it meant this one moment with his daughter.

"And I'm so glad you're my daughter."

"We might not all have a happily ever after, but can we try for a happy for now?"

"Yes. Yes, we can. I've never been happier in my life. Come here." He folded her in his arms and she climbed into his lap, resting her head on his chest. He rested his head on hers. They cried together until Laramie fell asleep in his arms.

For a moment, he pictured her as a three-year-old. Needing her father to shield her from life's hurts. Even if he hadn't had that opportunity, now at least he could shield her from her adult hurts. Her first broken heart. Her first crush. High school graduation. College, even.

Gratitude filled him. He picked her up and carried her to bed, Lauren meeting him at the doorway.

Laramie stirred and said something. He tucked a strand of hair behind her hair and placed her into bed, then quietly escaped before she fully woke.

He shut the door behind him. Lauren stood at the table, three coffee cups steaming from the table. "Guess we won't need that third tea."

"Oh, I don't know. I could probably drink two if it'd help me sleep." He pulled her into his arms and rested his forehead on hers.

"Is everything okay?" she asked.

"Things couldn't be better. You raised her so well. She's charming, creative, and she's got a good head on her shoulders."

"Is she still angry?"

He pulled away and smiled. "Not at me."

She tilted her head, put on her best glare face, and thumped his chest. "Because you're so charming and creative."

"I am," he said, then pulled her into his arms again. "No, she's good. She's not angry. She's understanding. We had a good talk. A good cry. And everything is going to be okay."

"That's good. So I think that means you're staying here tonight."

"I'll sleep on the couch."

"What? You don't want your daughter to know we're sleeping together?"

"Not until we're married."

She laughed and swayed her body with his, but he didn't bother telling her he was serious. He planned on proposing, and soon.

He hated that Laramie had been subjected to violence and cruelty at such a young age, but Lauren had done her best at shielding her from it all. He wanted his daughter to know true love did exist and parents could live happily together. For now, and forever.

CHAPTER EIGHTEEN

LUKE STAYED two nights in a row. They had a fun-filled day of shopping for school clothes, then dinner and a movie at home. Lauren worried what kind of influence it had on Laramie, but she was too excited to disappoint. She bounced out of bed the next morning, eager to cook breakfast. They grilled everything outside.

Lauren sipped her coffee as Luke stood at the grill with Laramie, helping her to pour the pancakes on the pan. Love swelled her heart. Low clouds fogged the sky, the clammy heat on her skin crawling down her spine. Even though they sat on the patio under the porch, the heat of the day crept over them.

She wondered if she should give them father/daughter time, but also recognized family time was also important. What would it be like to be a family? After Luke's imprisonment, she never dreamed such dreams. Could she afford to now?

They chattered and ate, but Laramie switched the conversation around and scraped her plate clean. "So what was it like in prison? Was it as bad as everyone says?"

Lauren's stomach flipped and her heart did a dip, dip, dip. Eyes wide, she judged Luke's reaction, shocked at her daughter's question.

He didn't even blink.

"Worse."

His chest puffed out, but his face didn't flush and he didn't flinch. He swiped a hand over his face, and Laramie leaned forward in her chair. Her gaze remained laser-focused, almost impenetrable, and it struck Lauren how her daughter's curiosity could be dangerous in other circumstances.

He shot a wink Lauren's direction and continued. "I mean, everyone thought I was a child killer. Everyone wanted to kill me. And most tried. But I held my ground, and someone new always came around for them to beat up. They learned to respect me, and many came my way when they wanted help with their own problems."

Laramie shuddered, and Lauren held out her hand to grip her daughter's arm, but she shook her off. "I'm okay, Mom. This doesn't terrify me. Besides, you do this kind of work for a living."

"I do," Lauren agreed. "But I'm older, I've been through a lot more experiences, and—"

"This isn't going to give me nightmares or anything."

"Well, what if the memories give Luke nightmares?"

Heat flushed her face. She shouldn't have said it, but she needed to make her daughter understand not all questions were appropriate, even if you were family. Laramie blinked, her chin juddered, her focus on Luke.

He held up his hands. "It's okay. I won't have nightmares. I've been through a lot and became tougher for it."

Laramie bit her lip in a smile and threw out a child-punch to his shoulder. "Yeah, let's see how tough you got."

"Oh, yeah?" He contracted his bicep and patted the muscle. "You wanna see how tough I am?"

Her precocious daughter sat back in her seat and folded her arms. "Mm-hm."

"Laramie," Lauren warned, but they were both all smiles. This is what fathers and daughters did. Teased, wrestled, challenged. They had missed out on the best of that, but no point in ruining a good mood now.

He mock-punched Laramie's jaw, then dropped his arm. Lauren admired his upper torso and pictured her hands on him later.

"So how many friends did you have in prison?" Laramie asked.

"Well, I definitely learned how to keep my enemies close. But I had good friends. Guys who had my back in the worst of moments."

"Did you get beat up a lot?"

"Hey, I just told you that."

She shrugged and chewed her lip. "Sorta."

"Maybe a time or two in the early days. But I was tough and knew how to defend myself."

"Laramie, it's time to shower now," Lauren said. As much as Luke said he didn't mind, she didn't want to force him to relive the nightmare from their daughter's questions no matter how bad she wanted to know for herself. It cut her to know how much pain she had caused him, how much pain he experienced in prison. Even if he didn't discuss it or display it in the warmth of his eyes.

"What are we going to do today?" Laramie asked.

"I don't know," she said.

"Can we go to Luke's?"

Lauren did need to at least take him home for his car. She had to go back to work tomorrow, and Laramie started school in three days.

"I want to go swimming again," Laramie said when nobody answered.

"Fine with me," Luke said. "I need to get back home anyway. We can grill a steak outside."

Laramie jumped from her seat and started stacking the dirty dishes in her arms. Luke opened the door for her, carrying the rest of the dishes. Lauren's heart swelled, happy that Laramie had accepted Luke. Accepted? She was more like enamored.

They spent the day in the lake, then the evening grilling steaks and s'mores.

Laramie chattered on about her plans. "I've got the community pool in our neighborhood, but it isn't near as cool as the river."

"You have to come to work with me tomorrow, Lare."

Her daughter shifted, full body, to her. "What?"

"I don't feel comfortable with you staying home alone until Clint is caught."

"What am I supposed to do in your boring office all day? Color?" She spat out the word as if it was a punishment. Laramie once loved to color.

"I'll set up the laptop for you to watch movies."

"She can stay here with me," Luke volunteered.

Laramie's entire face lit up, mouth jutting into a smile.

"We can go fishing and swimming, but you'll have to learn to hook your own worm." His eyes gleamed.

Laramie clapped her hands. "Okay!"

"What about your job?" Lauren asked him.

"I'll take off. I'm part time and as needed, and we aren't busy. It'll be fine." He reached for her hand and squeezed. Heat slithered through her at his touch. She should be afraid of letting Laramie stay with him. Afraid because they were growing too close, and what if something terrible happened again?

No sense in worrying about it now. No matter what might happen between them, Luke deserved time with his daughter, and she deserved her father.

Luke released her hand, leaving a void. He stood. "Speaking of worms, I've got to go check on them."

"Yes!" Laramie jumped from her chair. "Come on, Mom. You've got to see the worms."

Lauren followed them down the steps. Luke switched on the faucet and grabbed the hose, walking to the side of the house where an old refrigerator had been created into a worm bed. He opened the freezer portion and scooped out some kind of feed, the opened the door.

Laramie stood on one side of him, Lauren on the other, and he shifted aside the newspaper.

"You want to feed and water them?" he asked Laramie.

"Yes!"

He handed her the scoop and when she poured, worms slithered to the top.

"Oh my goodness," she exclaimed. "That's so cool."

"You don't think it's creepy?"

"Ah. Maybe a little."

"You sure you can handle one of them tomorrow when we go fishing?"

"I sure am gonna try."

He laid the newspaper back over the worms. "Now add a bit of water. They don't need much, just wet the paper."

As Laramie sprayed down the worms with the hose set to shower mode, Luke wrapped his hand behind Lauren's lower back and pulled her close. She smiled at him, her heart pooling to her feet. She didn't fight the enjoyment, no matter how much her fears buzzed her mind so loud her ears rang. She enjoyed this moment and every moment together they had while it lasted.

They tended the garden, and Laramie helped him pick

peaches from the tree. The sun descended and the evening wore into night. They went inside.

Laramie spending the days with Luke was a fabulous idea. She could stay with Luke and continue their bond. Luke told them they could stay the night if Lauren didn't mind getting up and driving to work. Since Lauren hadn't brought extra clothes, she could get up early and run home to get ready. Laramie had brought extra because of her swimsuit, and Luke gave her a large t-shirt to sleep in. He had a couple of spare toothbrushes in the cabinet.

They watched a movie until Lauren could no longer keep her eyes open. She had to get up early the next morning with enough time to run home and get ready for work.

"I'm sleepy, too," Laramie said. "Goodnight, guys. Love you."

Lauren followed her to the spare bedroom to tuck her in, and as soon as she walked back out into the living room, Luke wrapped her in a bear hug then kissed her.

"I've been wanting to do that all evening," he whispered.

"I've been wanting you to do that all evening."

"I'm glad it's finally time for bed."

"But you're sleeping on the couch," she teased.

"That's what Laramie thinks, but we'll be way up before she is."

They slipped into the bedroom, Luke's hands all over her. He kissed her as if branding her, the heat of his tongue gliding across her skin.

Did desire have a smell? Smoke? Musk? The deep salty exaltation of cocoa or the tang of red wine Lauren loved to sip in the evenings.

Or was it more of a sound? A boom, a crash, a blast, or something subtle? Like the *thump, thump, thump* of a pulse.

Luke lifted her around his waist and carried her to bed.

He trailed kisses along her neck, nipping and tugging. She determined desire had all of those things, and more. The taste of sweat, whisper of skin, and the sight of bodies shadowed in the nightlight from the bathroom.

They pulled apart long enough to remove their clothing, then he lay across her on the bed and slipped inside her.

She opened for him, savoring his length, then planted her palms on his ass to pull him closer. His fiery skin branded her palms, his breath wisped across her ear, then his voice stamping that final fall.

"God, Lauren."

She rocked with him, arching her hips up and meeting him thrust for thrust. Spasm after spasm of pleasure hit her. Even when she thought it was over, it culminated again, until the final rapturous release.

They breathed heavy together. He moved off to the side and pulled her close. She snuggled into his chest and listened to his heartbeat. In the aftermath of love, she wondered if she was making a mistake by falling for him again.

———

Luke looked forward to the morning. The alarm buzzed. Lauren stirred. He reached over her to hit snooze and cuddled her in his arms.

"Mmm," she muttered. "Good morning."

"Good morning to you, too."

"Can we sleep in today?"

"Sure we can."

She raised up in bed. "I wish."

He leaned up with her, eager to have a taste of her before she had to leave. He lifted up her shirt to display her pert breasts. They had both slept in clothes last night in case

Laramie woke up and roamed the house. Even though his bedroom door was locked, they didn't want to take any chances.

He suckled on her nipple as it beaded in his mouth, his cock already rock hard.

"How about a quickie first?" he teased.

"I'm definitely up for that, as long as you can promise me a cup of coffee afterward."

"Absolutely." He planted kisses across her breasts.

He pulled her shirt over her head and traced his fingers down her body to tickle her lower stomach. She squirmed, and he nipped her neck. The sweet subtle taste of her pulse against his tongue was enough to nourish him for the next century.

He slipped his finger under her shorts and into her moist heat, his cock pulsating and screaming for release.

The mental bars confining him—tougher than the ones he lived with for the past twelve years—disintegrated a little each day he spent with Lauren and his daughter.

He wondered if it was too soon to ask her to spend the rest of her life with him. Or should he ask Laramie's permission first? He had no idea what the right thing to do was, but he wanted to include her in their plans together.

He slid into Lauren's heat and relief weaved through him, unwinding the knots in his gut.

They came together, pulsating their desire in silent breaths. And after lying together for a bit, Lauren shifted the covers aside and rose.

"I've got to get up before I fall back asleep and am way too late for work."

"Okay," he grumbled. "I need a quick shower before Laramie wakes up. You wanna join?"

"Tempting. But we know where that will lead. I'll shower

at home so I don't have to put dirty clothes back on. You sure y'all will be okay today?"

"Positive." He couldn't wait to spend the day with his daughter. "As long as she doesn't squirm too much at the worms and the fish," he teased.

"It's still early, so you have time to shower. She usually sleeps past ten during the summer."

He saw Lauren off with a cup of coffee on the go, then quickly showered and dressed. He sat outside with his laptop and the sunrise. He had started his story with pen and paper, but now finished by typing out his thoughts, reliving the memories of prison and the bars that confined him for so long. His heart opened as he reminisced the good and bad times.

Most of those bad times had been the memories of Lauren, the inability to say goodbye, to grab her gaze and sway her with the mental connection they shared.

He typed out his thoughts, his fears, his memories, refusing to let fear stop him from sharing his story.

———

Luke Release Day

In prison I lay awake at night dreaming of Lauren, seeing her in my thoughts, hoping for her to visit, but week after week, year after year she never appears.

Today is release day. Twelve years of this battle, and I'm about to be a free man.

I blow out a breath and step outside.

My sisters and father greet me, though my heart aches at who isn't here. Mother had long ago passed away. I miss her all over again.

Lauren isn't here either, but why I had even hoped she would be?

I thought Lauren and I had a connection. I thought if I dreamed hard enough, she would see the truth and the truth, literally, would set me free. After a few years, I gave up hope she'd ever come see me in prison. In her mind, I was the man who murdered her sister. I tried to keep up with what was happening with her, but even my sisters lost connection and knew it was too painful for me to continue to try to reach out to her.

The best thing I could do for our dead relationship was to prove my innocence. But after a while I even gave up on that.

But it has finally happened for me. I long for Lauren even now, but vow to never see her, never reach out to her. For all I know, she still believes I'm guilty. No sense in stirring up old ghosts. It's time to start a new life.

Maybe I shouldn't go home, to the place this all started, but I want nothing more than to enjoy the property I grew up on along the river. To relish in my solitude. After a while, I urge my family to go on about their business and return to their lives. And they sense I want to be alone.

I plant a garden. I fish. I swim. And I work part time on cars because I'm afraid if I remain in solitude, I might never want to get out again. Experts say you should be social, so it's probably best I see people occasionally. Jim, my boss, is a great guy to work for. He was close to my family. He practically is family.

Imagine my surprise when Lauren shows up on my porch a few months later. I had just thrown some steaks on the grill and was relaxing outside. Thunder booms around us, heightening the storm brewing in my heart. I won't say she was there to threaten my life or even take my life, but I think she damn sure wanted to. At this point, maybe I even wanted her to.

She was still angry. I saw it in her eyes, the way she squinted and glared, and the vein popping down her hairline. I felt it in the aura she projected. But I had long-since given up, so I didn't bother begging her to listen to my story.

When I learned I had a twelve-year-old daughter, I cried. Tears of pain, tears of regret, and tears of unimaginable joy. I had created another living being with the woman I loved, the woman I would always love even if I had to let her go. I learned you can love someone, your heart can break a dozen times, but you can still go on. Still move forward. And I vowed to move forward, one step at a time.

A lot is still to be done. My life is a work in progress and I cherish each day. How do I end a story that isn't complete, and I hope won't be complete for many years to come? As I write this, the real murderer is still out there. Clint. My best friend at one time, and the man who destroyed my life. I don't hold grudges and I don't wish him death. There are things worse than death, as the cold walls of prison can attest.

All those years in prison weren't full of misery, as you've read in my story. I had some decent times and I feel I changed people's lives. I was there for a reason, maybe many reasons, and I found peace. Getting to know my daughter was worth every experience, even the bad. Each day is a new day. Each morning I step outside and watch the sunrise, and each evening I watch the sunset.

Something I thought to never do again.

LUKE TYPED *The End* and saved his work, then thought about texting his sister Charlotte that he finished his story. But he wanted to tell Lauren first. He wouldn't share it without first sharing it with her and having her approval. She was a large part of his story, the biggest part of his journey. He liked writing, and it was a growing talent he never thought to enjoy. His words were raw. He worried they might too raw for his and Lauren's growing relationship, but he'd take the chance.

He drained his coffee, and Laramie joined him not too long after.

"Good morning, sleepyhead."

"Morning," she grumbled but she was all smiles. "Can I have a cup of coffee?"

"Are you allowed to have a cup of coffee?"

"Mom lets me have some during the summers and weekends when I don't go to school. But we put a lot of milk in it."

"Okay. Let's go get you some. I need more anyway."

She made most of it herself, and he was proud at her proficiency as a young child. They went back to sit outside and enjoy the sunrise, despite the climbing heat.

"It's going to be a hot one." Laramie's gaze flickered toward the river.

"Yep. Might be too hot for fishing."

"No way. Never too hot for that."

He sipped his coffee. "Well, the fish like to eat early, so we best have breakfast and go out there before they go off into a cool spot for their nap." Chances were, they had already done that, but Luke knew a few good fishing holes to try.

"We don't have to do anything fancy for breakfast," Laramie said. "I'm good with some toast and eggs this morning."

"Perfect."

They went inside and had a quick breakfast and before long, they were in the Jon boat and casting their lines. Laramie squirmed some, but she didn't ask for help and she didn't back down. He was enamored by her strength for one so young.

He paddled far away from the crime scene, and was grateful she didn't look that direction or ask any questions. Her face beamed when she caught a few fish, and he was amazed at her patience. His chest expanded with light and strength and contentment.

He was fishing with his daughter, a daughter he'd never have known existed if he hadn't been released. Making memories, as if they had all the time in the world.

Some of her mannerisms reminded him of Lauren, some of him. The way her nose tipped up a tiny bit, her chin elevated and proud, but not vain, was like a miniature version of Lauren when she had just accomplished an adventurous feat. Her tiny ears were definitely Lauren's, but her eyes were so much like his and the way she chewed her lip as she hooked the worm and put laser-focus on her longing reminded him of his younger days. When he had been eager and trusting and open to explore what the world had to offer.

Luke would do anything to keep his daughter safe. And yet a murderer roamed the streets. Had even been to his property. Luke couldn't go to school with her. Couldn't stand sentry over her room all night while she slept.

His stomach tightened. No way would he ruin their good times with his vicious thoughts. They stopped on a rock at the riverbank and had a picnic, then went back on the river, paddling mostly instead of fishing.

"Can I try paddling?" she asked.

"Sure." The area had an undercurrent, but nothing swift and nothing to take too much of her energy. He worried she might drop them and they'd be stuck in the middle of the river, but he didn't tell her so and wouldn't dare take this from her. He kept one paddle and gave her one, and helped when she wasn't looking.

"Whew," she said after a few minutes of rowing. "That's tough."

She handed him the paddle and relaxed in her seat, her attention on everything around her. He dreamed of one day taking her motor boating on the lake.

"You getting tired?" he asked.

"No, this is great. Just need to rest a second."

He stopped paddling and dropped the oars in the boat. Water slapped against the metal, a harmony that put him at ease. He watched as Laramie removed her cap, fixed her hair under her, then toss him a smile as she situated the shade bac over her head. She peered out over the river, her lips curled in thought.

Sometimes, he forgot how young his daughter was. She seemed so bright and spirited but was also mature for a twelve-year-old. But then her young spirit appeared, the innocence and vulnerability only a child could display. His heart rumbled. He longed for her to feel safe with him. But had she felt safe with Clint? And look what kind of monster Clint was.

"I hated Clint," Laramie belted out of the blue.

His skin prickled. How had she read his mind? "Do you have telepathy or something?"

She frowned. "Tele-huh?"

"Can you read people's minds?"

Her nose crinkled. "Wouldn't that be cool?"

"I was thinking about Clint," he admitted.

"Great minds think alike." She patted her head and smiled, then clasped her hands in her lap. "But I thought I should let you know."

"Did he ever... do anything to you?"

She shook her head, and he held his breath for her answer. "No. Just gave me the creeps. I mean, I guess when I was younger he was okay. Part of the family. Like a weird uncle nobody likes, you know? But as I got older, I didn't like him."

"Did you ever have to stay with him alone?" he asked, wondering about their history.

"Yes. When Mom was busy and he babysat. Or he took me swimming and even fishing when I was younger. And he picked me up from school occasionally to help Mom out. Or drop me off somewhere, things like that."

Cold chills swarmed down Luke's spine. She had been so vulnerable. And if Luke hadn't been released and the truth had never been discovered, Clint would still have access to her.

"He and your mom never dated?"

"No. But he wanted to. Mom kept her distance, too. She just doesn't realize it. He obviously wanted more though. I'm glad she never did."

He was glad, too.

"You ready to head back?" he asked.

"Yeah. We better get these fish home. Lots of work to do if we're frying them tonight."

He didn't mind the work, especially if his daughter was involved.

"Oh yeah? You gonna help me skin some fish?"

She beamed at him. "I don't mind supervising."

He chuckled. He fingered the small multi-tool pocketknife he planned to give Laramie. He'd already asked Lauren for permission, and she agreed. He didn't want her hurt, but he wanted her to be able to protect herself. He pulled it out of his pocket and handed it over. "I have something to give you first."

"Cool." She took it, and her smile spread at the dark pink camouflage.

"It's a multi-tool pocket knife, but you have to be very

careful with it." He showed her the basics and how to be safe about opening and closing each tool.

"Is this in case Clint ever comes after me?"

Blood drained from his body, and he almost regretted the tool. He didn't want her to know of his fears. "Not just."

She put her arms around him. "Thank you, Dad."

CHAPTER NINETEEN

LAUREN FRETTED on how Luke and Laramie were enjoying their day, but she was too busy to check on them. When Luke texted her a pretty please grocery list to include frying oil, onion rings and hush puppies, a smile lifted her heart. Things must have gone well.

Luke met her outside and greeted her with a kiss, then helped her carry in the groceries. She wondered what it would be like to do this every day, come home after a hard day and be greeted with a kiss from the man she loved.

"How did it go?" she asked as she unloaded groceries. Laramie pulled out the frozen onion rings and hush puppies and put them in the freezer.

"Fun. I caught a lot of fish and have been supervising Luke while he cleans and cuts."

"She's a good fisherwoman," Luke said.

Lauren nodded, wondering if Luke caught his name that fell across their daughter's lips, and wondering when or if she'd ever call him dad. That was her decision, and she wouldn't push it.

Soon, the crackling of the oil, the smell of corn meal,

spice, and oil, and the memories of being out here with his parents during their weekly fish fries assaulted her. Her muscles kinked, throat punctured with heat and unshed tears. Laramie chatted on like normal. Lauren's mind spun with details of Luke. Them in their younger days, dancing under the stars, making love in the moonlight near the rocks. She'd loved his parents, but their relationship had ended when hers and Luke's had.

"Mom?" Laramie asked, pulling her back into the present. "Did you hear a word I said?"

"Yes, you were paddling and it was tiring and you stopped and had a picnic and went far down the river. Did you go all the way to the slab road?"

"No, but we should try that tomorrow, right Luke?"

"Sounds good to me."

"I said this is a good place for a birthday party, to bring out all my friends. And maybe if Luke and I can catch some more fish between now and then, we can fry fish and stuff."

"That's fine as long as it isn't cold." Laramie's birthday was in March, eight months away, and the weather was iffy that time of year.

"Probably too cold to swim," she said. "Maybe we could have a summer party."

"We'll plan that," Luke said. "Soon. Maybe within the next two weeks before the summer ends but once school starts. How does that sound?"

"Sounds amazing," Laramie exclaimed.

"That is, if the parents of your friends will let them come to a prisoner's house," Luke joked. Laramie screeched and popped him on the arm, but Lauren's gut twisted. Those words were probably truer than any of them wanted to admit.

They ate outside. The sun went down, and Laramie fell asleep on the chair outside. Luke carried her to her room, then they applied more bug spray and sat outside for one more glass of wine.

"Thanks for letting Laramie stay today," Luke said. Crickets chirped, cicadas buzzed, and distant coyotes howled.

Lauren shivered and rubbed her hands over her arms. "She had a good time. It gets eerie out here at night."

"Are you ready to go in?"

"Not yet."

Luke pulled her close, and she crawled into his lap. "I'll protect you from any Chupacabra."

She nestled her ear on his chest and relished the strong beat of his heart. "I hope this chair is strong enough to hold us."

"It'll hold."

They cuddled together in silence for a while, his breathing long and relaxed. At the point where she wondered if he had fallen asleep, he spoke.

"She called me dad today."

She lifted away and looked at him. His eyes sparkled, his smile broad and relaxed. Her limbs lightened. "She called you dad?"

"I gave her the pocket knife tool. She hugged me and said thanks, Dad." Tears gleamed in his eyes. "I said you're welcome and finished rowing home."

Her body tingled in warmth and contentment. She massaged his chest. "That's awesome. Wow."

He swiped a hand over his face. "I have more news."

"Goodness. Okay."

"I finished my memoir."

Her thoughts scattered all over the place, the tingle in her body turning to doubt. She hadn't been expecting this. "Oh, yeah?"

"I haven't told anyone else yet. I have an agent, and my

sister, Charlotte has agreed to help with marketing. The deal is good. It would put Laramie through college. I want you to read it before I accept the offer."

"You don't have to let me read it."

"I want you to. You're a large part of my story. And I can't accept the offer without your approval."

"You haven't accepted the offer?"

"No. I have an agent, but I haven't signed any publishing contracts yet. I wanted to finish the story first."

"Luke..." she said. A bird warbled, a breeze whistled though the trees, as if miming her thoughts, her true feelings.

What would it be like to have the world read his story? *Their* story? She didn't know it would be as simple as paying for Laramie's college, although she was grateful for the offer. Would the dynamics of their relationship change if the entire world knew their history?

"I'll read it," she agreed, curious about the story he hadn't yet told but also glad he found comfort in writing.

He nodded. She shifted in his lap and finally stood, growing uncomfortable.

"You're bony," he joked.

She slapped him on the arm.

"Come on. We'll go inside. I need to shower this bug spray off." He took her hand and grabbed their glasses, then escorted her inside and locked the doors behind him.

After a prolonged shower—full of lovemaking—they lay in bed and he gave her a binder with all the printed pages from his story. He gave her a pen in case she wanted to make him any notes and watched her read until his breathing grew heavy. She admired him while he slept. Tears burned her eyes and slipped down her face.

She read, and her breath whipped out of her in large hushed but choking sobs. She didn't want to wake him, so she bit down on her hand to stay silent. He was a good writer. The angst of his story potent on the page, their memories so real and true. Tangible, as if he had cut his heart open for everyone to see.

Not just their memories together, but his memories. His first day in prison, his first fight that left him bloodied and bruised. Even his last fight where he had gained respect from the others. Stories he wouldn't tell his daughter when she asked. Stories he lightened when he'd told her. The story of being falsely accused, of losing his mother, and finally losing his time in a world with no compassion. Getting out of prison and learning he had a daughter, developing a relationship with his daughter and the constant pressure of the real murderer on the loose.

He even briefly mentioned sex and how easily trysts could be found in prison. Not sex with other men, but sex with females until even that was no longer a priority for him.

Her heart ached. She couldn't sleep, continued reading pages until she finished, then found his handwritten note.

Dear Lauren, thank you if you've made it this far. I wanted you to be the first to read this. I wanted you to mark anything about our lives together you didn't want shared. And I also wanted you to know the man I am today. Prison changed me. Maybe not for the better and maybe not for the worst. But I wanted you to know, in case you read this and change your opinion of me. In case you no longer want to be together, no longer want to give our relationship a try, and no longer trust what you thought you knew about me. If I do share my story, you deserve to know before anybody else. I hope our story together doesn't end here.

WHEN LUKE WOKE the next morning, Lauren was gone. He surged out of bed and stopped at the door as starbursts erupted behind his eyelids.

He closed his eyes and clutched the door, his breath whooshing out of his body in choking sobs. She'd read his story and left him.

Once he'd regained his bearings, he rushed to Laramie's room. His chest expanded, throat thickened when he found her asleep in bed.

He strolled to the coffeepot and checked his phone to find the text from Lauren. *Had to get to work early this morning. Left a note in your notebook about the story. Have a great day and text me later!*

He breathed out his panic. She hadn't left him. She'd trusted him to stay with Laramie, trusted him enough to leave them both asleep while she slipped out the door to work. Worry kinked his muscles. What if Clint had been hiding in the bushes and waiting on her?

He sent her a good morning text, relieved when he got a quick response. She was at work. She was okay. Clint hadn't kidnapped her on her way.

Would this worry ever end?

He found the binder on the bedside table, her handwritten note on top. His pulse flopped through his chest, ripping his gut and diving to his feet.

Dear Luke: If anything, my opinion of you has strengthened. I'm sorry for what you suffered, what I put you through. I can't even imagine those days you endured and how everybody you loved abandoned you. I may never forgive myself, but I hope you will. I love your story and your writing, and I think you should share it. Maybe it can help somebody else. Although there will always be bumps along the way, I definitely don't want to end our story together.

He returned outside and drank another cup of coffee while he emailed his sister and his agent to let them know he finished his story. Charlotte called within five minutes. "Oh, my goodness, Luke. I'm so excited it's done. When are you going to email it to me?"

"I guess I could now." Even though the entire world might read it soon, it was difficult to attach and send to his sister. "There. Just did."

"I should be home at the end of August. Maybe sooner. But definitely by the time your story is published so we can start the publicity."

Okay, that scared him. Publicity, sharing himself and his story. Talking at the conference was one thing, but traveling the world and sharing his story was different. No matter how hard he tried to heal, his wounds were still raw.

"Hold on," he said. "It'll probably be at least a year before it's even published. Or at least that's what the agent said."

"You can't ever start your marketing campaign too soon."

"Maybe I should reconsider."

"No way. Don't you dare."

His sisters didn't know yet about Laramie. But they would soon. Charlotte would freak when she read it in the story and knowing her, she'd read it after they hung up. And then he'd hurt Adrienne's feelings if he didn't tell her.

"There are things you will learn about me you might not want to know," he said. "Things that will shock you, anger you, and disappoint you. Make you scream, maybe even at me. But also make you wonder why I haven't told you."

"Luke, you know I love you. And I know how hard sharing your story is. You will never disappoint me."

"Well, let me know what you think once you've had a chance." They ended the call, then he emailed Adrienne. Might as well not exclude his other sister.

Finished my memoir and thought you'd want to see it. It's the first draft, so please don't share. Love, Luke.

Laramie woke, and after breakfast, she begged to go out

on the Jon boat again. "I want to paddle more but this time maybe get out and swim, too," she said.

"That'd be fun, but you still have to wear your life jacket," he said, earning a pout from her, but not an argument.

He tensed when a vehicle pulled into the driveway. The tires crunched against the gravel drive, and he viewed the front camera from the outdoor monitor. One lone police SUV stopped, and two officers in plain clothes stepped from the vehicle and approached his front door.

Lights weren't flashing, but that meant nothing. They hadn't flashed the first time he'd been arrested, either.

"Who's that?" Laramie, who stood beside him, asked.

"Go to your room while I find out."

He went through the house to the front inside instead of walking around. Might as well not make this easy for them.

Should he text Lauren? Warn her of the officers, who were likely here to arrest him on suspicion of murdering the child he'd found on his property. Never mind the game camera with the photos of Clint. If the investigation was anything like last time, the pictures had likely been destroyed.

Relax. Nothing at all was like last time. Clint's father was dead and had no influence on this investigation. That revelation didn't keep the concern from tightening his chest. He didn't want Laramie to see him arrested, but maybe if he went quietly they wouldn't cuff him. They'd have to take Laramie with them to the station for Lauren to pick her up.

He was steps away from the door when they banged on it. They had their badges displayed when they opened it, but no guns, no warrant, and no hostility. Recognizing them from the other day, he nodded.

"Gentlemen."

Their guns were clipped to their khaki pants, but at least

they weren't pointing in his face. He wasn't even sure why he expected that.

"Mr. Fuller," the bald one said. He didn't remember their names.

The officer went for his pocket. Here came the warrant. Laramie approached, her footsteps anchoring dread in his gut. Anger fueled him. Anger at these officers for doing this now, in front of his daughter.

But before he said anything, the officer continued in a hushed voice, as if it wouldn't reach Laramie's ears. "We wanted to do a walk-around at the crime scene. Take more photos and walk along any path Clint might have taken to see if we can find any evidence."

His ears rang, mind racing to catch up to their words. They weren't here to arrest him?

Laramie huddled near him, and he regretted she had to be here, see these officers even if they weren't here to arrest him. Chances were, with her mother's job, she had seen cops before, but he wanted to protect her from all wrongdoing.

The officer to his left nodded. "Laramie. How you doing?"

She held out her hand. "Officer Stanton. I'm great. What brings you here?"

"Uh." His gaze shot to Luke. Luke stepped aside to give them entry.

"You guys want to come in a moment?" he asked, wondering how well Laramie knew the officer.

"Love to, but we got work to do. Laramie, we're here to roam Luke's property, but we'll try not to get in anybody's way, okay?"

"Are you going to look at the crime scene?"

Luke's heart lurched. His young child was way too smart for her own good.

Stanton—that was his name—nodded. "We are."

"Cool. Well, watch for snakes." Laramie waved and shuffled backward.

"Will do." The officer held out his hand and shook Luke's, then Laramie's. The other tipped his hat. "If you don't mind, we'll drive down there."

"That's fine." At least they were in an SUV so the chances of getting stuck were less than in a patrol car. And since it hadn't rained in a while, the property should be fine.

After the officers had gone, Luke shut the door and considered new plans. He didn't want to be anywhere near the cops, and the best area to put in the boat was near the crime scene. It had been easy to ignore yesterday, but with a sheriff's vehicle stopped nearby and voices carrying, even his house was too close.

"I'm thinking we should go do something in town today," Luke said. "Watch a movie and have lunch somewhere? Or we can go to Castle Springs and have a burger and kayak."

"How about Enchanted Rock? That'd be fun and I haven't been yet this year."

His breathing loosened, happy Laramie was eager to do something else. "Yeah, it would. Let me call your mom and make sure it's okay."

She scoffed. "You're my dad. It's okay."

He laughed and rubbed his knuckles over her head, rejuvenated at her words. It was the second time she'd called him her dad, even if she hadn't actually given him the title. "Would rather make sure. Why don't you put on some hiking shoes while I pack us up a lunch?"

"I can help make sandwiches."

"Sounds good."

He called Lauren and disappeared into his bedroom for privacy. "Hey, Lauren. Sorry to bother you at work."

"It's okay. Is everything okay?"

"Yeah. No, it's great. Some officers came. At first I

thought they were here to arrest me, but they just wanted to look at the crime scene." He slapped a hand over his forehead at his blubbering. That hadn't come out at all like he'd wanted.

"Oh, Luke." The way her words rushed out of her, concern edged with fear, warmed his blood.

"Kind of ruined the mood for us to go swimming. Laramie suggested Enchanted Rock."

"That would be fun. It's hot out there."

"You don't mind?"

"No. I'm jealous I can't come, but that sounds fabulous. Text me when you get back?"

"Will do."

He packed an ice chest full of water and sandwiches and a bag of sunscreen and other snacks.

"Can we drive with the top off?" Laramie asked.

"Absolutely." He'd do anything for this little girl.

CHAPTER TWENTY

Lauren was minutes away from meeting the parents of the child found on Luke's property. Since it hadn't yet been determined where the crime had been committed, and she had been kidnapped in another jurisdiction, they were going with where the body had been discovered.

Which meant they were Lauren's victims to handle. Brian offered to let someone else handle them, but it was her job. Plus, she wanted to. Brian gave her a chance to discuss the victim's part of it alone, then he'd talk to them about the investigation.

Although Clint hadn't been found, they were taking his case to the grand jury on Monday. And Lauren started the paperwork for the victim assistance program to help the family with their needs. She'd read the file this morning for the first time, and dread pumped through her veins. She couldn't avoid the pictures. She needed to know, needed to understand, and a sick sense of curiosity urged her.

Tamra buzzed her office. Lauren's heart skipped a beat, and she answered in a shaky breath. "Yes?"

"The Pattons are here to see you." Tamra's voice was

soothing, like a calming cucumber scrub on a rotten sunburn. Although nothing comforted Lauren.

"Thank you. I'll be up in a moment."

She stood, but her knees wobbled. She had to get control of herself before she faced the Pattons. She breathed in and out, in and out, and visualized success. The Pattons were hurting way more than she was right now. She had to be strong for them.

She walked down the hallway, hamstrings aching as if she'd done a hundred heavy-weighted squats. Phones buzzed, voices carried, but the only sound she heard was the *whip whip whip* in her ears. She inhaled and exhaled in long staccato breaths.

She passed Tamra's doorway, tossed her a smile, stopped at the main door that led to the reception area where the Pattons waited, and let out one more long breath. She opened it, and a calmness took over.

"Mr. and Mrs. Patton?"

The woman blinked and smiled a fragile smile, her eyes large and puffy. The man, who had been holding her hand, dropped it and rose first. He was tall, with a long gray but nicely trimmed beard. The woman was half a head shorter. Her lips trembled, and she stood and clutched her hands in front of her. Her hair—probably once a beautiful auburn brown—was now mousy and pulled into a tight ponytail. Dark circles lined her eyes.

"I'm Lauren Cooper, victim coordinator."

They shook hands and followed Lauren to her office.

"Would you like anything to drink?" she asked. They were already shaking their heads before she got the offer out, but she continued. "Tea? Coffee? Water? Soda?"

"No, thank you," Mr. Patton said. His name was Abraham and it fit him. He was strong and fatherly, probably self-assured at one time until his whole life had been brutally changed. She preferred to call him Mr. Patton, and he hadn't offered otherwise.

"I know this is a very, very hard time for you, and I'm not here to promise you we'll make it any easier. But there are things we can do, steps we can take to make things easier. Our district attorney will be in later so he can talk about the case for you, but for now I wanted to discuss our steps and answer questions."

"Why hasn't that killer been arrested?" Mrs. Patton asked, her voice sharp and slicing through Lauren's resolves.

"They're still searching for him."

"I mean the man who was released from prison and free to murder our daughter." She buried her nose in her hand, but kept her face tilted forward and eyeballed Lauren. "They found her on his property."

"Yes, ma'am, but there was no evidence of his involvement."

She should have taken up Brian's offer to have someone else handle these victims. This was a huge conflict of interest.

Mrs. Patton dropped her hand and scooted forward. "Well, we heard nothing except that the man found her on his property. And he was recently released from prison for murder."

Lauren cringed. She thought Brian intended to keep that out of the media, but she needed to check the status. The press would hover like buzzards around him, and she didn't want Laramie anywhere near that.

"Mr. Wimberly will discuss that with you as soon as he's done with his other meeting. But he can't go into great detail, as it is still under investigation."

Mrs. Patton balked, her husband shushed her, and Lauren rose from her chair with a quick, "I'll see if Mr. Wimberly is ready," before she fled out the door.

They weren't interested in anything the victim's program

might offer. They only wanted revenge, and right now their revenge was pointing toward Luke.

She knocked on Brian's door and when he bid her to enter, she did so with a hand over her heart. "The Patton family is ready to see you now."

"Everything okay?"

Her chin quivered, her eyes growing heavy with the thick syrup of tears. "Not really." She didn't want to break down in front of her boss, but he was way too easy to talk to. She waved a hand over her face. "I should have taken you up on your offer and had someone else handle them."

She hated to admit that. Her job was tough, and she was the only victim coordinator in the office. She should be able to face any tough victim.

He rose from his seat and approached her. "Did something happen?"

"They weren't interested in hearing about the victim's program. They were only interested in knowing when Luke would be arrested."

His brows shot up like missile-launches in the sky. Instead, those missiles launched straight to her chest.

"Luke?"

"They think he did it since he found the body on his property."

"You told them that?"

She shook her head. "No. I thought you did."

"I haven't released that information."

His admission eased her, but not near enough. "Well, somebody did."

"Dammit." He ran a hand over his face, which was reddening in anger by the second. A good read on Brian's stress or anger level was his facial color, and red was never a good sign. "Give me a minute while I call the sheriff. Then I'll be in your office to get them. You can stay in the meeting or leave. Your choice."

"If you don't mind, I'll let you handle it."

He nodded and turned away, his steps short and fierce to his desk. He grabbed his phone and waved at her, then she walked out the door.

Could she postpone going back into her office?

When she walked in the door, Mrs. Patton was balling. Her husband offered Lauren a weak smile. She noted they'd already found the tissues.

"Mr. Wimberly had one more phone call to make and he'll be right in."

The woman tossed her napkin to her lap. "We're obviously not his priority."

She understood the woman's anger. Had felt it herself and nothing erased the pain.

"I'm sorry you feel that way, but the phone call has to do with your daughter's case. He's getting all the information he can so he'll have it when he meets with you."

The woman harrumphed and blinked her eyes, a furious chopping of her lashes up and down along her lids.

"I know how hard it is," she said. She would never make comparisons, but an offer to share sometimes helped the hurting victims. "My sister... well, she was murdered, too."

Mrs. Patton let out a long and shaky breath. Lauren didn't go into detail about who or how, but she hoped her admission brought the woman back to reality, at least until she left this office and returned to her empty home.

"I'm so sorry," she said.

Lauren nodded. "I wanted you to know I understand. And I know the long road ahead of you can't be eased by any words. But we are here to help you, and we are here to make it as easy as possible. We have assistance programs and all kinds of things we can do to help."

A knock at the door sounded, then Brian poked in his head. Although Lauren finally felt like she was about to make headway, she stood and waved him in.

He breezed in and introduced himself, then escorted them to his office, leaving Lauren bereft in his wake.

He had given her a choice to accompany him, but she'd go stir crazy sitting in his office while he explained the case and they accused Luke. Her head pounded at their visit.

While waiting, she checked the Internet and social media, her entire body weakening and collapsing at the news. She had checked last night and found nothing, but now they knew about the body on Luke's property. Thankfully, they hadn't placed her with him. Not that it would matter, she'd gladly stand by his side this time, but she didn't want Laramie affected. And some comments were harsh.

She tried calling Luke, then Laramie, then sent a message to Luke. *The press knows about the body being found on your property. Be careful.*

She paced and waited for Brian's meeting to end, grabbing a quick sandwich at the deli down the street. Eager to know Brian's schedule for the rest of the day, she strolled to the front and asked Tamra.

"He had a meeting at three, but he buzzed me earlier and told me to cancel it and schedule an office meeting with everyone. Sorry, I thought you were in the meeting with him. Otherwise, I would have come and told you."

"It's okay. Thanks. I let him handle them alone."

She texted Luke again and sent a message to Laramie to have Luke call.

Her skin clenched when Brian's voice trailed down the hall, their footsteps birthing a wide angle of anxiety as they moved past her door and never glanced her direction. Voices carried in this office, and he said goodbye and *be in touch*.

Seconds later, he was standing at her door. She jumped from her chair.

"How did it go?"

He stepped in her office and shut the door. "Okay. They're at the anger stage of their grief, at least she is. She wanted to hang Luke, but I showed her the evidence of Clint. She broke down several times, but she's doing okay."

Okay. What an overstatement.

"Any idea how they found out about Luke?"

"I don't know, but I intend to find out. The sheriff is asking around on his end, too, in case it came from his office. Get to the conference room while I round everyone else up."

Everyone entered in clusters until finally, the room was full of impatient staff members who had too much to do than to sit around in an unplanned meeting. Brian got to the point and spoke of the leak to the press.

"Everything we do here is confidential," he reminded everyone. "Everything," he stressed again. "That means no talking to the news media, ever. All questions should be routed to me."

"Yeah, even inner office," Tamra spouted.

Brows puckering, he turned to Tamra. "Do what?"

"I don't know how you can think anyone in this office would have said anything, considering we don't even know what's going on."

His laser-focused gaze pinpointed Tamra. "You called Lauren on her day off to tell her the body was found on Luke's property, did you not?"

Her face blanched. "Lauren works here. I thought she'd want to know."

"Well, now the media knows." He held up his hands as voices started hammering out defensive tactics. "I'm not saying it was anyone here, but if so I'd like to talk about it and if not, I want to make sure everyone is aware. This is a highly sensitive investigation and probably won't be ending anytime soon, especially until we find Clint. I'll work on a press release now so the public can be on the lookout and everyone can stop eyeing Mr. Fuller. He's not our guy. He wasn't twelve years ago and he isn't today."

Lauren's shoulders sagged, grateful for Brian's words but sore over her coworkers. Brian believed in Luke's innocence, and he fought for his beliefs, but her coworkers were frazzled and anxious, upset over being accused. Was one of them responsible for spreading vicious rumors, even if partly true?

"I SAY we get back to your house and jump in the river for a few minutes to cool off before cooking dinner."

Luke tossed a grin at Laramie and turned on the county road to his home. "I say I love that idea."

They'd had fun today and had walked for miles. He was impressed at Laramie's fortitude. The sweat that had poured off his forehead and down his back had turned sour, and neither of them smelled so great.

"You probably need a bit more sunscreen. Your face is getting pink."

She giggled. "Yours, too."

"What the..." Vans—about six of them—were parked along his fence line like predators waiting to attack. One minute their day was perfect with plans for a perfect evening, and suddenly the news media.

"Duck," he told Laramie.

"What?" She squinted at the upcoming chaos. Catastrophe —the only way Luke viewed this situation.

"So the news media doesn't see you. Duck."

"Oh."

She crouched over as he sped past and he hoped and

prayed they didn't recognize him and considered him a guy who lived on this road who was going home.

His gate was closed. The cops must have closed it when they left because he rarely did anymore. He obviously needed to start again. At least that was keeping the news vans out of his driveway.

"What's going on?" Laramie's words were muffled, her face planted in her lap at an uncomfortable angle.

"You can get up now."

The pressure in his chest eased as he continued along the road and nobody followed. Thank God he'd put the Jeep top on before they left for their trip. The windows had been rolled up, the AC blowing, and his windows were tinted enough to make it difficult to see who was driving.

He drove toward town, checking his phone once he stopped at the intersection. The ache in his body grew deeper when he saw Lauren's text. He pushed the phone icon to call her.

"Hey," she answered, her voice quick and breathy.

"Hey. I got your text."

"About the news knowing?"

"Yeah. Got it later than I should have. Guess I didn't have service then I didn't see it when it came through. Laramie and I just drove past my house. About half a dozen news vans are waiting for me to get home."

"What?"

He winced at her screech.

"We're okay. They didn't notice us. I'm driving to your work so I can drop Laramie off, but I'll make sure I'm not followed."

"Why don't you meet me at the house? I'm leaving work now."

"Sure, okay. See you in a bit."

He ended the call and peeped at Laramie, who scrutinized him.

"It's okay," he lied. Would it ever be okay? Would he ever be able to have a normal life?

She shrugged. "Yeah, so I guess the news knows you found a body on your property, and now they want to attack you."

He nodded, a lump forming in his throat.

"They probably think you did it." Her matter-of-fact statement rolled that lump to his chest.

"Most likely."

"Well, I know you didn't do it."

"Thanks." His voice was rough, an undertaking to weave through the distress. He was all too familiar with what it was like to be accused—it sucked—but his main concern was Laramie and how this affected her.

"Guess that means we won't be swimming in the river," she said.

"Probably not. I'm really sorry."

"It's okay. It's not your fault. We've got the community pool to cool off in." Her nose crinkled, and he didn't have the heart to tell her he wouldn't join them. The last thing Lauren and Laramie needed was to be seen with him.

Lauren hopped out of her vehicle when he pulled up in the driveway behind her. She waved, then went to Laramie's side and opened the door.

"Hey, doll. How was your day?"

"Amazing!" She slid out of the Jeep and shut the door. "We had a lot of fun exploring on the rock."

Lauren tossed him a smile and planted a hand on Laramie's shoulder as they walked to the front door. The cool air of the house tingled his skin, an invasion of his heat and sweat. His pulse battered against his ribcage as if he'd run a two-day marathon with no rest.

"I wanted to go swimming in the river," Laramie said. "Do you think I could swim at the pool?"

"Not right now, baby. I don't want you to go alone."

Laramie shrugged. "Okay, I'm gonna take a shower then."

"We can still grill burgers," Luke offered, then cringed. Maybe he shouldn't have offered without first talking with Lauren.

"Okay, cool. Be back."

Once Laramie had disappeared in her bedroom and he heard the shower running, he let out a long, exaggerated sigh.

"I'm so sorry." Lauren walked into his arms and he held her, their bodies swaying together. "I met with the victim's parents today and found out they knew about her being found on your property. We don't know how it happened, but they were insistent that you killed her."

His breath whooshed out of him.

"Brian talked to them about the evidence. He held a press release and told them he can't release all the information on our investigation. He released Clint's picture in hopes he'll be spotted."

"Why did that take so long?" he grumbled.

She pulled out of his arms and rested her back against the kitchen counter, and he stood in the middle of the room, his legs weak and achy.

She shrugged and shook her head. "I don't know."

"Look, it's best I leave. We'll grill burgers tonight if you're okay with that. I already promised Laramie earlier. I might find a hotel for the night—"

"You can stay here," she interrupted.

He put up a hand to stop her words. "No. Neither of you need to be seen with me until this all dies down. I don't want anyone targeting your home. We don't need to be seen together. She'll be starting school the day after tomorrow."

His voice cracked. He would miss the first day of school—the first day of his experience with her school. He knew what it was like to be under the spotlight and he didn't want that for his daughter.

"Luke," Lauren said, her voice wispy and fragile, severing the thin hold he had on his emotions.

The shower shut off. He blinked away the burn in his eyes. Lauren turned away and rummaged through the freezer, pulling out meat and switching on the faucet. She placed the meat in a bowl and ran hot water to thaw the patties.

Luke sent a text to his attorney—the one he'd had in prison and the one who still represented him but not the same one who had helped sentence him to life. He needed to meet with Randall soon, discuss the book contract and what happened next.

A book could either help him or hurt him, but he was ready for the truth.

CHAPTER TWENTY-ONE

Despite all the preparation for the first day of school, Lauren scrambled through the house to get there on time. She had overslept, largely thanks to her late-night phone call with Luke. He was upset he couldn't be with them, and he had already missed years of firsts, but he insisted on keeping a low profile until the announcement of his book and a subsequent press release.

Her stomach tightened when she dropped Laramie off. "Keep your phone with you at all times. And don't forget I'm coming to pick you up. Don't leave the school. Don't—"

"Mom," Laramie interrupted. "I know. And I don't think Clint will kidnap me on my first day of school, so don't worry so much, okay? Love you," she added as she opened the door and hopped out.

"Love you. Have a good day," Lauren called after her.

She was a basket case most of the morning. At eleven, the principal called. "Hi Ms. Cooper. I just wanted to check with you and check on Laramie. I know it's a tough time for you, but I thought Laramie would be at school all day today. And she hasn't been properly signed out to leave the school."

"What are you talking about? She hasn't left the school."

"Okay." She sensed the confusion in his voice, and fear rose. Her knees wobbled as she stood. "She was here for her first three classes, her third period being PE."

Panic clawed at her temples. "Call the police!"

"Oh, then. We'll check the security footage at or near the school. We'll check with friends and parents, even get them out of class to ask if they've heard from her. Someone found her phone outside the gym as if she'd dropped or tossed it."

"She'd never toss her phone."

"She wouldn't have run away again?"

She wanted to jump through a phone warp and punch away the condescending voice of the principal, but Brian walked into her office, his face screwed into a frown.

Dizziness seized her power, igniting a fire so ferocious, it foamed her stomach, her chest, her thoughts and reactions. Burning, boiling, barbing her limbs. But then the pain dissolved, heightening to a level or resistance that left her numb. "She wouldn't have run away. Call the authorities. Have everyone on high alert. And lock down your school in case there's a threat."

"Ms. Cooper—"

She hung up on him and planted her face in her hands. The school knew to be on the lookout for Clint, and she had trusted them with her daughter's safety.

She was close to falling apart, but she kept one hand firmly grounded on her desk. "Brian, call the cops now. Please. Laramie is missing from school and I dropped her off myself this morning. I'm expecting victims this morning but I've got to go home and check to see if she's gone back."

Brian snapped his fingers and barked orders to people in his office. Someone called the cops. Another would go by Lauren's house and check. The entire office buzzed with activity.

"I refuse to believe she ran away again." She used quotes for *again.* "We have to find her."

"We will." Brian stepped forward and put his hands on her shoulders. "We will," he said, this time with more authority to ground her.

It didn't help. Her whole body shook. Her mind whirled. Clint was out there somewhere. Her faith in law enforcement finding him had dwindled.

She needed to call or text Luke. She didn't believe Laramie had skipped school, and she would never, ever toss her phone. Her phone was an attachment to her. Sure, she wasn't allowed to use it after school and only for an hour after homework was done and dinner was eaten and never at bed, but she loved that phone like an extension of herself.

"We'll cancel your meeting today and shut down to the office to help you find her. Don't worry about a thing."

She nodded, her chin quivered. Everything was too surreal to process his words. Her mind swam through a struggle of doubt and fear. Of *what ifs* and *what nots.*

Her daughter was missing. *Missing.* But any movement was tangled up in the past and the future. The uncertainties. Her breath struggled to reach her chest. Each inhale like a lifeline to the next exhale.

"But I want you to stay here. We've got people out there looking for her. You're in no shape."

His words pounded through her reserves. "I can't stay here and just wait."

"You're not just waiting. I want you to make a list of every place she might have gone. And I want you to make a list of anywhere Clint might take her if Clint has taken her."

She shook her head, tears blinding her. A force of strength building in her. Because how else could she manage another breath? Another thought?

"Did they have a favorite hangout? Did he take her for ice cream at a certain place? Fly kites somewhere? Something?"

"No, no," she murmured. Her mind raced. Clint *had* taken her daughter roller blading or for ice cream or to the county fair when she couldn't go. Clint had been alone with her daughter on more than one occasion since she was a wee child. And now this? She couldn't fathom it. Clint wouldn't harm her child. Would he? No matter how many children he had harmed before. He had plenty of opportunities before now.

Yes. Yes he would, and that thought spurred her to action.

She washed her hands over her face and contemplated those places he might have gone. They had already investigated him and his properties since his last victim was found. They had searched records of him and his family members and so far, the only property in his name was his own and his grandparents.

An officer came in, his expression set in poker-stone. "Mr. Wimberly?"

Brian turned. "Yeah?"

"May we see you a moment?"

Lauren charged forward. "What's going on? This is my daughter. I have every right to know."

Brian held up his hand, blocking her. "I'll be back with you in a moment. I won't keep any secrets."

Lauren gritted her teeth and would have said more if Luke hadn't surged through the door. Eyes wide, face pale, hair haphazard all around his face.

"Where's Laramie?" he demanded.

Her stomach dropped.

"I got a text from an unknown number. Said I have your daughter. I called 9-1-1. Tried calling you. Tried calling the number back."

She ran to him and clutched his hands. His body shook,

neck corded, skin tight and sallow. He was barely holding it together, so she forced herself not to break down.

Their eyes met and held, gaining strength from each other. She laid her head on his chest and told him everything she knew. Which wasn't much.

He let out a harsh cry and almost collapsed. They clutched each other.

Clint had been like a brother to Luke. Lauren had trusted Clint with Laramie. She'd seen him angry, but never had she seen him violent. He was charming and cool, but Laramie said he creeped her out. She sensed something in him nobody else had.

Moments passed. She listened to Luke's heartbeat and let it be her anchor. She was about to go check on things when Brian and an officer stormed in. Lauren broke apart from Luke's comforting embrace.

Brian returned holding a plastic evidence bag. "We found this on Clint's property."

When Lauren saw the necklace in the bag, air whooshed out of her lungs, her head nearly popping with pressure. "Laramie's necklace." The one she had helped Lauren create at summer camp.

Her knees buckled, but Luke gripped her and held her into his chest again. Her biggest fear had come true.

"We have officers stationed at his house, his grandparents', the school, your house, even Luke's house," Brian continued, but his voice droned. None of that mattered. They had to figure out where Clint had taken her, where he had taken all his victims.

CHAPTER TWENTY-TWO

Anger and fear clutched Luke's mind, fueling his guilt and regret. Anger at the cops, the prosecutors, but mostly himself.

He'd spent most of his time with Clint as a teen and hadn't recognized the signs of a sociopath. Sure, he'd been selfish, insensitive, and sometimes heartless, crude with no regard to how his behavior affected others. He had been a mastermind of charm. No one expected him to be such a brutal killer.

So why had they expected Luke to be?

A question he'd never had an answer for and one he no longer had time to dissect. Everyone knew the truth now, but it was too late.

Clint had Laramie and so far, no evidence Clint let anyone live after he took them.

The reality tore at his gut. He let out a cry but quickly stifled it. Lauren's boss and others hovered around, eyeing them both as if they were about to let out a shitstorm of crazy.

And he just might.

The room cut off his breathing, confining him, the pounding in his head like nails in a coffin. He had to get out of here. Had to be moving, doing something. Prison walls closed in on him.

Where had Clint liked to hang in their younger days? Maybe a special place. He had to have a special place.

Luke wanted to wrap his hands around his neck and watch the breath squeeze out of him, the life fizzle out of his eyes.

Luke whirled around and raced for the door as if his life depended on it.

"Luke," Lauren yelled, barreling behind him. "Luke," she said again, reaching for him.

He stopped in the hallway and turned. Curious eyes beaded into them, small pellets of concern that stung. Sure, people wanted to help, but he wished they'd stop hovering.

"Where are you going?" she asked.

"I've got to get out of here. I've got to be doing something."

"What do you think you'll be doing?" she asked as if she was questioning to find a way out of the anguish in her mind.

"I don't know. But I can't sit here and wait for someone else to do their job." He paused. "Look, we know Clint isn't holding her for ransom. He isn't miraculously going to call and ask for money or freedom. So for us to be waiting here, wasting our time—"

"Wait for me. I've got to grab my purse."

Lauren left to grab her purse but was back within seconds. She grabbed his arm, and they rushed out the door. Once the sunshine and humidity hit, he had no idea what to do next or where to go. He walked toward the Jeep and stopped, squeezing his eyes shut.

Officers were stationed at her house, the school, Luke's property. Not enough for Luke. He'd search every place they'd ever been, every place Clint ever wanted to be, even if the cops had already done so.

"I've been thinking about where Clint hung out as a kid, but nothing comes to mind except his grandparents' house."

Lauren laid a hand on his shoulder and squeezed. "They've gone over that place a dozen times."

He pinched the bridge of his nose. Memories assailed him, mouth souring, stomach curling. Something niggled at his memories. A dark, smelly room that he'd stumbled open once when they had been out bike riding.

"Fuck." Heart thudding, he opened his eyes and jumped into the Jeep. With the door and top off, it was an easy in and out. "Fuck!" He pounded his hands on the steering wheel and fired up the engine, ready to face danger head-on. Ready to face Clint. Ready to kill him.

"What is it?" Lauren raced to the passenger side and hopped in.

"How much did they search?" He pulled away and raced toward the house in question.

"They said they searched all over. Even had dogs. They went over the storm cellar, but no signs. They have officers in the area. Why?"

"When I was a kid and we were out bike riding one day, I stumbled over a root cellar. Separate from the storm cellar. It's almost impossible to find if you don't know where it is. I've only been once. Clint hated it, was scared of it, and claimed his grandparents covered it, and we never talked about it again. Remember the tree house?"

"I do. They searched that, too."

"Part of that tree house covers the entry to the root cellar."

"I never knew about it."

"Most people don't. Fuck." His heart slammed against his ribcage, but he maintained his focus. He had to concentrate to keep them all alive. He flipped on his hazard lights and honked at a car easing out in front of him.

"It's okay, it's okay," Lauren reassured him. She dialed her phone and told the chief the news.

"There are officers already there and they are sending backup," she told him once she hung up.

His tongue curled.

"Obviously he told us to stay put," she said.

"That's not going to happen."

"Of course, it isn't."

The sirens blared, and they arrived on the property. Luke shifted the Jeep in four-wheel drive and drove through the pasture, his pace much too slow for his wellbeing.

The chief waved and raced after them. The Jeep was slow enough, and Luke slowed even more to give the chief time to jump into the back.

"I thought I told you to stay put," the chief groused.

They bumped and bounced through the pasture. "Do your guys have any idea where they should go?"

"They found the tree house and the entry."

Luke pulled to a stop near other police SUV vehicles and he and Lauren slid out of the Jeep. An officer approached, his hand up. "Stay back." He looked mean and raw. Tough. Tall, buzz cut, piercing gray eyes. So why was he standing there doing nothing?

When Luke asked, he got a terse reply. "We went down and almost got shot. Now, we're waiting on SWAT. We've tried talking to him."

Lauren gripped Luke, and he held her so she wouldn't fall. "Is Laramie down there?"

"We believe so."

Lauren raced toward the hole in the ground and fell to her knees, digging at the dirt. "Laramie!"

Luke was surprised the officers had found it. They had

removed the covering, and the opening was only large enough for one person to get in and out of. Luke had only been in it once, and a built in rope ladder was the only means up and down. He wondered how Clint got his victims in and out.

"Laramie!" Lauren screamed.

The chief grabbed her before the gunfire shot out of the ground.

"Clint!" she yelled. "Stop this madness. Please. She's your godchild. You helped raise her. Please!" Her voice cracked, and the chief held onto her so she didn't fall. Luke shot forward and took her, freeing the chief. She fell into his arms, her fingers tightening around his biceps to hang on.

Luke would kill Clint, even if he had to spend the rest of his life behind bars. Although prison was the best punishment, he didn't deserve to ever see the light of day again.

———

Luke's arms did not comfort her. She pulled away and fell to her knees again, crawling to the hole in the ground. Her breath constricted, mind reeling in desperation. Someone, she wasn't sure who, warned her to keep away in case of more gunfire.

But that was her daughter down there, and she had to get to her.

Luke stooped beside her. His face constricted, tension lining his jaw. But she wanted to be the one to jump down there and pummel Clint.

The chief handed them each a helmet and a vest. "Wear this," he commanded, and helped her put it on. Her entire body shook.

"Laramie!" she cried again, falling to her knees once she was in the garb to protect her from bullets.

"Mom." The voice was faint, as if speaking through a cube.

"Laramie!" Tears blubbered around her throat. "Clint. I'm coming down there. Exchange me for her!"

"Come on down, Lauren." His voice slithered over her skin.

"Ma'am," an officer called to get hold of her. She brushed him off.

"I'm coming down there, Clint. Don't shoot."

"Ma'am," the officer said again. "SWAT will be here within minutes."

"Then they can save me instead of her. I'm going."

The officer's hands trampled over her legs in an awkward attempt to cover her with resistant garb. He muttered about this being foolish. "Can't believe the chief is letting you do this. Can't believe the DA is."

They couldn't keep her from protecting her child.

"Come on down, Lauren." Clint's voice made her toes curl. "But I promise you if anyone follows, everyone is dead. Laramie is first."

Brian handed her a gun. "Take this. Keep it concealed."

Lauren nodded, her entire body heavy tingling in dread. She took the pistol and stuck it behind her waist. All the garb she wore, along with her long shirt, concealed it, but every movement slipped it down her back.

She stepped backward through the hole and found footing on the stairs. "It's just me."

"Lauren," Luke said, trying to stop her. She didn't listen. Officers surrounded him as if to protect him from himself or from doing anything rash.

"Oh, Luke, you poor sucker," Clint called.

"Stay here," Lauren told Luke, already crawling her way down the stairs. "It's me," she told Clint in case he didn't recognize her with the garb, and she faced the concrete wall on her way down the ladder.

She reached the last rung and jumped off. She turned and held up her hands, spotting Laramie immediately. Clint cocked his gun, the click a catastrophic ricochet in her ears. She halted.

"Don't move another inch."

Lauren coughed. The smell was damp and musty. Lights from below streamed as if a colander was placed above them to strain the light into the darkness. Dirt covered a spacious concrete floor.

Laramie was tied to a chair in the far corner. Her eyes were wide, face pale. Clint stood behind and to the side of her, his gun pointed at Lauren.

"Nice get up you've got there."

"Just trying to protect myself."

"Against what?" He planted a hand over his chest. "Mwah?"

"We're doing the exchange now, right?" she asked.

"I never agreed to an exchange."

"Yes. Me for Laramie. Let her go free."

"Mom," Laramie muttered. Her daughter's voice tore Lauren's stomach in knots.

Nothing mattered but Laramie. Keeping her safe, keeping her alive. If that meant Lauren's life, so be it.

"I never agreed to that," Clint said. "I just wanted you to come down here. You want to be with your daughter so much. So let's be together. You can watch her die."

She shook her head, the fury and helplessness of the situation quivering in her bones. Laramie's trembly lower lip focused her. She must do something to protect her daughter. To protect herself. Dozens of law enforcement stood above her, but these steps put them in a vulnerable position. A rope ladder tied to the wall offered the only way to walk down.

Up to her to get them out of this alive. And she would. Clint had been a huge part of their life. She would use that to her advantage. Manipulate, control. Whatever she must.

"Has he hurt you, Meemee?" she asked, Clint's nickname for her daughter Laramie hated now that she was older.

Laramie shook her head. "No. Just scared."

Clint waved his gun. "Come on over closer, Lauren. You can get in on the action."

Lauren inched forward. She had to get closer to Clint to get them out of this situation. Zip ties around Laramie's ankles and hands had her stationary.

"Why are you doing this, Clint?" She plodded forward. Each step closer made her an easier target. She might be covered in bullet resistance, but her face was easily exposed. He could seriously injure her in her shoulder and arms, too. She kept her head down, helmet toward him, to at least make the gunshot less brutal.

Unless he killed Laramie first like he'd threatened. But each step forward made him an easier target, too.

Her fingers itched to get the pistol from her waist and shoot. Why had the officers let her down here? She was in way over her head. But Laramie needed her, and she would do anything in the world for her daughter.

Even die.

"Lauren, look at me. How can I explain myself if you don't look at me?" His voice, like a venomous snake waiting to strike. Flat. Graceless. The charm long since gone.

She tilted her head and blinked at him. "Okay. Please explain. Why?"

Officers surrounded Luke. To protect him, or them, or Clint he wasn't sure. Unbelievable. They let Lauren go down there alone to face Clint and now were standing around as if nothing was happening. Many of them, including the chief and Brian, studied their phones.

His body screamed, mind whirling and twirling, knots chaining his gut to his chest. A stagnate mix of feculence and fear filled his nostrils. Nausea rolled in his throat, but he clamped it down with determination.

He'd get down there even if he had to jump.

He raced toward that hole in the ground, the one symbolizing his prison sentence. Because what might happen to Lauren and Laramie was worse than spending life in prison. Or dying. He'd rather die himself than let anything happen to them.

None of this would have happened if they had left him in prison. He doubted Clint would risk taking Laramie.

Would he?

"Luke." Brian grabbed him by the shoulders and pulled him back up. He was a big man, a strong man, but Luke had faced much bigger and much stronger. He stood with him. He didn't want to take anyone down, especially in the crosshairs of dozens of men with guns, but he'd take that risk. He had to get down there and help since no one else wanted to.

"Luke," Brian said again. "We have eyes on Lauren."

His words didn't register. "What?"

"We tagged a small camera to her vest. She isn't alone down there. We're watching her right now, figuring out how to make our next move."

The words stung him like tiny pins pricking holes in his skin and brought breath back into his body. His knees buckled, but he continued to stand strong.

"Let me see."

Brian held a tablet toward him, but didn't hand it over. So that's what they had been looking at this entire time.

Lauren stood facing Clint, inching closer. Clint held a gun, but it pointed at the floor. From this angle, he couldn't see Laramie.

"Does—" His voice cracked. He cleared it and tried again. "Does she know?"

"No."

"You should have told her. She could have maneuvered to make sure we could see different angles, ways to sneak inside."

"We didn't want him to suspect anything. And if she knew, she might act differently. She's carrying."

"She's..." Luke shook his head, disbelief tingling his chest. "You gave her a gun?"

"Yes."

"So, you don't want her to know she had a camera, but she has a gun?"

"She's highly capable with that gun. I've seen it myself."

Clint was capable of killing. They'd all seen that.

They studied the tiny screen. Clint and Lauren spoke, but the sound was too muffled to hear what was being said. Luke should step away and let the officers handle things, but that wasn't going to happen.

He'd spent the last twelve years giving up his rights and control and wasn't about to any longer.

She turned at an angle where they saw Laramie, and the weight of his chest caved in. All the breath he'd been holding on to gushed out of him, only to stay out, unable to draw in another. When he finally did, his entire body starved for more.

Laramie was tied to a chair, her hands in front of her, but she moved and shifted. His breath froze when he saw why. She used the small knife to free her hands while watching Clint, who was too involved in a conversation with Lauren to consider the child a threat.

"What is she doing?" one officer murmured.

Once her hands were free, she unbound her feet and waited for the opportunity to strike. Clint's gut clenched. Lauren moved again, cutting Laramie from the frame. But the scream pitching through the tablet screen clutched his heart, and the video turned back to Laramie to show her on Clint's back, fighting him with the small knife.

"Fuck this," Luke said, grabbing the gun out of an officer's belt.

"SWAT is here! SWAT is here!" the chief bellowed.

Luke didn't care. He stepped through the opening facing forward, his gun drawn and ready.

Clint threw Laramie off, and she fell to the floor with a grunt. He didn't even notice Luke tripping down on the ladder. His breath swayed when Lauren grabbed the gun from her back and shot at Clint.

———

The gunshot missed Clint. Hate and fury ate away at his face. He lunged forward and knocked the gun out of her hand, pushing her down to the ground. Her head struck with a resounding thud, except the helmet protected her. She blinked. The heavy weight of the garb and his hands shackled her.

Laramie screamed and ran forward again, but he knocked her away. His hands were around Lauren's throat. She jabbed his eyes, but he fought too hard and she was too weak. Spots formed above her eyes. Another gunshot resounded, but she had no idea where it came from. Everything slowed. She tried to call out for Laramie to warn her to flee and find somewhere safe, because as soon as her breath was gone, he'd go after her daughter next.

She struggled, thrashed, strained to find breath and

suddenly, breath. Free, clearing breath. She coughed and rolled on her side, aching for air but worried he had gone to Laramie. She clutched her throat, searching, but spots fogged her vision.

Then she saw Luke, squaring off with Clint. Clint no longer had his gun. She had no idea where he'd put it, and he'd thrown hers off. But Luke had one pointing at him. She crawled on the ground, meeting Laramie's eyes, who stayed huddled in the corner.

"Get out of here," she yelled at Laramie, but her voice was too scratched to make sense.

SWAT rappelled through the opening, in one of those lines she'd only seen in the movies. Then another, then another. Soon, three garbed men, along with Luke, faced Clint.

"What a nice surprise," Clint said, his whole face screwed into a clownish smile. He was enjoying this.

"Hands up where we can see them."

"Am I under arrest?" he asked, but his voice was light and jovial as if he thought this was a joke.

Lauren crawled toward Laramie, but it felt like she was on the other side of the ocean. So far, too far.

Clint reached behind him and grabbed a gun. She screamed at the same time she reached Laramie and folded her in her arms. Laramie buried her head in her mother's chest as Lauren continued to watch the scene unfold.

His hands came forward, but gunfire resonated in the entire cavern, shaking the area like an earthquake. Clint went down, his pistol dropping, his body drooping, his life already gone.

TIME FROZE. A wave of uncertainty hit Luke then too much

happened at once. He focused on Lauren and Laramie, but they disappeared. Officers surged in, took his weapon, and rushed him out. His legs shook, and he made his way up the ladder and out into the open air.

Open air. Lungs drew deep, painful breaths, barely holding on to reality. What was reality anymore?

His control collapsed when he laid eyes on Lauren and his daughter. They were alive. They were okay. They huddled together until they saw him, then Laramie scurried forward and threw herself at his chest.

He folded her into his arms and held out an arm for Lauren. She joined, and the three of them held each other in a circle, heads bowed into each other, their breaths mingling, growing stronger.

"I love you," Luke said as he held them. "I love you both, so much. Don't ever, ever, ever scare me like that again."

Laramie giggled, a soft whispery sound full of nerves and released fear. "I'll try not to." She pulled away from him, but their arms remained on each other. "You saved me. That pocket knife you gave me, I used it to cut away at my ties."

His chest dipped, pulse caved, and he pulled her back into his embrace. He let the tears fall.

Clint could never hurt them again. No matter what happened in life, Clint could never hurt him or his family ever again. Maybe it wasn't justice that he didn't have to suffer the long years in prison and got off easy with a quick death, but his death lightened Luke, the heavy dread relieved.

Their hell was over. Finally over.

He released them, but kept them within arm's length. He had to see them, had to breathe in the sight of them. Earlier, he thought he'd never have another chance.

"We love you, too," Laramie said, her words tugging at his heart. "And I'm glad you're a part of my life."

"I hope I'll always be."

ANGELA SMITH

Laramie nodded, a fresh bout of tears falling from her eyes. She smiled at her mom, then back at him. "I have a feeling you always will be."

Lights flashed around the scene. EMS checked them, then they were released. They were allowed to go home but were warned they'd have to give statements later.

"We have counselors if you need them," Brian told Lauren, his gaze rolling over Laramie.

She nodded and rubbed his arm. "I'll let you know if we do. Thanks so much."

He hugged her and patted her back. "I'm so glad you're all safe. Go home and rest. Take a few days off." He pulled away, then shook Luke's hands and held it. "Taking an officer's weapon is a crime." He slapped Luke on the back with his free hand then dropped his hold on the other. "But I don't think it's anything you have to worry about. You okay to drive?"

Luke nodded. He was ready to get out of here and get his girls out of here. Away from the scene, the flashing lights, the cops, and the memories.

Once they were in the Jeep, Laramie dug in Lauren's purse and let out a whoop.

"My phone. My blessed phone!"

Luke winked at Lauren and laughed. Laramie was okay.

They made it to Lauren's and would worry about the little things later. The fact her car was at her work, they were all a mess and wanted food and a shower. For now, Luke wanted to sit with them and take it all in.

Laramie's phone rang, jostling them.

She jumped up. "Oh, that's Tiffany. Do you mind if I take it?"

"No. Go ahead," Lauren said.

"Hey girl. Yeah, yeah, I'm okay." She continued talking and disappeared in her room.

Luke gathered Lauren in his arms. "I guess that means we're alone."

She snuggled closer. "For a little while, anyway."

"She'll be on the phone a while."

She tilted her head up at him, her smile igniting life into his heart as if he hadn't truly lived.

He would gladly give twelve years of his life for this moment, for their future moments.

He cupped his hand behind her neck and pulled her close to kiss her. Every bad thing escaped out of him, his entire being filling with pleasure. And hope.

"I meant it when I said I love you."

Her face beamed, and she curled her fingers in his hair. "I love you too, Luke. *We* love you. Very much."

He slipped from the couch and got on his knees. He pulled the ring box from his pocket. He'd stored it there every day for the last week, waiting for the perfect opportunity to pop the question. He'd imagined a beautiful date, the stars shining brighter than the lights strung up over his porch. Wine, music, dancing. But it was the perfect opportunity, and he wasn't about to miss it.

He pulled the box from his pocket and opened it. She gasped at the two rings.

He slid one glittering ring onto her shaky finger. "Will you marry me?"

"I… I… yes… yes." Tears bubbled out of her, mingling with his. He sat back on the couch and wrapped his arms around her.

Pulling away, he placed the box with another ring in his pocket, then explained. "The other ring is for Laramie. Not an engagement—too silly—but a promise to love and cherish her until the end of time."

"She'll love that."

He wiggled his brows. "I say we get pizza. Some wine. And I'll give it to her over pizza."

"A grand idea. But I say we sit here like this for a while and give her time to process this with her friend."

"You're just looking for an excuse to hold me a while longer."

She giggled and traced her finger over his cheek, eyes, and throat. "I sure am."

When Laramie came out of her room, she smiled at them and bounced forward, her face tired but refreshed. "Whatchadoing?"

His heart swelled with gratitude. She was fine, she was strong and would overcome. Another reason he was so glad Clint was out of their lives for good. Made it easier for Laramie to get back to her life.

Forget waiting on pizza. He was ready to tell her now. He waved her over, and she sat with them.

"We have something to tell you." Luke pulled the ring box from his pocket.

This moment was worth waiting through a lifetime of darkness, because now his life burned brighter than ever and he wondered, if he hadn't spent time in prison, if he would take his life too much for granted to appreciate these small moments.

He opened the box, and Laramie squealed, then looked at her mom if she expected her to take it.

"It's for you," Luke said.

She clapped a hand over her heart. "For me?"

He pulled it out of the box and slipped it on her finger. "For you. A promise of a lifetime of love and laughter and happy moments. A promise to be your father and a dad. And a promise to love and cherish your mom for eternity so you will know the true meaning of relationship."

Tears blubbered out of her. "Are you guys getting married?"

He nodded and grabbed Lauren's hand to show Laramie the ring. "We're getting married."

She fell back on the couch and shrieked, hand over heart. "Yes! My dream has come true!"

He rubbed his knuckles over his daughter's head and touched his nose to Lauren's. "So has mine. So has mine."

T*he* E*nd*

AUTHOR'S NOTE

Thank you for reading Dark Justice! I hope you enjoyed reading about Luke and Lauren as much as I loved writing their story.

This was a hard subject to write on many levels. My twenty-one year career at a prosecutor's office has taught me so much, but not near enough to truly know the ins and outs of the criminal justice field and every shadow of gray that the system encounters. I apologize in advance for any mistakes. DNA has come a long way and still has a long way to go, and years of research continues to teach us!

Not only that, but it was a very emotional book for me too.

I would love to know what you think. Authors thrive on reviews. It's a necessity for their careers because it's hard to get noticed without them. May I ask you to please leave a review?

I also hope you'll explore more about me and my books. You can visit my website at www.loveisamystery.com. Also, be sure to sign up for my newsletter to stay up to date with

AUTHOR'S NOTE

what's going on in my world, get free books, learn fun facts, and participate in surveys and giveaways! You can sign up at www.loveisamystery.com/newsletter.

Thanks again for reading. Until next time!

Angela Smith

ABOUT THE AUTHOR

Angela Smith is a Texas native who, years ago, was dubbed most likely to write a novel during her senior year in high school. She always had her nose stuck in a book, even hiding them behind her textbooks during school study time. Her dream began at a young age when her sister started reciting 'Brer Rabbit' after their mom read it to them so often. She told her mom she'd write a story one day and never gave up on that dream even though her mom was never able to see it come to fruition. By day, she works as a certified paralegal and office manager at her local District Attorney's office and spends her free time with her husband, their pets, and their many hobbies. Although life in general keeps her very busy, her passion for writing and getting the stories out of her head tends to make her restless if she isn't following what some people call her destiny.

Find out more at www.loveisamystery.com.

OTHER BOOKS BY ANGELA

Burn on the Western Slope

Fatal Snag

Final Mend

One Last Hold

One Wrong Move

Solace

Liberation

Dark Ride